ZARA DUSK

A Court of Verity and Lies

Copyright © 2023 by Zara Dusk

All rights reserved. No part of this publication may be reproduced, stored or transmitted in any form or by any means, electronic, mechanical, photocopying, recording, scanning, or otherwise without written permission from the publisher. It is illegal to copy this book, post it to a website, or distribute it by any other means without permission.

This novel is entirely a work of fiction. The names, characters and incidents portrayed in it are the work of the author's imagination. Any resemblance to actual persons, living or dead, events or localities is entirely coincidental.

Zara Dusk asserts the moral right to be identified as the author of this work.

First edition

*This book was professionally typeset on Reedsy.
Find out more at reedsy.com*

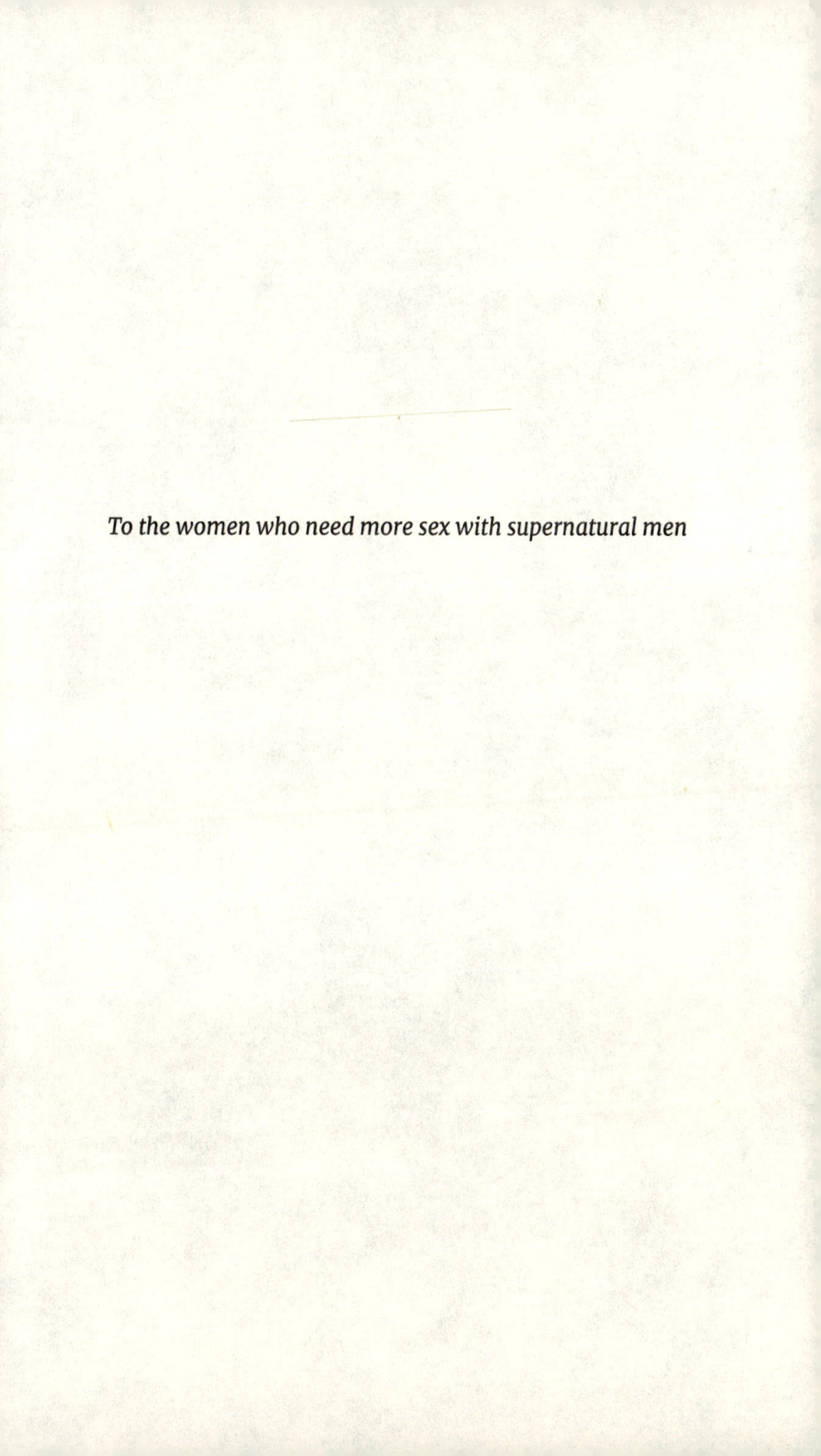

To the women who need more sex with supernatural men

Contents

Foreword	iii
Gabrelle	1
Gabrelle	9
Gabrelle	16
Gabrelle	24
Thorne	31
Gabrelle	38
Thorne	44
Thorne	49
Gabrelle	54
Gabrelle	62
Thorne	69
Gabrelle	75
Gabrelle	84
Gabrelle	91
Gabrelle	98
Thorne	105
Gabrelle	111
Thorne	118
Thorne	124
Gabrelle	131
Thorne	139
Gabrelle	147
Gabrelle	153

Thorne	160
Thorne	165
Gabrelle	171
Gabrelle	178
Gabrelle	185
Thorne	191
Gabrelle	196
Thorne	202
Gabrelle	211
Gabrelle	216
Gabrelle	224
Gabrelle	230
Thorne	239
Jayke	246
Gabrelle	252
Thorne	260
Gabrelle	266
Epilogue	274
Free novella	279
About the Author	280
Also by Zara Dusk	282

Foreword

This book has some dark elements. If you're concerned, you can find the content warnings at https://zaradusk.com/content-warnings

Gabrelle

A door banged open, jolting me from my thoughts. After stealing a final glance at the magnificent blue lake, I sculpted a smile and spun around to see who had barged in.

And there was Ronan, decked out in his usual all-black attire, exuding princely charm with his raven-black hair and eyes. He had a way of capturing attention, even among the fae.

He strolled across the Lakehouse's large open-concept living area and squeaked open the floor-to-ceiling glass doors, joining me on the deck.

"Looking stunning as always, beauty queen," he said in greeting.

I suppressed a sigh. Lately, I had noticed that Mother always greeted me with a comment about my appearance. Being from House Allura, renowned for beauty, it came with the territory. But hearing the same style of 'hello' from one of my best friends in the world was tiresome.

Still, I'd never admit it. So I carefully crafted my face to match my carefully crafted outfit. "Of course, moody. It's kind of my thing." I brushed a lock of dusty-pink hair over my shoulder and picked an invisible speck from my crisp white jumpsuit.

His laughter swept away my annoyance like magic. "Not

your only thing." His good vibes infected me like a happy virus, courtesy of his House's magic. Ronan, the contender for the House Mentium throne, had this uncanny ability to rub off his moods on everyone. Irritation had no chance when he was cracking jokes.

"You're also very good at coming second behind me in challenges," he said with one of his famous smirks.

Raising an eyebrow, I countered, "Hardly, moody. I outperform you in every trial Gaia throws at us." That wasn't entirely true, but I couldn't let my friend get away with his nonsense. Better a small lie from me than a massive ego on him.

Ronan scoffed playfully and crossed the deck in a few strides, his long legs effortlessly covering the distance. Leaning against the railing, he gazed out at the lake. I followed suit, mirroring his relaxed stance, basking in the comforting warmth of the sun on my upturned face.

We fell into a companionable silence, the kind that only years of friendship can forge, as we stood side by side, gazing out at the vast lake. When Neela, the heir of House Flora, had first arrived with her human-level vision, she mistakenly assumed the water stretched on indefinitely. It took a few weeks for her fae senses to fully return before she saw the distant shore.

Tall pine trees hugged the lake, their tops stretching high into the sky and filling the air with the fresh smell of pine. It added to the chill vibes of the place. "It's more than just a Lakehouse, isn't it," I said.

This place had witnessed countless hours of joy for me. It was the one sanctuary in Verda City where the other heirs and I could escape from the prying eyes of the lesser fae and find some relief from the responsibilities of being next in line to the thrones.

Gabrelle

A door banged open, jolting me from my thoughts. After stealing a final glance at the magnificent blue lake, I sculpted a smile and spun around to see who had barged in.

And there was Ronan, decked out in his usual all-black attire, exuding princely charm with his raven-black hair and eyes. He had a way of capturing attention, even among the fae.

He strolled across the Lakehouse's large open-concept living area and squeaked open the floor-to-ceiling glass doors, joining me on the deck.

"Looking stunning as always, beauty queen," he said in greeting.

I suppressed a sigh. Lately, I had noticed that Mother always greeted me with a comment about my appearance. Being from House Allura, renowned for beauty, it came with the territory. But hearing the same style of 'hello' from one of my best friends in the world was tiresome.

Still, I'd never admit it. So I carefully crafted my face to match my carefully crafted outfit. "Of course, moody. It's kind of my thing." I brushed a lock of dusty-pink hair over my shoulder and picked an invisible speck from my crisp white jumpsuit.

His laughter swept away my annoyance like magic. "Not

your only thing." His good vibes infected me like a happy virus, courtesy of his House's magic. Ronan, the contender for the House Mentium throne, had this uncanny ability to rub off his moods on everyone. Irritation had no chance when he was cracking jokes.

"You're also very good at coming second behind me in challenges," he said with one of his famous smirks.

Raising an eyebrow, I countered, "Hardly, moody. I outperform you in every trial Gaia throws at us." That wasn't entirely true, but I couldn't let my friend get away with his nonsense. Better a small lie from me than a massive ego on him.

Ronan scoffed playfully and crossed the deck in a few strides, his long legs effortlessly covering the distance. Leaning against the railing, he gazed out at the lake. I followed suit, mirroring his relaxed stance, basking in the comforting warmth of the sun on my upturned face.

We fell into a companionable silence, the kind that only years of friendship can forge, as we stood side by side, gazing out at the vast lake. When Neela, the heir of House Flora, had first arrived with her human-level vision, she mistakenly assumed the water stretched on indefinitely. It took a few weeks for her fae senses to fully return before she saw the distant shore.

Tall pine trees hugged the lake, their tops stretching high into the sky and filling the air with the fresh smell of pine. It added to the chill vibes of the place. "It's more than just a Lakehouse, isn't it," I said.

This place had witnessed countless hours of joy for me. It was the one sanctuary in Verda City where the other heirs and I could escape from the prying eyes of the lesser fae and find some relief from the responsibilities of being next in line to the thrones.

Ronan glanced at me, then back at the lake. "What do you mean?"

"The Lakehouse, how it changes and grows for us. Becomes part of us...or we become part of it." There was no doubting that the place reflected our needs and personalities.

"Like Alara's dungeon?" Ronan asked. When Leif found his mate last month, the Lakehouse changed overnight. It grew her an underground stone bunker where she could retreat and feel safe.

"Exactly."

Ronan shuddered dramatically. "The tomb of hell. I hate going down there. It feels like being buried alive."

"Hell yeah, wolves and their stone fetish," I quipped. Leif Caro, the House Caro shifter, loved anything made of stone—just look at his monstrous marble den. I closed my eyes against the warm sun. "The Lakehouse is more than just a place to hang out. It's a training ground for when our time comes to rule. We have to figure out disputes and adapt to each other. It's like a mini realm for us to practice in."

Alara could retreat to her den when she needed to, but ultimately, we all had to figure out how to get along and reconcile our differences.

Ronan looked across the water. "One fae's tomb is another fae's refuge."

I playfully nudged him with my arm. "Good Gaia, are you turning philosophical, moody? That's the most profound thing you've ever said," I teased.

He nodded wisely. "Yes, I am extremely intelligent. Don't forget good-looking and sexy."

I raised an eyebrow. "Let's not get carried away now." He chuckled, and I leaned casually against him, enjoying this moment of friendship. "I love it here," I said.

Ronan must have detected some wistfulness in my voice. Hell, I'd been jumpy all morning. He placed a hand over mine on the deck railing, his hand pale against my dark skin. "You don't have to go to Fen, you know. We can figure out another way."

His words hung in the air as starlings twittered in the trees. In the distance, two bow waves glided toward us from the lake's far side. I knew exactly who was causing them. "Leif and Alara are coming," I said.

I watched the two wolves swim closer, their forms cutting through the water with impressive speed. But they just reminded me of why I had to go to Fen. "I have to go, moody. The Stone of Veritas is the only way to kill the Shadow Walkers. And it's is in Fen."

Ronan squeezed my hand. "Somebody else could go. It'll be dangerous, and I don't want to risk losing you." Ronan was a good friend. There had been a time I'd thought he might be more than that, but that had long passed. He wasn't right for me, I knew that now. Foolish comments like that just proved it.

I bit back my sigh. "The rest of you heirs have irritated Thorne Sanctus so thoroughly that he wouldn't let you set foot in his Court." I ran a hand through my long, curling tresses. "It has to be me."

"We could send somebody else," he insisted.

I gave him a withering stare and was pleased to see him wither beneath it. "Come on, moody. We need a direct line to the Prince of Fen. A washerfae isn't going to cut it. Pretty sure they won't stash the Stone of Veritas in the laundry room."

I might not be the queen of self-awareness, but I wasn't

fooling anyone, especially not myself. Those jokes about hiding the priceless artifact with the laundry? Just my way of masking the fear gnawing at my guts.

Ronan began to speak, but I stopped him with a decisive nod. "I'm going, moody. I don't want to hear any more on the subject." No turning back now.

Ronan's expression still carried a note of worry, but I brushed it off, focusing on our pals closing in. The bow waves had already reached our shore, and two soaking-wet wolves sprang out of the lake, water cascading from their fur. They made quite the entrance. Leif, a colossal silver wolf with a shaggy head and a long pink tongue that was best avoided, and his proud mate, Alara, a smaller dark orange wolf, strutting alongside him.

The two wolves shifted into their fae forms, as naked as babes. I'd seen Leif's dick approximately seventeen-thousand times, but he'd gone shy since his mating bond had snapped into place. Or at least protective of us all. The mating bond evoked horrendous jealousy for several months following the honeymoon, so it was for my own safety that Alara didn't spot me looking at Leif's big swinging schlong.

In any case, Leif had taken to storing spare clothes beneath the deck so he and Alara could dress before they came inside.

Leif trotted up the stairs to the deck wearing light-gray sweatpants that highlighted the silver in his flashing eyes and long silver hair. He was bare-chested, and Alara held his hand possessively, her orange eyes and hair flashing in the sun. I was careful not to look too long at him—the she-wolf had sharp claws. I didn't love it, but I could handle this odd situation for a few months until the jealousy of their bond faded.

Alara didn't scare me—I had years of warrior training behind me and was a skilled fighter—I was more concerned about hurting her if we came to blows. She and I bonded quickly after we met. Something about her called to me, and I even helped to bring her and Leif together, in a strange way, by slipping her a key to a cell he'd locked her in. Perhaps Gaia had been guiding my hand.

In any case, I viewed her as a friend. I cast her a smile. "Good morning, Alara. And wolf boy."

The orange-haired shifter broke into a grin. Wolves loved their hierarchies, and Alara seemed perpetually amazed—and secretly pleased—at how we heirs ribbed her beloved alpha.

"It is a glorious morning, isn't it!" Alara said, beaming, still glowing from her mating bond.

"Morning, beauty queen," Leif said, teasing me right back. It was fair enough, but it still stung. Even my closest friends judged me for my physical appearance, saw my skin-deep appeal, and measured me by my beauty. Even though they were just joking, it was tiresome.

Being alluring had its benefits, and I used them well. But I longed for more. Perhaps I would marry a blind fae when the time came, someone I could be sure didn't love me for my looks.

I etched a smile onto my perfect face. "If you've come for food, wolf boy, I'm afraid Dion isn't here yet. Maybe your mate can whip up something delicious for you."

Alara blanched. "No way. I can't cook. Even if I could, I wouldn't."

Leif got defensive on his mate's behalf. "Yeah, Gabrelle. She's my fuck toy, not my chef."

Alara scowled, playfully thumping his chest, though her grimace quickly transformed into a mischievous grin as her fingers traced across his bare skin.

It was amazing how easily Alara fitted in with our group of heirs. Her easy banter came naturally, not just with Leif but with all of us. But the end of their intense post-honeymoon period couldn't come fast enough, so I could resume my close friendship with Leif and get to know her better.

The front door banged open again—honestly, my fellow heirs barely had a scrap of fae dignity between them. While I preferred a more composed entrance, they had perfected the art of door-slamming and corridor-stomping.

The heir to House Dionysus and the heir to House Flora were not natural friends, so when they appeared together, I raised a questioning eyebrow at Ronan.

"Neela thought they should spend some more time together," he explained. For somebody newly arrived in the realm, Neela had a good natural grasp of our politics. Most of the tension in our group of heirs was between her and Dion, and her response was to get to know him better, which was the perfect solution.

"Oh, shit, dude," Leif said, spinning around. "Why'd you let the grumpies out together? They'll bring down the whole vibe."

I stepped through the floor-to-ceiling glass doors into the lounge room, where a scent of woodsmoke met me, and studied the new arrivals closely. They didn't appear irritated, so I supposed their friendship-date went smoothly. Neela's spiky sky-blue hair and pixie-like features were a strong contrast to Dion's black curly hair and tall frame. But both fae were smiling, so that was good.

Like all Magirus, Dion's hair and eyes changed to the color of his most recent meal, so I could only assume he'd just downed a plate of licorice. Or coal.

"Morning, lovelies," Alara said, grinning and still holding her mate's arm as he led her inside. "Well done for not killing each other."

Neela huffed a laugh.

Leif bounded across the floorboards to his buddies and licked them in greeting, earning a light slap from Neela, a grin from Dion, and a possessive growl from his mate. Alara trotted across the room and swept up Leif's hand in hers.

"What's for breakfast?" Leif asked Dion.

Dion grinned at the thought of cooking. Nothing pleased him more than spending time in a kitchen, and the Lakehouse larder was always well stocked. He marched over to the fridge. "Let's see, I could m—"

Chatter and laughter echoed all around, but a strange knot tightened in my gut, a weird feeling that something big was about to go down. A storm was brewing, ready to unleash chaos. "Hold up," I interjected, brushing off any objections with a dismissive wave. "The Court is expecting us. We can't be late."

Neela had already crossed to Ronan's side, her spiky-blue hair just reaching his broad black-clad shoulders. "She's got a point," the Floran princess said. "Being late is not an option. This shit is major."

Normally, wolf boy and wolf girl would disagree with anything that came between them and food, but Leif just whined slightly and didn't voice an objection.

My gut turned into a pit of writhing vipers. When Leif Caro didn't put up a fight about food, shit was about to go down.

And this time, it was going down on me. So to speak.

Gabrelle

The Court of Verda insisted that we face them to explain our intentions regarding the Shadow Walkers and the Stone of Veritas. It wasn't a pleasure to visit. The place was a hotbed of drama and betrayal, even with our parents wearing the crowns. Or especially because it was them.

Stepping foot in the Court of Verda wasn't on my wishlist. But at least I had my friends by my side as we entered its intimidating gates. Ronan and Neela on one side, Leif and Alara on the other—Leif now wearing more than just sweatpants—and Dion trailing behind. Liz, Neela's serving fae, even showed up in her green braids and practical pocket-studded overalls, though I wasn't exactly clear on how she could assist us.

The Court was the centerpiece of Verda City, its sprawling marble corridors and gilded archways reflecting the light of a thousand stars. Yet, concealed within those grand walls, hidden passageways veiled in dark mist whispered tales of treachery. It was an odd mix of welcoming and threatening, and I did my best to steer clear of this place whenever possible. The sense of forbidding always outweighed any semblance of welcome.

To enter, we passed beneath a line of ancient statues of winged fae, their eyes seeming to follow us as we walked.

Legend had it that the figures would not permit entry to any who sought to harm the Court, but it had been lifetimes since the statues were last activated, so I didn't know if their defense was rumor or fact. But they certainly cast an eerie mood, and passing beneath them felt like stepping into a cemetery.

Ronan put a reassuring hand on my shoulder, but the fear coursing through him just penetrated me further, so I shook his hand off and strode ahead.

Once we stepped inside, it was like entering a whole other world. Fancy-pants courtiers waltzed on marble floors, pretending they didn't have emotions. The air carried hints of jasmine, honey, and fancy incense, but underneath it all, you could practically taste the fear. Maybe Ronan's anxiety was rubbing off on the rest of us.

"Would somebody cheer moody up," I said calmly, hiding my irritation. He was meant to be here to help, not infect me with his emotions.

Neela cuddled his arm, and the sensation of walking to my doom lessened, but it didn't dissipate. It couldn't because most of the fear came from within.

I pushed back my shoulders and approached the throne room. "You've got this, babe," Leif said, and Alara came and rubbed herself against me like a house dog. I didn't even bother to push her away because, in her wolfish way, she provided some comfort.

The double-height doors swung open as we approached, acknowledging the future leaders of the realm, and we stepped into the circular antechamber. A flurry of controlled wind lifted us up toward the ceiling, which I knew was just an illusion. As we passed through the illusion of a roof, Alara and Neela ducked and held their heads while Ronan and Leif chuckled. Clearly, they hadn't warned their partners what to expect.

I was too wired to even smile. My heart pounded, and I found it difficult to keep my facade of calm.

Mother had taught me many lessons, most of which I despised. Like how to use my beauty for gain. How to use my inner magic of Lure to force others to do my will. But one lesson I would forever be grateful for was how to school my emotions. My skill at hiding my feelings had earned me the nickname ice queen, which I was proud of and far preferred to beauty queen.

But here, entering the throne room from below on a blast of wind, disappearing through the enchanted ceiling, passing through magical wards designed to make us feel uncomfortable, my emotions were higher than usual, and I had to struggle to maintain my mask of disinterest.

As the wind died away, I muttered a quick spell to smooth out my hair and clothes—they were my armor, and I didn't want to enter battle without them. After the rush of wind, the air was so still that it seemed to hold its breath. The silence was oppressive, the only noise a faint whisper of someone taking a sharp breath. Neela or Alara, no doubt. Liz hadn't been allowed inside the throne room, and the rest of us had visited before. But it was still impressive.

We gathered in the middle of the room, encircled by five thrones. The five thrones were stately and regal, each one slightly different but equal in grandeur. They radiated power and authority, and the fact that they formed a circle was a big "equality" statement.

My eyes landed on Mother, seated on the Alluran throne, which was elegantly curved and aesthetically balanced, constructed from wood that seemed to defy gravity. And there she sat, with that empty smile she'd taught me to wear like a disguise. "Good morning, daughter," she said silkily, crossing her legs. Her eyes twinkled with approval that I'd smoothed out my hair and clothes and didn't look as disheveled as my companions—but, thank Gaia, she didn't voice her approval. It was nice to be greeted by something other than a comment on my appearance.

The throne beside Mother's was golden and heavy, studded with gaudy jewels. Dion's father sat atop it, his hair pale blue this morning, his jaw square, and his expression stern. He nodded at his son and raised an imaginary glass, and D returned the gesture.

On the other side of Mother was the Mentium throne, a masterpiece of interwoven cobalt and gold, which twisted around in a tornado of blue and yellow, showcasing opposite emotions. Ronan's father greeted his son but ignored Neela, who shrank beside me. Curious. I would have to question them on the dynamics of their family relationship, which had clearly changed since Neela arrived in Arathay.

The other two thrones sat heavy and empty. The Floran throne, a marvel of twisting wood that seemed to grow directly from the marble floor, looked dead without its ruler. And the Caro throne, a gold-veined marble behemoth, looked large and lonely without Leif's mother upon it. Those two empty thrones told our plight more eloquently than words ever could.

Five monarchs. Two already dead. If one more died, leaving a minority alive, all five thrones would be passed on to the heirs. To me and my unfortunate friends, and none of us was ready.

"Speak," King Dion Dionysus said. D's dad had the same name as him, which must make things confusing at Solstice.

GABRELLE

I exhaled slowly, demonstrating how very unflustered I was. "As you know, we have discovered that the Shadow Walkers can only be killed by an artifact known as the Stone of Veritas."

We didn't need to explain the threat of the Shadow Walkers. They had swept across the realm from the East, hailing from the Shadow Isles, consuming the souls of shifters to multiply and breed. Leif's mom, Stella Caro, had been killed by them. Her empty marble throne was evidence of their threat.

And now, they had moved on from shifters and were attacking the general fae population. A Shadow Walker attack left its victim a walking husk who had to be put down by family and friends, then salted and burned.

"Go on," King Dionysus said, waving a hand impatiently.

I tilted my head unhurriedly. "We have discovered that the Stone of Veritas is in the Realm of Fen. And we intend to find it. We are only here as a measure of courtesy to inform you of our intentions."

King Mentium's voice was deep and harsh. "You are here because we summoned you, faeling. Your Alluran charms hold no sway in this Court, and you'd be well advised not to use them."

The equally spaced thrones arranged in a circle gave the impression of equality among the monarchs, but I knew better. Everybody in this room knew better. The monarchs had a ranking set by Gaia, resulting from years of trials. And Ronan's father, King Malachi Mentium, ranked highest.

But I had dealt with his son's tantrums for decades, and I could handle the father's. "How clever of you to point out that I'm not yet Ascended," I said, responding to his use of the term faeling. "But I am twenty-five years old and will ascend in three months. It is widely accepted that I will ascend into

Lure, like my mother, and that I am highly gifted in this magic. So it would do you well to afford me the respect I'm due."

As courtly threats went, this was only lightly veiled. I told the highest-ranked king that after I was an Ascended Lure, I could use my magic to make him do whatever I wanted. And the best part was, it was absolutely true.

Lure ran strongly through my veins. I could already force almost anybody to do almost anything, even against their will. If I chose to ascend into that power, I would be unstoppable.

Everybody expected me to choose Lure, like Mother. But I despised it. I despised the power it gave me over others, despised the way I saw Mother use it on the weak, despised how closely linked it was to Beauty.

So I had every intention of ascending into Stealth, like my father. But King Asshole didn't need to know that.

A proud smirk played on Mother's face for an instant before she wiped it clean.

I brushed a perfect lock of hair over my shoulder. "So, as I said, we are here to inform you of our intentions. It is best for the realm if the three remaining monarchs remain under the heavy protection of the Court rather than venturing to the Realm of Fen to retrieve the Stone of Veritas. But, of course, you are most welcome to join me, King Mentium."

The king scowled at me for a few long moments before turning to Mother and remarking, "She is just like you, isn't she, Chantelle?"

The compliment curdled in my stomach. My mother was a manipulative bitch and the last fae I wanted to be anything like. Yet the comparisons kept rolling in.

Mother smiled lightly, a plastic expression for a plastic heart. "Yes, Malachi, she is."

GABRELLE

I bit back the snarl that threatened to spill past my lips. I hated the comparison to my mother, but I refused to let it show. Instead, I kept my face smooth and my voice even as I spoke. "So, will you join me on my quest for the Stone of Veritas, Your Highness?"

King Malachi Mentium considered my question for a few moments, glancing around at the other monarchs before settling his gaze back on me. "I will not. But I will offer you the Court's blessing."

"How useful," I said sweetly with such a serene expression that the king couldn't be sure if I was being a bitch or sincere. I definitely wasn't sincere.

"Be warned, faeling," King Dionysus said, mirroring his co-monarch's derogatory term. "The Realm of Fen is dangerous, full of traps and trickery. Watch your back every damn second."

Beside me, the younger Dion tilted his head. "Trickery? But nobody can lie in that realm, right? Seems pretty straightforward to me."

Dion's father stared at us, power roiling through his gaze. "There are more ways to lie than with words, princes and princesses. You would all do well to learn that lesson."

Gabrelle

The kings and queen finally released us, and we dropped through the illusioned floor like stones before being caught by a rush of thick wind and gently placed on the marble of the antechamber beneath the throne room.

"Holy fuck," Leif said, stumbling into Alara, both catching each other before they tumbled to the marble floor.

"Efflanio levitas," I muttered to smooth out my hair and clothes from another tumble through a whirlwind. My jumpsuit was still crisp and white, with not a speck of dirt.

Neela was on her butt on the floor, scowling, but she cheered up when Ronan yanked her to her feet and planted a kiss on her forehead.

I exchanged a look with Dion. Spending so much time around loved-up couples was exhausting. I was even glad when Liz rejoined us as we swept out of the antechamber because she evened up the numbers.

"Well, that went swimmingly," I said, the sarcasm dripping from my words. Alara's face was pale, and she clutched at the hem of her dress as she walked. "It was bloody terrifying," she whispered. "Why didn't you warn me, city dick?" she demanded of Leif.

Neela rolled her eyes. "Come on, wolf girl, we've faced much scarier shit than that." The Floran heir turned to me. "That was rockstar, by the way. I love watching you demolish those assholes."

I smiled at her warmly, feeling a genuine emotion for once. "You're not so bad at it yourself."

Neela glanced at Ronan, who had been the ultimate asshole when they'd first met, and she'd put him in his place and kept him there ever since. "I know," she grinned. "Thanks."

"My dad's not an asshole," Ronan grumbled.

I shot him a look but didn't say anything. It wasn't the time or place for an argument. We had bigger problems to deal with. Namely, finding the Stone of Veritas before the Shadow Walkers took over all of Arathay. As we walked down the marble halls, I considered our options. We could try to sneak into the Realm of Fen undetected, but the chances of that were slim. Our current plan, as shaky as it was, was the only option.

"I'm going to leave straight away," I said.

The others stopped mid-stride and stared at me. Alara's eyes widened, her mouth forming a small O of surprise. Neela reached out to grab my arm, but I stepped away, determined to do this now. "There's no point delaying any longer. The Prince of Fen's mourning period finishes tomorrow, and I intend to be his first visitor. To pay my respects for his dead mother, of course," I said, winking.

"And to find the Stone of Veritas," Dion said.

The others exchanged worried glances, but no one argued with me. We all knew it was the right choice, we just didn't want to admit it out loud.

"What about your Ascension?" Ronan asked.

I'd turned twenty-five last month—and had a masked ball at the Mirror Palace to celebrate. So at the next Ascension rite in Verda, I would come into my full power. I flicked a lock of dusty pink hair over my shoulder. "The next Ascension rite isn't for three months, moody. I'll be back well before then."

His black eyes burned into me. "Promise?"

"Promise."

We returned to the Lakehouse, except Liz, who returned to the Rose Palace. My packed bags were waiting for me in the lounge room at the Lakehouse, rays of afternoon sunlight slanting in through the floor-to-ceiling windows and gilding them.

My friends were silent as they watched me cast a spell to propel my luggage before me.

Neela darted in and hugged me, and Alara squeezed my arm. Leif whined as I stepped onto the moonway and began my journey to Fen alone.

The walk through the moonways took an eternity, beginning with the one to Ronan's house, then the long one that headed northwest. To reach the truth-telling realm, I had to cut through a corner of Brume, and by the time I got to the border between Brume and Fen, my feet were aching. I would have to travel from here on standard pathways because moonways didn't last long in Fen—their magic dissipated over time as the swamplands shifted and moved, so they were too dangerous to attempt. I would have to travel to the capital city of Isslia the old-fashioned way.

But that could wait until tomorrow. Night had fallen, and a chill ran through me. I wrapped my cloak tightly around me and started walking through the fog of Brume, heading north. The moment I crossed from Brume into the Realm of Fen was like plunging into cold water. My shivering intensified, and I immediately wanted to unburden every secret in my heart. I looked around for somebody to talk to, so I could blabber like a fool about every thought that crossed my mind.

It was impossible to tell a lie within the borders of Fen. That was a fact, for the local fae and for tourists too. But the locals had natural immunity to the most potent effects of the realm. Whereas for most visitors, it was impossible to keep truths bottled up. Just practicing the restraint of not speaking was a challenge in this complicated realm.

Thank Gaia I was alone because I'm sure my face was contorting under the pressure of keeping my thoughts bottled inside me. To distract myself, I focused on my surroundings. A massive forest stretched before me as far as the eye could see; ancient trees that had seen generations come and go stood tall and proud. One of the trees looked like a kindly old gentlefae, and I opened my mouth to tell it that I longed to be respected for something other than my beauty.

I just caught myself in time. Years of practicing at being an ice queen with no emotions were finally coming in handy, although my resistance to the realm's lure was shaky at best.

I made my way along a winding path, battling against my tongue every step of the way. I ended up in a village nestled among the tees. As I got closer, the sound of music and laughter reached me; it seemed to be coming from an inn near the center of town, so I headed toward it. After a few wrong turns, I reached it. The feeling of being lost was so foreign and unusual—mostly, fae had internal maps of every place we visited. But none of my friends had ever been to this village before, so they couldn't transmit me the map.

I walked into The Dripping Icicle, this cozy old tavern buzzing with activity. The sign above the door creaked as a light breeze brushed by, showing off a freshly-painted picture of an icicle over a flame. Inside, the air was filled with the scent of ale and the smoke from a crackling fire in the corner. The place had a handful of folks scattered around, either sitting at tables or leaning against the bar. It definitely had a more down-to-earth vibe than where I usually hung out. Taking a deep breath, I walked up to the bar where an older fae with bright red hair was serving drinks to her customers.

"Good evening," I said when she looked up. I planned to leave it at that, but my mouth ran away under the effects of the realm. "I am Princess Gabrelle Allura, one of the five heirs to the thrones of Verda, and I intend to visit with your crown prince and—"

I managed to cut myself off abruptly, but only by slamming my hand across my mouth.

The bartender grinned at me. "Don't worry about it, love. Folks from out of town always spill their load to me. I'm used to it. What are you plannin' on doin' tomorrow?"

Some nearby conversations had died down, and I could see I was the subject of a joke. The locals all wanted to hear whatever truths I was ready to spill. Especially since I'd just admitted to being a Princess of Verda, which was completely unplanned.

I squared my shoulders, summoning every ounce of emotional control I possessed. Other foreigners may be unable to hold their tongues, but I was Gabrelle, the ice queen. Speaking slowly, so I could run every syllable past my cerebral cortex, I said, "Tomorrow, I shall travel to Isslia."

There. I was practically sweating with the effort to keep myself from sharing anything else. The patrons looked at me hopefully for a few more moments, then lost interest and turned aside, resuming their conversations.

The female behind the bar looked me up and down. "Spent a

bit of time here, have you? That's impressive control. Almost like a native."

Determined to improve my control even more, I slowly opened my mouth. "Thank you." I tried to make it sound leisurely, but it was a far cry from my usual ice-bitch self.

The female chuckled. "Name's Lida. I own the place. Drink?"

With a sigh of relief, I nodded. "Yes, please." The words came out stunted and forced, but at least they weren't followed by a confession of how I wiped myself after taking a shit.

Lida pulled down a bottle of amber liquid from the shelf and poured me a generous measure. She set it in front of me with a smile. "You don't look like a beer drinker, and I'm fresh out of Dionysus wine, so this will have to do."

She was teasing me, but she wasn't far off. I would have preferred a glass of refined wine, but I would make do with rough whiskey.

I didn't have to search far for my currency; Verdan coins weren't much used in Fen, so I'd brought a purse. I handed the fae a silver coin stamped with a large, creepy eye that symbolized truth and vigilance, the twin values of the realm.

Lida smiled down at the coin. "You'll be after lodgings too, will you? I've a room upstairs that will do you nicely. What's the most you will pay?"

What was the most I would pay? What an odd negotiation tactic. I had no intention of confessing how much I would spend for a night. I opened my mouth to bargain, but the whiskey loosened my control, so I said, "I'll give you the entire silver purse for one night in your inn."

The female threw back her head and howled at the ceiling in laughter. "Goodness, you are a desperate one!"

Fuck. Now I'd admitted that I would give this female

everything I had just to relax in a comfortable bed, she would take me for all I was worth.

But she surprised me by saying, "I would have accepted as little as a tin penny. Would you be happy to settle for a silver coin?"

"Yes," I practically shouted, my control spent. This was the oddest negotiation I'd ever participated in. Rather than me starting low and she starting high, we'd reversed the roles. I'd confessed how much I would spend, and she'd told me how little she would accept.

Goodness, navigating through the truth-telling realm would be trickier than I expected.

I stared longingly at the half-measure of whiskey remaining in my glass.

"Wanna finish that drink, love?" Lida asked.

I nodded. "Yes, but I don't want to loosen my tongue any more than it already is. I like your hair, by the way." I clapped a hand across my mouth. My ice princess cool was evaporating fast.

"Shoot it, then run," Lida told me. "Here's the key to your room. It's on the top floor. I've already sent your bags up."

This bartending lesser fae was a useful guide for navigating the truth-telling realm. I nodded at her, slammed the drink, and bolted for the door. But just as I reached the exit, I couldn't help yelling, "You're wonderful" to Lida before I could get clear.

I wasn't in the habit of confessing my admiration of anyone, and certainly not lesser fae from other realms.

Goodness, I had a lot to learn about control.

Upstairs, the little bedroom was adequate. It had a snug charm, complete with a softly glowing fireplace to take off the night's chill. Best of all, the door had a sturdy lock. I fell into the bed with relief, and despite my racing thoughts, I was asleep within moments.

But when a loud crash sounded outside my door, I woke with a thudding heart.

Gabrelle

I jolted awake at the thump on the door, my heart racing as I heard someone fumbling with the lock. I sprang up from the bed and reached for the dagger I had stashed under my pillow. The door finally gave way with a creak, revealing a tall and sturdy male. He was lightly lined with wrinkles and had a rugged look, with unkempt hair and a scraggly beard. His sinister aura made me uneasy.

He scanned the room before his eyes settled on me. "Well, well, well. What do we have here?" he said with a deep and gravelly voice. "A little princess all by herself in a dingy tavern. Ain't that a sight to see."

Clutching my dagger tightly, I held my ground and demanded, "Who the hell are you? What do you want?"

He chuckled, taking a step closer to me. "Relax, princess. I ain't here to hurt you. At least, not unless you play hard to get. I heard that a pretty little thing was staying here, and I figure I'd have a go on her." His brown eyes were hooded with lust as he took me in. "They weren't joking, either. You're the sexiest little meal I've ever seen."

The male lunged at me, and his stale beer breath coated my skin in the moment before I ducked aside. I had the advantage of many years of hand-to-hand combat training. And sobriety.

I ducked under his outstretched arm and aimed a swift kick at the back of his knee. His leg buckled under him, and he stumbled forward, crashing into the bed. I took advantage of his momentary confusion and lunged forward, plunging my dagger into his side.

He let out a guttural cry of pain, but I didn't stop there. Twisting the blade, I yanked it free, a sick satisfaction washing over me as his blood stained the sheets. He crumpled to the ground, clutching his wound as he gasped for breath. I stood over him, panting and trembling with adrenaline.

"I'm not a damn meal," I spat at him. "And I will not be intimidated by the likes of you."

"You fucking bitch," he roared, anger and pain igniting his eyes. "You're gonna pay for this!"

I put my bare heel into the knife wound in his side and leaned my weight onto it. "You should have thought twice before trying to take advantage of me," I said, my voice cold and emotionless. "Now, I suggest you leave before I finish what you started."

He glared up at me with hate-filled eyes, but eventually, he staggered to his feet and stumbled across the room.

"Wait," I called, and he sagged against the doorway. This was an excellent opportunity to experiment with the extent of my powers in this realm.

I'd only been in Fen once, and that was before my skills with Lure had developed. So I had no idea if I could use that power here or if it counted as lying and was forbidden by Gaia.

I laced my voice with coercive power. "Apologize to me."

I studied the fae to see the effect of my magic. When I attempted to Lure fae with strong minds, I could see the struggle in their eyes as they attempted to fight my commands.

They never succeeded, but at least they tried.

Not this male. He stood upright and turned to face me with a slack jaw and vacant eyes. "I'm sorry for trying to take advantage of you."

Arching an eyebrow at his robotic response, I smirked. Good. It seemed like I could still use my compelling powers in this realm. "Apologize for being a weak and pathetic man-slave."

"I'm sorry for being a weak and pathetic man-slave."

I had little use for this male, but there was one more experiment he could help me with. I slanted my eyes at him. "Are you married?"

"Yes, princess."

I smiled wickedly, letting him see the plan form on my face so he could begin to panic. "Tell me a lie," I compelled him with Lure. "Tell me you aren't married."

He couldn't ignore the command. Yet he couldn't lie. He opened his mouth to speak, but his tongue appeared to be locked. His face turned red, and he began gurgling, foaming at the mouth until spit ran down his chin. It was a pleasure to watch such a prick suffer.

But I didn't want to kill him. That would be difficult to explain away. "Stop," I commanded, and he immediately relaxed, his face returning to its usual egg-white color, his breaths ragged.

"Go home and be good to your wife."

"Yes, princess."

"Now get the hell out," I commanded, and he stumbled away, slamming the door shut. I let out an explosive sigh. I wasn't sure how big of a mess I'd found, how big of a problem it was that I'd just beaten and stabbed a local, how difficult that would make it for me to leave the village.

GABRELLE

I tossed and turned in an uneasy sleep, plagued by dreams of a burning village and a crumbling kingdom. As the morning sunlight streamed through the window, I woke up with a start. I could hear voices coming from the common area, and I quickly got dressed in a pair of designer jeans with an off-the-shoulder shirt and a leather jacket.

I joined the other patrons of the tavern for breakfast. The local farmers were finishing off big breakfasts of steak, eggs, and ale. I ordered a bowl of plumple porridge and a muddy coffee and kept to myself.

Lida, wiping the table with a rag, caught my attention. "Did you sleep well?"

My natural reply of "Yes, fine" thickened in my throat before I could utter it, growing into a spiky ball that lodged in my flesh. The harder I tried to force the words out, the colder the spiked ball in my throat became until I could barely breathe.

"Relax, princess," Lida said with a chuckle. "We don't usually ask questions like that round these parts, but I was trying to make you feel at home."

The barfae wandered off to serve another customer, and I was forced to reconsider my feelings toward her. I had no doubt she was trying to make me choke on a small lie, not make me feel at home.

Tossing my payment of Fen silver on the counter, I made my way out, levitating my bags along. Moonways were of limited use in Fen because the safe roads kept shifting and changing as they fought back against the perilous swamps. A moonway along a safe track one day might pass through a deadly swamp the next. So it was safer to use the roads.

Which meant a long, boring walk to Isslia.

The road twisted through the swamp's deadly heart, carving

a narrow path through the trees and reeds. Giant toads, striped and green, eyed me from the muddy track. They were bigger than true dogs and as nasty as croconads. They could swallow a faeling whole—and they often did.

I cast a spell around me to warn of any predators that might sneak up on me. My spellwork wasn't amazing, despite all the lessons we heirs received. I was pretty good at the easy ones, like smoothing down hair or removing spots of dirt from silk, but for combat, I relied on my bow and arrow or Lure.

But neither of those was useful against a threat I couldn't see. Hence the warning spell bubble. It made my skin tingle and the back of my neck itch, which at least kept me alert.

I spent the day walking, trying to avoid the mud underfoot and attempting to ignore the swamp's manure perfume.

An osquip set off my perimeter spell, sliding through the mud with its long neck and short alligator body. Its rough scales were the color of old bone. It was a predator, but a lazy one, preferring to wait by the road for an easy meal to wander by rather than hunt.

I skirted it slowly, hoping it wouldn't notice me, but it whipped its head toward me. Its mouth opened impossibly wide, revealing rows of jagged teeth, and it lunged at me with a roar.

I shifted to the side, leaping over a log and pulling out an arrow from my quiver within the space of a breath. I loosed my weapon and hit the creature in its right eye. It wouldn't kill it, but it was enough to keep it occupied while I scurried past.

I patted down my leather jacket and muttered an incantation to vacuum the mud off my jeans. I sighed dramatically, although nobody was around to hear it. I was Princess Allura from Verda. I did not like to scurry.

GABRELLE

After hours of staying alert, enduring aching feet, and a blister forming on my big toe, the swampy land gradually transformed into a more solid terrain. At last, I reached Isslia, the capital city of Fen.

The last time I'd been here, I'd been brought by Mother's Fliers. But this time, I had insisted on making my own way, which was clearly an idiotic mistake, and not one I would make again.

I cleaned myself off and then made my way to the Court, a sunken circular building that looked like a giant had squished an ice cube into the mud.

The entrance was downright absurd and drove me nuts. You had to leap off the solid ground into the central hollow, and if Gaia was feeling generous, you'd float down gently to the central area ten floors below.

The point was that in throwing yourself at Gaia's mercy, you shed dishonesty, and by floating down past all those windows, you opened yourself to inspection. It was all very well, but it was almost impossible to fall gracefully, so all you really shed was your dignity, and all you opened yourself to was ridicule.

Nevertheless, I leaped into the air, confident Gaia would catch me and let me drop gently. I landed with more of a thud than I wanted, but I quickly muttered "Efflanio levitas" to ensure my hair settled elegantly. I was here to petition the crown prince, so I needed my armor.

A severe-looking male with a straight spine and narrow lips greeted me. "Good afternoon. What is your business here?"

I swallowed my sigh. Clearly, it would be too much to ask for a cordial welcome. "I would like a polite welcome and a warm drink," I snapped. "I am Princess Allura, and I have been walking all day."

Straight-spine tilted his head, keeping his expression neutral. "What is your business here, Princess Allura?"

If it didn't ruin my chances at finding the Stone of Veritas, I would Lure this prick to fetch me a warm meal and a Healer. Instead, I placed a careful smile on my face. "I would like to see Prince Thorne Sanctus."

Straight-spine nodded. "Follow me. I will find out if he is willing to receive you."

He'd damn well better be.

Thorne

Before their deaths, my mother and sister lived in the Ice Palace, but I preferred to sleep in my chambers within the Court of Fen. My rooms were on the highest floor of the Court, just below ground level. From my balcony, I could see all the way down into the circular pit, ten stories deep and a hundred yards across.

The grand structure was underground to protect against frequent ice storms, although the skies were clear today. On bright days, the pale bluestone of the circular walls glistened like ice, and the looming statues shone.

It was too early for anybody to be out in the central courtyard, which was still cloaked in shadow, but windows around the pit blinked on as fae awakened for the day.

A knock sounded on my bedroom door. "Come," I commanded.

Staven Jeffers, a fae as old as time with wrinkles on his wrinkles, entered the room. His yellow hair was fading white, and he moved slowly as though his years were sandbags. "The prisoner is ready for interrogation," he said.

Let her wait, I thought dismissively. I had no desire to rush and meet with the prisoner.

I was already dressed, wearing ice-blue robes as befitted the crown prince, but I was in no rush to meet with the prisoner. I took a leisurely breakfast, then a long walk through the Court, letting her stew in fear.

Then, after lunch, I pushed back my blue-black hair to ensure the scar that ran across my left eye down to my jawbone was clearly visible. It tended to intimidate.

The Interrogation Chamber was a comfortable space, softly lit by wall sconces of faelight, encouraging prisoners to relax. The walls were painted a soft green, with a hammock strung up on one side and comfortable beanbags in bright colors throughout. A large U-shaped couch filled the center of the room with plush cushions and inviting armrests. A large bunch of flowers on the coffee table wafted a sweet perfume.

We wanted prisoners to relax. After all, this room was warded with complex spells that were boosted every week by the realm's most potent Weavers. It was the only room in Fen where one could speak a lie.

I pushed into the room and nodded briefly at the large mirror behind which my observers sat. The prisoner was a young female with long wavy hair of the purest gold. She turned her burning golden eyes on me.

"Good morning, Preya," I began, crossing the room to where she lounged on the couch and settling into a seat across from her. "Is that your real name?"

"Yes," she said unhesitatingly.

Preya was from the Realm of Verda, also known as the Realm of Greed and Excess. Fae from Verda were liars and reprobates, without a single moral among the entire population. Verdan fae would sell out their own mothers for a shiny gold coin. That was the reason my political enemies used them as spies.

"Have you been in Fen for long?"

The female blinked at me and flicked a lock of golden hair behind her shoulder. "Look, are we just here to chitchat? This room is nice and all, but I'd really prefer to take my leave."

I smiled, pushing aside my ice-blue robes and leaning forward on one black-clad knee. "Of course you would. I just want to ask you a few questions first. Then you will be free to leave," I lied.

The lie tasted like ash on my tongue. It tasted like sin. Like I'd sold my soul to the God of Death, Mortia.

She relaxed at my words. She didn't know the secret of the Interrogation Chamber. She didn't know this was the one place in Fen you could lie.

She leaned back against the purple cushions of the couch, spreading her arms along the backrest. "Okay, shoot."

I asked about her activities in Isslia, where she spent her time, and where she laid her head. Small questions with inconsequential answers. Soon, her natural reflexes as a lying Verdan kicked in, and she told her first lie. It spilled from her lips as smoothly as honey, and her golden eyes sparked as soon as she realized it.

She could lie. She felt powerful.

Time to move on to the bigger questions. The ones she would refuse to answer in any other room in Fen.

"Do you work for Erevan Reissan?" I asked.

She only paused a moment before her dishonest lips moved in their well-greased lies. "No."

Erevan was my political rival. I was the Crown Prince of Fen, but only on a technicality. My sister, Arrow, had been trained for the role from birth. So with her untimely death and then my mother's, my political rivals were circling me like coyotes.

"Have you ever met with him?"

Her lies flowed like wine. "No, I have never met Erevan Reissan or any of his friends and family."

I leaned back in my seat, studying her carefully. Her lies were seamless, as I knew they would be. It was time to push her a bit more. "What about the night of the fire at the Ironworks? Were you there?"

She hesitated for a moment before shaking her head. "No, I wasn't."

But her eyes flickered slightly, betraying her. Closing on the truth, I leaned forward, locking my gaze with hers. "Preya, you realize that lying to me will not end well for you?"

She smirked, a cocky grin on her face. "I can't lie in Fen, remember. It's impossible."

I grimaced, feeling my scar pinch across my face. "Indeed, Preya. Welcome to Fen, where lying is not an option," I stated, my voice dripping with a dangerous undertone. Pausing for a moment, I relaxed back, a cold smile playing on my lips. "In fact, lying here is punishable by death."

Her eyes darted to the door. "Uh-huh."

"Did you know that?" I asked.

"Yes."

"What a shame."

She glanced up at me, her golden eyes clouded in confusion. "Why?"

I stood then, flaring out my ice-blue robes and heading to the door. "Walk with me," I commanded.

We stepped through the door, me with my lying prey in tow. As soon as we were in the corridor, through the intricately woven spells that isolated the Interrogation Chamber, the natural order of the realm was reestablished. We could not lie.

The air in the corridor held a tinge of burning wood, an ominous reminder that justice in Fen came with a price.

"Tell me again," I said casually. "Do you work for Erevan Reissan?"

Without hesitation, believing herself immune to the realm's magic, Preya opened her lips to lie, and the truth spilled out. "Yes. I work for Erevan to spy on you. My mission is to find some dirt on you that will prove you unfit to rule, so he can take the throne next month."

The syllables bubbled out of her mouth like she was a rabid dog, and as soon as she could stop herself from talking, she clapped a hand over her mouth, her golden eyes wide.

I smiled coldly, my anger simmering just beneath the surface. "Thank you for your honesty, Preya," I said, turning to face her. "However, as you know, lying in Fen is a capital offense. And you just admitted to working with my political rival to undermine me."

She backed away from me, her eyes darting around as though looking for a way to escape. "Please, let me go. I didn't..."

I gestured to the guards who had been waiting outside the Interrogation Chamber. "Escort her away," I commanded, my voice frosted with ice. "Ensure a swift execution."

Preya screamed as the guards dragged her away, her golden hair flying out behind her. As soon as she was out of sight, I leaned against the wall, my heart beating fast. I hated that I had to use the Interrogation Chamber to get to the truth, hated that I had to tell my own lies. But in a realm as dangerous as Fen, the truth was always worth the cost.

Guilt pressed against my skull, but I shoved it aside. I was the Crown Prince of Fen, and I had a duty to protect my fae and my realm from any threats, no matter the price. I would do what it took to keep my throne, even if it meant sacrificing a few liars.

Lost in my thoughts, I walked briskly down the corridor. The mourning period for my mother was over. It had been a long month of sitting in my grief and wallowing in the feeling of loss, trying to figure out how to proceed. She was gone. Arrow was gone. And I was supposed to lead.

But now, in the blink of an eye, the official mourning period was over, and I had to push forward. Had to find a way through the political maze and get myself onto the crown, as Mother wanted.

I pushed open my bedroom door and found Staven Jeffers already inside, standing hunched beside a marble statue of my mother.

"Yes? What is it?"

Staven gestured toward a basket filled with sweet pastries and hot tea—a traditional way to end mourning in Fen. They honey-spiced treats smelled delicious, and my mouth watered.

"Your Highness," he said formally. "I have come to inform you that the mourning period for your mother has ended." He paused for a moment before continuing in a softer tone. "And your first visitor arrived moments ago."

Visitors were strictly forbidden during mourning, but now the floodgates were released, I anticipated a deluge of well-wishers and sycophants.

"Who is the visitor?"

"Her Royal Highness, Princess Gabrelle Allura from the Realm of Verda."

My mouth dried up, and my appetite fled. My first visitor was a lying royal brat from the biggest den of dishonesty in all of Arathay. She was here to demand something of me, I was sure. A favor. A squirming request. A deceitful demand.

Anger bubbled through my veins. If it didn't start a fucking war, I would find an excuse to execute her too.

Gabrelle

The thin-lipped, straight-spined, rudely-spoken male informed me that Prince Sanctus would see me in half an hour and demanded that I wait on a wooden chair in a draughty corner. He didn't even offer me a glass of water. At least it gave me the opportunity to change into a more appropriate outfit—a white sleeveless gown with a high collar that was both sexy and modest. But I hated having to change in a public restroom.

By the time the serving fae returned to collect me, I was in a seriously foul mood. My ice bitch self had melted, burned away into steam, and I was ready to shout at whoever I met.

But my realm needed me to do better than that. Needed a cool-headed negotiator, not a hothead. So I took a deep breath, exhaling the fire in my veins, and channeled my inner ice queen. I'd freeze the molten fury within me, presenting a flawless facade of cool, calm control.

"Wonderful," I said from beneath my mask of contentment. "I am so pleased I can finally meet with him." That, at least, was no lie.

The serving fae led me along a white marble hallway to a vast, austere throne room with a long walkway leading to a dais in the center. Pillars of smooth bluestone reached a ceiling decorated with a mosaic of intricate snowflake patterns. On the platform stood an imposing throne of solid ice, its arms and legs shaped like icicles. In front of it stood a pedestal with a single book, its pages bound in frost.

The crown prince sat atop the ice throne. A ragged scar ran down over one eye all the way to his jawline, a raw, blistered red that stood out against his light tan. His hair danced between blue and black as he moved his head, watching me approach.

Walking up to that ice throne gave me the chills. I had to fight the temptation to wrap my jacket tighter around me for some warmth. "Good afternoon, Prince Sanctus," I said with a supernova smile. "I am Princess Gabrelle Allura, heir of House Allura, contender to the Alluran throne in the Realm of Verda."

I might as well go for my full title. Pricks like the Sanctus prince liked theatrics.

"I know who you are," he snarled, not even bothering to gift me a smile. "What I don't know is why you've come here. Although I have my suspicions."

My cold hard fury helped keep my tongue in check. It allowed me perfect control over my words, despite being in the babbling realm.

I cocked my head. "What an unusual choice of word. Suspicions. It almost seems as though you don't trust me." I let my smile grow. "I certainly hope that isn't the case." My tone was light, and I intended to set up banter between us and build rapport. After all, I volunteered for this mission because I was the only heir who didn't have a terrible relationship with Thorne Sanctus.

"Do you really?" The prince asked. "What reason could I possibly have to trust you?"

Damn, this trust-building conversation was going south fast.

In a last-ditch attempt, I flicked a lock of my long, wavy pink hair over my shoulder in an orchestrated mannerism I had perfected over the years. I glanced away, allowing the prince to look me up and down and absorb my physical perfection. "Well," I said, giving him ample warning that I was about to look back at him so he could avert his gaze. "You are a crown prince, and I am a crown princess. We will jointly rule Arathay at some point in the future." I smiled again, though his blue-black gaze was murderous, and he showed no signs of being swayed by my charms. "You and I both know what it is to be born to greatness. We have a lot in common and good reason to trust one another."

I felt proud of that little speech. My anger was the perfect antidote to the realm's tongue-loosening magic, and my words navigated the political landscape without speaking a single lie. We had good reason to trust one another, that was true enough. No need to mention the full truth that I didn't trust him an iota.

He did not look impressed. "Do you really think I will fall for such a cheap ploy?" He sneered. "You can talk all you want about trust and commonalities, but it doesn't change the fact that I am not stupid enough to be taken in by flattery or pretty words. You have come here with some other purpose than just visiting."

My jaw clenched, but I forced my face to remain calm. "That much is true," I said carefully. "I came here to present my condolences on the loss of your mother. I represent Queen Allura and the other ruling Houses of Verda in giving you our sincere condolences."

The prince's eyes glittered dangerously as he leaned forward, resting his elbows on the arms of the throne and folding his hands beneath his chin. "And you weaseled your way into my throne room on the first day of the mourning's end. How convenient."

His tone was clipped and sharp, and although he tried desperately to keep up the regal façade, he had poor control over himself. He was rude and unsophisticated, and I couldn't bring myself to respect him. I certainly couldn't tell him he would make an excellent ruler, for Gaia wouldn't allow me to lie.

"There's nothing convenient about it," I said airily. My anger was being pacified by his roaring rage, and with every display of my control, I pissed him off further. I was loving it. "We know your Fen customs, and I timed my visit perfectly."

His scowl darkened, and his entire body tensed. His scar stood out red and angry against his light brown skin. "Suspiciously well," he spat.

Diplomacy might be required to deal with this rude brat, but I still needed to put him in his place. "Oh, dear prince," I said, feigning disappointment. "Is 'suspicious' the only word in your vocabulary? I expected better manners of the Crown Prince of Fen."

He leaned forward, his scarred face twisted into a sneer. "Manners don't get you far in this realm, princess. We care about more than just sex and coin, which may shock you."

"Very little shocks me," I said, making a show of inspecting my perfectly manicured fingernails. "Particularly not low-grade insults worthy of a tawdry bar."

"It's not the grade of the insult that matters," the prince said darkly, "but the worthiness of the recipient. And you, my lady, are worthy."

My jaw fell slightly before I could regain control. How dare he insult me so boldly? What kind of an animal was he to tear down a visiting princess who was only here to pass on the condolences of her realm? My careful mask only slipped briefly, and I was sure he didn't notice. But it took me several seconds of deep breathing—and calmly pretending to inspect my cuticles—to find my voice.

This prince was the epitome of rudeness, boorishness, and poor breeding. He didn't deserve to be in my presence, let alone sitting on a throne while I stood on aching feet.

"I wish I could tell you that your hospitality outshone my expectations," I said carefully, making sure to speak the truth. "But it has met them exactly."

The prince seemed to be on surer ground now that we were trading barbed courtesies. He leaned back in his ice throne, and the angry red scar subsided. With a sweep of his arms, he swept his ice-blue cloak behind his leg, revealing rough black pants and a very I-don't-give-a-fuck attitude toward fashion. "Your method of passing on your condolences is rather unorthodox," he remarked calmly.

Dammit. I'd lost the upper ground in this conversation. I'd started out as the more relaxed fae, but now I was flustered and losing the battle of wits.

Plus, I was losing sight of my real reason for being here. Sure, I represented the Realm of Verda in giving condolences to Prince Sanctus on the loss of his mother, but I was also here to butter him up, become his best buddy, and convince him to hand over the Stone of Veritas for the good of the fae realm.

This prick was unlikely to do any of those things. And he didn't strike me as the type to give up anything for the greater good. He was just an entitled brat who'd missed all the lessons on courtly manners. "That was an error on my part," I said. "I never intended to be so clumsy at providing you with solace."

Sanctus leaned his elbows on the icicle armrests of his throne. "Is that an apology?"

That felt like a trick question. I hadn't meant it as an apology, but if I said 'no,' the rude dick would accuse me of not being sorry. But I couldn't say 'yes' and still speak the truth. I sat on the question for a few moments before replying, "I apologize, Prince Sanctus."

His response was like a slap in the face. "I do not accept your apology, Princess Allura."

Again, my composure was shaken by his rudeness. Twice within ten minutes, the carefully constructed mask I'd spent a lifetime building had cracked.

But what he said next shattered it.

Thorne

The female before me was far worse than the one I'd just executed for lying and treason. The dead female merely aided and abetted a political rival to take my throne—the princess *was* a political rival, cunningly lurking in the shadows of power. Oh, the joys of royal life.

And her skills at deceit had been honed through years of training in the biggest cesspit of all—the Verdan Court.

"Your beauty doesn't impress me, princess, and your charms are worth nothing here." I declared, rising from my throne and descending the steps with a purposeful stride. I towered over her, adding an extra touch of intimidation to my presence. "You have lived your whole life skating by on your looks, getting everything your little heart desires, leaping from whim to whim with no regard for others. Well, my sweet little liar, I don't even see your beauty. I only see a fae's true worth. And, like every other heir from your disgraceful realm, you are worth nothing."

The simpering princess finally gave a response that was calculated and rehearsed. Her whole body shook for a moment, withering under my contempt. I'm sure she had never been spoken to like that in her entire sheltered life.

I was in a foul mood to begin with, but I'm afraid I enjoyed watching her fall apart. The princess from the house of beauty, with her perfectly coiffured hair, pristine white gown, manufactured expressions, and crafted movements. It all fell away from her. For one shining, brief moment, she was exposed to me, her flaws glowing and her mask shattered.

But just as fast, she regained her cool. She lifted her chin and stared right back at me, not a hint of fear in her eyes. "Your highness," she said, her voice calm and steady. "You judge me without knowing me. But that is to be expected from someone who only values power and strength."

I chuckled, finding her boldness amusing. "And what do you value, princess? Your precious beauty? Your courtly manners?"

"I value justice and fair rule," she replied, her voice unwavering. "I value peace. And I value hospitality."

I raised an eyebrow, yes, hospitality," I scoffed, rolling my eyes dramatically. "It's all about extravagant feasts and bottomless goblets, right? Just like every other degenerate from the Realm of Greed and Excess."

"Hospitality is not about indulgence but simple manners," she said, a hint of anger creeping into her voice. "Hospitality between realms is an aid to peace. But it is clear that peace is not high on your agenda."

"You, a pretty princess in a pretty gown, who is nothing more than a clotheshorse with a smile, you dare to lecture me on politics?" The balance between us was tilting again as my emotions overtook me, and her heartbeat calmed. She knew nothing of the political turmoil that threatened me, the creeping advances of Erevan Reissan, who wanted to boot me from the throne before I even sat on it.

She clearly grasped the shifting balance between us, too, as a leisurely smile crept over her face. "I am not some delicate flower to be dismissed and tossed aside at your whim," she said coolly. "I am a princess of Verda, trained in politics and warfare from the day I was born."

She let the implication of her words sit in the air between us like stale breath. She was born for the throne and had been trained for it. I was not. I was born as the younger brother of the crown princess. My parents never intended for me to rule and did not train me like my older sister, Arrow.

Princess Allura reached out a slender brown finger and traced it down the scar on my face, tracking the ridged tissue from my eye to my jaw and leaving a trail of ice on my skin. A faint passionfruit scent accompanied the gesture. "Arrow always made an effort to be hospitable," she said.

How dare this female touch me? How dare she come to my throne room and taunt me with memories of my dead sister? The sister who died in the Realm of Verda.

I smacked her hand off my face, barely able to contain my rage. "Arrow would become queen if she hadn't had the misfortune to visit your realm," I spat. It wouldn't be truthful to say that it was House Allura's fault my sister died, but I willed her to read that implication from my words.

The princess stared at me for a moment before she spoke. "Do not blame your sister's death on the entire realm, your highness. That would be unjust." Her voice was measured, but a flicker of anger in her eyes was intriguing.

"Unjust?" I repeated with a sneer. "You were there the day she died, were you not? You were at the Ascension party when the Shadow Walkers attacked."

Princess Allura's eyes widened, and for a moment, I thought I saw a flicker of fear in them. But it was quickly replaced by a steely resolve that I could almost admire if I wasn't so damn furious at her.

"I was there," she said, her voice low and even. "And the Shadow Walkers are part of the reason for my visit to Fen. It is now more important than ever for the fae realms to unite against our common enemy."

We stared at each other in the heavy silence that followed. Princess Allura's expression softened as she shifted her gaze away, her eyes becoming distant and unfocused. Her eyebrows drew together, and her lips pursed in concentration. There was a stillness to her body as she sunk into her thoughts.

Tension padded the air around us, making it thick. I steeled myself for her next words, expecting some grand declaration or announcement about the Realm of Verda's intentions. She seemed to be thinking of something, on the verge of asking an important question. But then she stepped back and bowed her head in a gesture of respect.

"Let us speak of more pleasant things," she said with a courteous smile.

Disappointment ticked my jaw that her words weren't more meaningful, but I'd had enough sparring for one day.

"Somebody will prepare you rooms to sleep in for the night." I hoped she was intelligent enough to understand the implication that I didn't want her staying any longer than a single night. "And somebody will bring you food," I added as an afterthought. "So you can't accuse me of being inhospitable."

As she walked away, I felt a strange pull toward her. It wasn't attraction but something else entirely. Perhaps it was the challenge she posed to me or the respect she showed in the face of my anger. Princess Allura was a puzzle I didn't want to solve.

Her hips swayed with each step, and, despite having traveled all day, her dress was pristine white and her brown skin as fresh as if she'd stepped out of a spring. That was her true weapon and her true armor.

But I meant what I said. I didn't see beauty, and I didn't care how attractive that female was. She was nothing but an emissary from the Realm of Greed and Excess, Verda.

I watched the door close behind her, then spun and headed in the opposite direction, my footsteps echoing in the vast hall. I skirted the ice throne, which I had no business sitting on until after the coronation, and headed toward the rear exit.

The Realm of Verda was a potential ally, but one that I didn't trust. The memory of my sister's death still burned hot in my chest. Memories of her flooded my mind, the sound of her laughter, the warmth of her embrace. She had been my confidante, my closest friend. And then she was gone, snatched away during an attack on Verdan soil. And I could never forgive those who should have protected her.

Thorne

To decompress after my day of irritating conversations and foreign spies, I went for a walk.

My rooms were on the top floor of the Court, just below ground level, with a private staircase that led me to the streets above, right into an alley behind a shop selling roasted nuts and spices.

As I exited through my hidden door, I closed my eyes against the warm sunshine and breathed deeply.

In Fen, we didn't have seasons, just eternal summer. It was always warm in Isslia, the sun bright and big and powerful, glittering off the buildings and streets. "Well, except for those occasional ice storms that hit us out of nowhere, coming from a clear blue sky and leaving pockmarks or gashes in any exposed flesh.

That was one of my favorite things about Isslia. It always threw off visitors, who kept scanning the sky for signs of an incoming storm, unable to grasp that they came without warning.

I liked that. The change was inevitable, unpredictable, rare, and slammed everybody equally.

Twilight fell as I walked, and the city of Isslia gleamed, a work of art crafted by a master engineer. The streets had a strange beauty as they wound around squat buildings of grey-white stone and bluestone, curving and turning like icy rivers. The city's protective walls, built to hold off the worst of the ice storms, were constructed of the same stone, but they stood higher and stronger than the other structures, a bright blue-silver in the twilight, a coat of armor against the elements.

My mind drifted to my sister and how she used to burst into laughter when I told her stories or playfully teased her about being too serious. The pain of her absence was still raw and heavy in my heart.

My mother was devastated, unable to move past the grief of losing a faeling, especially in such a vicious and violent way. She never recovered from the shock and passed away shortly after my sister's death. Killed by the Realm of Verda as surely as Arrow was.

My mother's death had been even harder on me than Arrow's. She had been the only one who truly understood me, the only fae who saw me for who I truly was. A large part of me died with her.

I rounded a corner and paused to let a creaking wagon pass. A faeling raced beside it, trying to outrun the clattering hooves of the horses, shrieking in laughter.

I was alone in this city. This beautiful city filled with enemies and rivals on every side. What should have been a smooth transition of power from my mother to my sister, who had trained her whole life for the role of queen, was now uncertain.

My mission was crystal clear, but it felt overwhelming: I had to do my mother proud and secure the Fen throne for our family.

And then, just as I rounded the next corner, I bumped into none other than Erevan—my biggest political rival for the throne. His face was a mask of disdain, and he stepped back, sizing me up. Then his mouth twisted in a smirk, and his butterscotch eyes glinted in the fading light.

"What are you doing here?" he asked in a low voice. He seemed to be enjoying himself, taking pleasure in this unexpected meeting of enemies. "I thought you'd be cowering inside, as far away from the common fae as possible."

He was trying to bait me, but I refused to take it. I stood tall and met his gaze with a level one of my own, tilting my chin slightly, daring him to challenge me.

But I had something over him today after my morning in the Interrogation Chamber. "I caught your spy from Verda, Erevan," I said abruptly. "She has been executed for treason."

His expression changed briefly before settling again into that contemptuous smirk that infuriated me so much. His butterscotch hair shone brightly under the setting sun. "Which one?"

I snapped my head around. "What?"

"'Which spy, Thorne?" His butterscotch eyes flashed with contempt. "You didn't think I only had one, did you?"

"How many spies do you have?" I demanded.

My enemy tutted as though he was reprimanding a naughty toddler. "Now, now, Thorne, surely you don't think I'll spill all my secrets just because you asked?" He folded his arms across his chest. "And you didn't even ask nicely."

Erevan was a smidge taller than me and was trying to intimidate me with his size and imposing presence. I couldn't afford to dismiss him because he came from an influential family with deep connections, and I was alone.

My mind raced as I frantically tried to remember my mother's lessons about handling political rivals like him:

remain composed and listen attentively to what they say without reacting too quickly or impulsively.

But my mother had never prepared me for dealing with someone like Erevan. He was too unpredictable, too dangerous. The tension between us was thick, like a storm cloud about to burst. I had to tread carefully.

I sucked in a breath, reminding myself to stay calm. "Tell me," I said through gritted teeth. "How may spies do you have?"

Erevan chuckled, clearly enjoying himself. "Oh, Thorne, you're so eager to learn." He leaned in closer, his breath hot against my ear. "But so lacking in subtlety or skill. I think I'll keep my secrets to myself for now."

My heart thudded as I fought to keep my cool. I knew I had to stay focused and not let him get the upper hand, but my rough day had worn away my defenses. "Is that so?" I said coolly, stepping back to put some distance between us. "Well, I have my ways of finding out, Erevan."

He arched an eyebrow. "Do tell."

I gave him a tight-lipped smile. "I think I'll keep my secrets, too."

Erevan's smirk faded as he considered my words. "Your secrets won't last long," he said, "I have more support than you do for the throne. I have family. I have connections and a lifetime of preparing for this coup. Plus, I have the common fae's favor. When the coronation occurs next month, they will support me as King of Fen. You don't stand a chance."

Erevan's words stung, but I refused to let him see it. Instead, I raised my chin defiantly. "We'll see about that," I said, clenching my fists. "My mother's legacy still carries a lot of weight in the realm. I won't let her death be for nothing. And I also have...other allies who might support me in this fight."

That word *might* was critical because, without it, Gaia would have clamped my lying words on my tongue.

Erevan's smirk returned, and I could see the moment he understood why I'd used the word *might*. He laughed, a low and mocking sound. "You don't have a choice, Thorne. You're alone. You have no allies, no backing. You're just a lost little prince who can't even keep his own mother safe."

My blood boiled. "I will make you regret those words," I said through gritted teeth.

Erevan smirked. "No, you won't."

I turned on my heel and strode away, my heart thumping. I could feel Erevan's eyes on my back and sense his satisfaction at getting under my skin. But I refused to let him see how much he had affected me. I kept my head held high, my steps measured and confident.

"I just wanted to smack that smirk off his face and prove to him, and everyone else, that I deserved the throne. Prove it to my mother. To Arrow.

Prove it to myself.

Gabrelle

A gaunt male with an attitude problem showed me to a plain bedroom on the fifth floor of the Court of Fen. "You will sleep here tonight," he grunted.

The bedroom was cramped and barely furnished, with just a single bed, a small closet, a desk, and a wooden chair with a stiff back. Dull red wallpaper lined the walls, and a single window let a triangle of light slant in from the afternoon sun, highlighting the dust particles that hovered in the air.

It was the worst place I'd ever been told to sleep—including last night's rural tavern with the rapey neighbors. I pulled myself up to my full height. "I would prefer to sleep somewhere else. Are there any other options?"

The spindly male looked at me blankly. "Not for you."

"I beg your pardon?"

"Not for you. The prince told me to bring you to this room and not to let you change to another."

"Did he now?"

"Yes," the male said blankly. "That's why I said so."

I heaved a dramatic sigh. "Well, don't let me keep you. Get out," I declared, dismissing the spindly male with a wave. If these pricks weren't going to be polite to me, then I wouldn't be polite to them.

I unpacked my clothes into the closet, inspecting each one as I did. The sunflower gown had a loose thread, so I repaired it absentmindedly while I looked around this awful room.

Prince Prick wanted me gone. He wanted me to be as uncomfortable as possible, hoping I'd complain about my treatment and leave.

Well, I wouldn't give him the satisfaction.

But nor would I spend more time in this depressing room than I had to. As soon as my clothes were unpacked, I headed out to the hallway to explore the Court.

The Court of Fen was more extensive than I had expected. It was a sprawling, multi-tiered circular building with dozens of rooms and chambers connected by narrow winding corridors and staircases. Every so often, I passed a heavy wooden door that led to the unknown. From time to time, a distant clatter of raised voices or the faintest whiff of incense greeted me as I explored.

With every turn and twist, the Court of Fen revealed more of its hidden treasures. The mundane walls gave way to intricate statues, and the worn tapestries whispered forgotten tales of ancient glory in hues of red and gold. Each corner held the promise of something new, a story eager to be unraveled.

Every corner I rounded revealed something new: a counter selling strange curiosities, an alcove filled with exotic plants, and even an abandoned library nook filled with dusty books that crumbled when I flicked through them. Everywhere secrets were waiting to be discovered and stories waiting to be told.

Hours passed as I roamed the Court's winding passages, searching for clues about the Stone of Veritas and also for a Healer for my blistering feet. I was happy to admit to the Healer thing if I got questioned.

Just when I was about to give up and retreat to my dreary room, a glimmer of light caught my eye. At the far end of a long hallway lined with portraits hung an open door; through it, I could see a wide chamber flooded with sunshine.

I was drawn to the room's beauty. Lush wool carpeted the floor, deep velvet chairs surrounded a grand fireplace, and flowering plants in ornate vases brightened the windowsills. And perched atop one of those chairs was a handsome stranger, watching me intently.

"Princess Allura," he said with a smile. "Welcome to Fen."

I looked at the stranger, his chiseled jawline and broad shoulders, with butterscotch hair that looked artfully tousled. Although I'd never met him before, I'd studied the realm's nobles and knew who he was. I tilted my head. "Erevan Reissan, I'm pleased to meet you."

His butterscotch eyes sparkled in good humor, reminding me of Leif. "You know who I am?"

"You think you're the only one who did their homework?" I responded, a smile playing on my lips. I tilted my head, allowing the sunlight to caress my cheek, accentuating my best features. "I know a thing or two about you, Erevan Reissan."

He rose to his feet gracefully and took my hand. "I am very pleased to meet you, too. May I call you Gabrelle?"

A pang of irritation ran through me because I preferred to be called *princess* by fae I'd just met. But in this instance, with Thorne Sanctus already against me, I could use all the friends I could find.

"Yes, you may," I said simply, enjoying the simplicity of truth.

"And you may call me Erevan. Please, take a seat, and I will organize some refreshments."

I sat on the velvet armchair with the best view of the corridor—a predator's instinct. "It is nice to be welcomed to the realm," I said quietly.

Erevan penned a quick note using paper by the door, muttered "Avem volare," then released the spellbird into the corridor, presumably summoning the refreshments. He sat opposite me and leaned forward so the material of his fine purple shirt stretched across his shoulders and biceps. He was at ease in his bespoke suit and wore it well. "Let me guess...Prince Sanctus was less than welcoming?"

I relaxed into my chair and slowly crossed my legs so the slit of my white gown opened along one thigh, noticing how he glanced at it. "Exactly. You obviously know him well," I said, laying on the compliments. After my horrific meeting with Sanctus, it felt wonderful to be back in familiar territory—flirting with a handsome fae captive to my charms.

Erevan's lips turned up in a smirk. "I know him well enough. We have...history."

"Interesting," I said, raising an eyebrow. "Do tell."

Erevan leaned back in his chair, crossing his arms. "Let's just say that we were once rivals for the affections of a certain lady."

I arched my eyebrows in surprise. "Really? And who won?"

Erevan winked. "I'll let you know when it's over."

I laughed, enjoying the easy banter between us. "Well, it's nice to know that not all fae from Fen are obsessed with power and politics."

Erevan's expression turned serious. "Don't be fooled, princess. We all have our own obsessions and desires. It's just a matter of whether we choose to let them consume us or not."

I studied him for a moment, sensing a depth to his words. "And what are your obsessions, Erevan?"

He held my gaze for a long time, and I felt a pull between us, a familiar longing on his part and attraction to my beauty.

The spell was broken when the refreshments arrived, and Erevan poured us each a glass of rich red wine and offered me a small plate of fruit and cheese.

"Dionysus wine?" I asked.

"Of course," he said with a grin. "Only the best for our visiting princess."

It was interesting to note how far we could push Gaia's restrictions in Fen. The Earth Goddess allowed flirtation, obviously, not ruling out platitudes like 'only the best,' though it was arguable if that was strictly true.

The sunlight streaming in through the windows began to fade, casting the room in a warm, golden glow. I felt comfortable with Erevan, possibly because he looked strikingly similar to Leif, although with more color in his skin and eyes.

Erevan and I continued chatting, and I learned that he, like Leif, was a skilled swordsman. But he, unlike Leif, couldn't exaggerate his skills, so I had more confidence in them.

The sun had set when we finished our wine and cheese, and Erevan stood up to light the globes around the room. As he moved around, his purple shirt strained against his muscles, and I appreciated the view.

He turned around, and I let him catch me in the act of admiring him.

"What are you thinking about?" he asked, grinning.

I uncrossed and recrossed my legs, reeling him in like a fish. I was in my element here, and I raised a shoulder sensually. "I'm thinking about you," I said smoothly, not dropping his gaze.

Erevan crossed the room in three strides and leaned closer, smelling of woodsmoke and leather. "You are the most beautiful fae I've ever seen," he said, his breath hot on my cheek.

I brushed a lock of curled hair behind my shoulder, smiling silkily. "Thank you." I'd heard that compliment a million times, and it had no impact on me, but I knew how to play to my audience. Besides, Erevan was an attractive male, and my ego needed a boost after being decimated by Prince Prick.

Erevan's eyes darkened with hunger, and he slid his hand onto my knee, sending a thrill through me. "You know, I have a private garden that I think you would find very interesting, Princess Gabrelle."

I raised an eyebrow, curious. "Oh? And what makes you say that?"

Erevan's fingers trailed higher up my thigh. It wasn't the most subtle move, but I allowed it. "It's filled with exotic plants that have certain... properties," he said.

Okay, now I really was intrigued. "Is that so?"

Erevan leaned in closer, his lips hovering over mine. "I can show you," he whispered before capturing my lips in a searing kiss.

I had to play this carefully. I melted into Erevan, enjoying his taste, but I needed to toy him along. Perhaps I would give in to some carnal pleasure with him later, but for now, I had to make a friend. And a powerful friend with a hard-on was the very best sort.

I pulled back from the kiss, playing up how breathless I was, letting my chest heave. I was still seated, and he was leaning over me, so my bouncing breasts were in his line of sight.

"Do you want me to stop?" he asked.

This was tricky. Usually, I'd say no, then make up some excuse, but I couldn't lie here in Fen. To buy myself time, I clasped a hand around his bicep, feeling the hard muscle. "We should stop," I said instead of answering the question directly. I rose to my feet gracefully, overplaying how flustered I was, smiling coquettishly. "I need to find a Healer," I said. It wasn't sexy, but it was a good exit card and had the bonus of being entirely accurate.

Erevan stepped back, blinking in concern as he scanned me. "A Healer?" He looked me up and down, searching for injury. "Why didn't you say so earlier?"

His concern was sweet. I brushed it away with a hand through the air. "It's just blisters from my hike through Fen."

His brow furrowed. "You didn't use Fliers?"

"No," I laughed. "But, trust me, next time I will."

This afternoon of flirting and drinking was exactly what I needed, and I felt a lot more like myself by the end of it. I allowed Erevan to escort me back to my room—which always made males feel good about themselves—and he summoned a Healer who easily dispatched my minor injuries.

"Are you sure you're okay to sleep here?" Erevan asked with a disgusted look at my tiny room.

"Yes, I want to," I told him truthfully. I wanted to throw Thorne's hospitality in his face and prove him wrong about what I could handle. "Before you go," I said, "do you know anything about a Stone of Veritas?" Hopefully, it would come across as an inconsequential question, and he wouldn't pay it too much attention. My heart hammered as I waited for his reply.

"What's that?"

"Have you heard of it?" I asked. After all, I was here to learn information, not share it.

"No," he said, and I suddenly recognized the value of Gaia's rules for Fen. He had just told me the truth, no question about it.

Erevan leaned against the doorframe, smirking. "I'm more interested in you." His scent intensified as he leaned in and snaked an arm around my waist, pulling me close to his chest. Desire pulsed through me, all the way down to my panties.

Maybe that carnal pleasure didn't have to wait.

Gabrelle

Erevan's kiss was like a lightning bolt, sparking desire through my veins. Fire blazed inside me, begging to be set free. His hands moved down my sides as we explored each other's lips, and damn, it was intense. Despite all the reasons this was a bad idea, I allowed myself to get lost in the moment.

But just as I felt myself giving in, I pushed him away. "No," I said firmly, feeling a tinge of guilt. That wasn't the kind of fae I wanted to be anymore—using others for my own amusement. Like my mother.

Erevan looked surprised but not offended. He stepped back and flashed a smile. "You might be the most interesting princess I've ever met."

"And you might be the only male I actually like in the entire realm," I told him honestly. "But I would like to be alone now," I said, carefully choosing my words.

"Of course," he said, then with a quick bow, he walked away.

After pushing Erevan away, I took a deep breath and retreated to the solitude of my dreary room. I sat on the bed—it was as hard as a rock, of course. I wondered if Erevan had imported it specially just to torture his guests. It probably came from the Isle of Hard Surfaces or the Realm of Pissed-Off Visitors. I flopped back onto it—gently because I didn't want to bang my ass—and stared at the white ceiling. At least no spiders or grobblebugs were scurrying about. Just a plain white roof that matched the boring room.

The one saving grace was the adjoining bathroom—it might have been tiny, but it was private. I took a hot shower and gave myself ten long, luxurious minutes to fall apart and feel like a failure before I pulled myself together, emerged, dried off, and dressed in my hunting leathers, ready to take whatever crap this Court threw at me.

As I stepped out of the bathroom, feeling refreshed and slightly less of a hot mess, I noticed a slip of paper peeking from under my door. Curiosity piqued, I picked it up and unfolded the note.

Would you like to join me for dinner? E.

"No, Erevan," I said aloud, my voice echoing around the empty room, "I would not. I would much prefer to ransack the castle looking for the Stone of Veritas."

There was a pen and paper in my luggage because it always paid to be prepared, so I fetched them and considered my reply.

Under normal circumstances, I would lie. No fae could speak a lie in Fen, but did that extend to writing? I wriggled my fingers, praying to Gaia they wouldn't suddenly twist in pain as I wrote my response.

I would love to, but unfortunately, I have a headache and need to rest this evening. Perhaps we could postpone until another time? xxx G.

As I penned my response, relief washed over me. No pain. No Gaia-be-damned agony. I'd found a loophole. I spun in a little circle, clutching the note to my chest. Perhaps I could claim I had a sore throat and only communicate via writing from now on. My little chuckle bounced around the sparse room.

Now for the most important matter. The Stone of Veritas was somewhere in this Court, and I needed to find it. Maybe it would be wise to wait until Erevan was off on some fae business and then search, but who knew how often he left? Screw it, I decided to take matters into my own hands—or rather, my own feet.

Peeking out the window, I saw guards patrolling the circular courtyard five floors below, weapons ready. I had to avoid the yard.

My heart pounded in my ears as I cracked the door open and cautiously peered into the corridor. No one in sight... yet. I cautiously stepped out into the hallway, tiptoeing with each step to ensure not even a breath of sound escaped me. When I reached the main hallways, I heard the clamorous clanging of swords as guards trained and courtiers whispering conspiratorially. I had no hope of getting past them without being seen—even dressed down in my hunting leathers, the heir to the house of beauty drew eyes.

To get through the crowd without being noticed, I needed more than just quiet boots. I had inherited Stealth from my father, and though my magic was feeble compared to his, with enough concentration, I knew I could make it work—if only for a little while. Perhaps I would ascend into Stealth at my Ascension in a few months, and my power would strengthen.

Taking a long breath, I focused on the power and summoned it. A wave of energy surged through me as my vision blurred and my body melted into nothingness. The sensation passed, and it was done. No ordinary fae could see me—at least until my spell faded away. But the cost was that my own vision had been affected too; my view of the world was now ethereal and blurry.

GABRELLE

On my earlier exploration, I had marked where Prince Prick's chambers were—on the highest floor of this underground building. Steeling myself for what lay ahead, I took the most direct route there, ducking around groups of courtiers and pressing myself against walls where necessary.

Slowly and cautiously, I made my way up the last flight of stairs to the prince's quarters, my heart thumping wildly. I had to be careful, avoiding the guard on duty and skulking along the dimly lit corridor. The enchanted symbols of wood and metal emitted a faint glow, giving me the creeps. Who knew what kind of eerie magic was lurking around here? The Stone of Veritas had to be hidden somewhere within these walls, and I had to find it.

With a trembling hand, I opened the first door and slipped inside. The gloomy chamber was illuminated by moonlight that filtered through tall windows overlooking the circular courtyard below. A large bed stood in one corner, covered with a thick velvet quilt. My Stealth vision was fading fast, so I frantically searched every nook and cranny, hoping to stumble on a hidden latch or loose board that held the precious Stone. My hands fumbled over every surface but found nothing.

Disappointed and desperate, I left the room and searched the corridor, trying every door. And then, finally, I hit the jackpot. I opened a door that led me into an impressive music room. My breath caught in my throat—all kinds of instruments lay around, including a grand piano. But what really caught my eye was the beautiful wooden faeboe. With my blurry vision, I couldn't see it clearly, so I stepped closer, captivated by its beauty. That's when I heard a sound coming from the shadows behind me.

I spun around to find a tall, broad-shouldered figure emerging from the darkness, his blue-black hair absorbing every damn bit of light in the room. Oh crap, it was the prince himself. He stared at me with icy eyes, his voice dripping with anger. "What the hell are you doing here?" My whole body froze—this could mean certain death if he discovered my true purpose. My Stealth had faded away, leaving me exposed and vulnerable.

I stepped back, desperately searching my brain for some excuse, anything that wouldn't make me sound like a damn thief. But no matter how hard I wracked my brain, I couldn't come up with a plausible explanation that didn't scream guilty as charged. The truth danced on my lips, itching to spill out as Gaia's realm magic made me long to speak, but I managed to bite it back. I wasn't about to confess to my crime.

The prince sneered, his voice dripping with disdain. "We've had our fair share of visitors from the Realm of Greed and Excess. The land of liars and cheats. But none have had the balls to break into my rooms and steal directly from me. You've stooped to a whole new low, little trickster."

Anger surged through me, and as the last remnants of my Stealth vanished, I saw the male before me with crystal clarity. "You're rude and uncultured, and you have no right sitting on the Fen throne or any damn throne in Arathay. I arrived at your doorstep tired and beaten down, and all you've done is insult me."

"I've done nothing but speak the truth," he roared.

"Speaking the truth doesn't give you a license to be a royal pain in the ass," I roared back.

Every piece of my composure shattered. My mask of politeness and calm had no impact on this coarse male—he had torn it away, stripped it from me, and destroyed it. I couldn't find the control I usually had over myself, my inner well of peace.

All I felt inside me was bubbling rage. "I came here to befriend you," I yelled, "and you have snapped my olive branch in half."

The prince's hands clenched into fists, his arms bulging with tension as he struggled to maintain control. "You came to befriend me because you want something from me," he snarled. "Do you deny it?"

He stepped closer, towering over me, blocking out the light from the wall sconce behind him, casting me into shadow. "No," I snarled. "I don't deny it. Nobody would want to be friends with you on the merits of your personality. You are un-fucking-likable. So obviously I want something from you. Did you think this was a tea party where we braid each other's hair and become besties? This is politics, you moron. I offer you something, you offer me something, that's how it works." I was shaking with rage, and the toxic words were spilling from me, unstoppable. "But you never learned much about politics, did you? Because you were never meant to be king."

I pressed both hands against his pecs and shoved him hard, taking a step back. He stumbled, but his jaw remained clenched, the scar on his face burning red with fury.

"You're a total dick," he snarled. "You'll make a terrible queen."

I huffed a humorless laugh, not bothering to deny it. "Even a dick can be a good ruler."

"You are a lying bitch," he spat, his eyes blazing with rage. Then, gesturing around the room, he added, "And clearly a thief. Fen doesn't need your friendship, and I sure as hell don't need your presence in my Court. So leave. Pack your bags and get the hell out of my realm forever. Or..."

A measure of control returned to me as I realized how badly I had messed up. This was a Leif-level screw-up, and that was saying something. I was here because I had the 'best' relationship with Thorne out of all the heirs, and now he was ordering me out of the kingdom. I hadn't lost control of my emotions this badly since I was a young faeling. I blamed Gaia's realm magic for loosening my tongue and, apparently, my feelings.

I squared my shoulders, desperately trying to regain some authority. "Or what?"

His blue-black eyes narrowed, a dangerous glint flickering within them. "Or I'll make you leave, little trickster. Dead or alive."

Fear gripped my heart, pounding relentlessly in my chest. This was the truth-telling realm. *Dead or alive.* He meant it.

With a predator's grace, he stalked closer, and the battle between us was about to reach a whole new level.

Thorne

I saw the moment the truth of my words sank into the little trickster's brain.

Leave the realm, or I will make you. Dead or alive.

The power of Fen's magic thickened in the silence that followed my words. She knew I meant every word of it. I couldn't lie.

If Gaia didn't think my mother and sister deserved life, then this lying bitch from the realm of liars definitely deserved death. And if she didn't leave my city, I would happily deliver it to her.

I snapped my fingers and called for a guard. A male in ice-blue livery appeared in an instant. "Take her back to her room. By force, if necessary."

The guard hesitated momentarily before crossing to the trickster princess and grabbing her elbow.

"Get off me," the liar yelled, throwing her elbow into the guard's gut. "I am perfectly capable of walking without your help."

The guard straightened up and looked at me, and I nodded my assent. "Let her walk, but ensure she returns to her room. And lock her in."

"I don't like you," the princess sneered before stalking out the door with her head held high. Her words had no impact on me. I didn't want friends, I wanted to rule in my mother's place and continue the family legacy.

As the guard guided her back to her room, the weight of the confrontation still hung in the air, lingering like an unspoken promise. Reluctantly, I heard her retreating footsteps, knowing that our encounter would continue to haunt me even in the sanctuary of the music room.

Princess Gabrelle Allura had the reputation of being disciplined and regulated, so I had expected more of her. Frankly, I'd hoped to like her. But her actions showed her to be a thief, her heritage showed her to be a liar, and her lack of emotional control was laughable.

The realm would be better off without her. All of Arathay would benefit from her death.

Adrenaline coursed through me all night, and I slept poorly. In the morning, I looked more ragged than usual, but I didn't bother to cast a spell to fix the dark circles under my eyes. Just as I never bothered to glamor my scar. Concealment was just another form of lying, and I valued nothing more than truth.

With the morning sun spearing angled light into the Court, I went to my music room. It was a sanctuary for me, where I could forget my troubles and simply enjoy myself. Music had always been an enormous part of my life, a way for me to express emotion and connect with others without having to be face-to-face. Music couldn't lie.

The room was filled with instruments from all over Arathay, from Ourea's lyres to Brume's flutes and from Verda's drums to Caprice's harps. All were tuned perfectly and ready for use. I lingered for a moment at the carved wooden faeboe I had acquired during my last trip to Fenwick. What had Gabrelle seen in it? Was she trying to steal it? More importantly, why?

I opened the grand piano and played a sorrowful melody. The keys were an extension of my hands as if they knew what notes would best express my emotions. Every key spoke its own language, allowing me to pour out my feelings without ever having to say a word. Each stroke became a release, a conduit for my inner turmoil as if the music held power to soothe my restless soul.

After playing for several minutes, I felt calmer and more at peace than I had since Gabrelle's arrival in Fen.

A throat cleared behind me. "Your Highness, it is time."

I sighed. The echoes of the last haunting chord reverberated in the empty music room, but the weight of responsibility hung heavy on my shoulders. Time to hold court. I stood and made my way through the building, reminding myself with each step of my power and place in life. Even though I was only a month away from being crowned king, I still felt like an impostor in my own home.

Arrow was born to rule, not me.

When I entered the vast throne room, the courtiers bowed their heads and moved aside, oblivious to the tempest that raged within me. Beneath the poised facade, my desire for power and the seething resentment fueled a fire that threatened to consume us all.

The period after the death of a monarch and before the coronation of the next was always strange, with odd rituals and uncertain behaviors. I was the interregnum ruler, but I was not entitled to sit on the ice throne. So I stood on the dais beside the throne, above the courtiers but still not their king.

The citizens of Fen were not used to grand speeches, thank Gaia. In other realms, the kings gave long soliloquies peppered with lies and half-truths, but Fen fae were more sparing with words.

"Welcome to Court," I boomed, then fell silent and watched the crowd. Most courtiers wore modestly cut floor-length gray, blue, or white robes, many with solid metal strips down the back to protect against sudden ice storms.

So the vibrant red gown with a dipping neckline and long split stood out like a lion among pigeons. Gabrelle Allura, flaunting her beauty as though that would impress me.

She beelined through the crowd, who parted for her even faster than they'd parted for me. Irritation prickled my skin, turning hotter and angrier as she approached, her long leg flashing out of that high slit with every step.

"Princess Allura," I spat. "I am not happy to see you. I thought you had left Fen."

She smiled, a creepy false smile that made me detest her even more. "No, Prince Sanctus—or, may I call you Thorne?"

"You may not," I snarled.

"Well, *Thorne*," she began, emphasizing my first name. "I decided to stay. I was advised that you don't have any grounds to eject me from the realm." She flashed a smile at someone behind me, and I turned my head to see Erevan grinning at her like a love-sick fool.

I should have known she was working with him, conspiring directly with my enemies. Perhaps she was the other spy from Verda that Erevan alluded to yesterday.

"Perhaps not," I growled. "But I believe you will undertake a treasonous act soon, and then I will have grounds to execute you."

The courtiers inhaled sharply at those words, clearly shocked that I would treat a foreign dignitary so poorly. Dammit. I had momentarily forgotten about my audience. This Gaia-be-damned princess was making me look bad in front of the most powerful fae in Isslia mere weeks before the coronation. I had to control my tongue, or I was playing right into Erevan's hands.

Gabrelle smiled sensually, a seductive grin that parted her plum lips perfectly. She knew she had the upper hand, and she loved it. "Goodness, Thorne," she said, deliberately pissing me off by using my first name again, "You aren't very good at diplomacy." Her lilting voice echoed around the room, ringing with truth.

I had to claw back some power in this conversation and restore my dignity in front of the courtiers. "No," I said, smiling despite my rage, "but I love my realm and would do anything for it."

The tension in the room crackled like electricity, the courtiers' eyes darting between us, captivated by the scintillating dance of power.

She waved a hand dismissively. "The same could be said of most fae here," she said, smiling seductively at the entire damn room, a calculated provocation that set my blood on fire. "But perhaps you have nothing more to offer the throne than anybody else."

Erevan stepped forward, and faelight glinted off his butterscotch hair. "And less than some," he boomed, drawing another gasp from the crowd.

Words held more power in Fen than any other realm, and the courtiers were lapping up everything the trickster bitch said. She tilted her head, exposing her perfect long brown neck. "Will you reconsider your position and ask me to stay?"

She had me in a stranglehold. She had a firm grasp on my

big hairy balls, and I could do nothing about it. I couldn't tell her to leave again, not when she cast my diplomatic skills in doubt. She was the future leader of another realm in Arathay, and I couldn't be seen dismissing her.

But I couldn't lie to her either. "I want you to leave," I said through gritted teeth, "but I ask you to stay until the Wild Hunt." That was a touristy celebration that brought a lot of visitors to the realm, so I could manage her presence until then. I held her dusty-pink gaze. "Please stay."

She threw me one of her false, bright smiles. "Can you guarantee my safety?"

"Of course not," I snarled. "Anything could happen to you, things beyond my control."

Erevan's voice boomed from my right. "Especially at the Wild Hunt."

For once, I was glad of his interruption because talk turned to the Wild Hunt of Fen. It was an annual celebration in Green Valley, a tradition that went back thousands of years. It was an outlet for the fae of Fen, an emotional release, a festival that helped keep us all in balance for the rest of the year.

It was a debaucherous event, where even I let myself loose. A Wild Hunt where some fae acted as sexual prey and others as predators, and nobody went home until it played itself out.

Gabrelle

I strutted out of that damn throne room, a smirk plastered on my face. Victory was mine, and Thorne Sanctus knew it.

When I reached my tiny, dreary room, I found a large package wrapped in sparkling silver paper with a large red bow and a note. *I heard you liked music. E.*

I unwrapped the package and found an exquisite faeboe carved from silver bowenelk ivory. I was accustomed to extravagant gifts from would-be lovers, but this was particularly interesting. Erevan had clearly heard the details of last night's escapades, right down to the exact instrument I'd been caught with. He must have spies working among Thorne's guards.

This meant Erevan had also discovered the lie of my headache, but he didn't seem too fussed by it. Clearly, he had more flexibility and resilience than the crown prince. Perhaps I could deepen my relationship with him at the Wild Hunt.

Smiling, I stored the silver faeboe on the desk. Prince Prick had allowed me to stay in the realm until the Wild Hunt, which gave me at least a week to search the Court's winding corridors and hidden alcoves.

Determined to uncover the truth, I spent the week avoiding Thorne and Erevan, focusing solely on my task. I even dared to enter the crown prince's quarters another evening while he was out, but I still found nothing. Still, the damn Stone had to be here somewhere.

As the Wild Hunt drew near, my frustration was off the charts. I was ready to let loose and tear this place apart. But the Hunt was a night for celebration, and I intended to let loose. Even better, the other heirs from Verda were coming. I needed to see some friendly faces. I put on my outfit, pulled on a blood-red cloak, and slipped outside, joining the throng of fae heading toward Green Valley. It was an hour's walk in the sunshine, and my mood was high when I arrived at the nearest town, Grunelle.

I had arranged to meet the other heirs at the best bar in Grunelle, a place called The Dragon's Fizzle, identified by a hanging sign of a cute dragon with a fizzle of black smoke wafting out of its nostrils.

Two bouncers were turning fae away at the door—this was the busiest night of the year, and the bar was packed. I sauntered past the line and flashed my sultriest smile at the bouncers. Both of them, a skinny male and a curvy female, went slack-jawed at the sight of me and ushered me through with a slight whimper.

The old-style tavern was crowded with fae from every realm, chattering and clinking glasses. Suspended balls of faelight caught the glimmer of brightly colored wings as tiny faeries flitted around the room and laughed from the rafters. I smelled ale, roasted lamb, and gallons of excessive perfume.

I spotted my friends sitting at a table behind a velvet rope. Each of them wore a long cloak that obscured their costumes for the Wild Hunt. Leif saw me first and bounded across the room, then licked me in greeting, a long sloppy lick that I wiped away on his sleeve.

"I'm so glad you're here, babe," he exclaimed. "You're like my favorite fae in the whole world, well, except Alara, obviously, and maybe Ronan, maybe even Jet, but you're like super up there, and I missed you."

"You're babbling, wolf boy," I said, "try to hold your thoughts inside."

"Can't, not here, not in Fen. It's so weird being here, isn't it? Like it just pulls all your thoughts out of your head and smashes them across everybody else's eardrums."

"Only for the weak-willed, darling," I said, tossing out a light-hearted insult, but it felt so good to be bantering with somebody who loved me instead of crossing swords with a prick who hated me. "It's really good to see you too," I admitted, and the wolf howled so loudly I had to clap my hands over my ears.

Leif towed me to the table, leaping over the velvet rope and landing on Alara's lap. She oofed and grinned, then threw me a happy wave.

Neela and Ronan were here too, but not Dion. "Food-based emergency," Ronan explained with a grin when I asked where the Magirus was. "He couldn't come."

Ronan and Neela both fell over themselves to tell me how much they loved me and missed me, the words tumbling out of their mouths like water over Foster River Falls. "You're so good at everything, I've always thought you were amazing, except when I first met you, and you tried to kill me. But since then, I've really loved you," Neela said, her face split into a grin.

Ronan kissed my cheek when I sat on the chair beside him. "You're so good at everything, honestly. Some days I worry you'll outrank me as monarch, even though I would never tell you that." He clapped a hand over his mouth, and everybody laughed. "You're amazing," Ronan said, the words popping out between his fingers and causing another round of giggles.

"There's one good thing about Fen," I said. "You really know who your friends are and who your enemies are."

Their ears perked up at that. "Enemies?" Leif said. "Don't tell me you've already pissed somebody off. That's my job. Don't take my job away from me," he pouted.

Alara patted her mate on the arm. "Don't worry, city dick, you still piss off a lot of fae."

He licked her hand happily. "Thanks, babe. I love you."

"I love you t—"

"Stop your irritating displays of love," I said, and they all looked at me in surprise. "Sorry, it's just that sometimes I feel left out," I confessed. Dammit, I put my glass of Fae Fizz firmly back on the table—I wouldn't take another sip. I'd forgotten how it lowered my defenses against launching truth bombs.

Ronan and Alara, who were seated on either side of me, reached out and one-arm hugged me, but Ronan undermined the effect by saying, "Yeah, I always thought you were jealous."

Time to change the subject. I crossed my legs, pulling my blood-red cloak across my lap. "Nice work getting a table, it's pretty busy tonight."

"Yeah," Neela said, "I suspect we got the table because we're entitled princes and princesses who might kick up a stink otherwise."

Leif whined. "No. It's because I asked nicely."

Alara scoffed, and Neela shook her head. "Nope. Definitely the asshole prince thing."

Leif whined again, so Alara fished a tennis ball out of her

pocket and passed it to him, which perked him up.

"You mentioned something about having an enemy," Ronan said. "That sounds bad."

"It is bad," I admitted.

"Well, as long as it isn't Prince Sanctus," Ronan said. "That would suck big time."

I glanced at him. "In that case, it sucks big time, as you so eloquently put it."

"Fuck burgers," Neela said. "You really screwed up."

Everybody piled on agreeing with her, and I wished the realm magic would ease off a bit with the honesty thing. But it was fair. I had messed up.

"Yes," I said, holding up a hand to quieten the noisy blaming still going on, "I messed up. Well, it was his fault. He's a total prick."

"That's true," Leif said. "When I met Thorne, he slapped me in the face. And not in a good way."

Neela spat out some ale and clanged her glass on the table. "Did you lick him?" she asked, frowning.

Leif whined. "Only a little bit."

"That might explain it," Neela said, wiping her mouth.

I leaned back and crossed my legs, surveying the heirs until they quietened down and I had their full attention. "Well, I didn't lick him, and he was still a prick to me. Then, last night, he caught me sneaking around his rooms looking for the Stone and threatened to kill me."

"Fuck!"

"Asshole."

"Holy Gaia."

"Yeah," I said. "I don't like him." I remembered how I'd spat those words at him and how their simplicity and honesty felt so damn good.

The chorus of support chimed in. "I hate him."

"He's an asshole."

"Should we kill him?"

Everybody snapped their attention to Leif at his question, frowning. "No, wolf boy, we shouldn't kill him," Ronan said. "That's a terrible idea. Even worse than when you suggested we drain the Requin Sea to kill all the sharks."

The silver-haired alpha whined. "But it would work. All the sharks would die." Even his mate looked at him askance. "Whatever," he said, shrugging. "I wasn't joking about the sharks. I mean, I wasn't just joking. I mean, the water thing, I wasn't joking. Fuck!"

Neela grinned. "You can't lie here, Leif. You can't pretend you were just joking." Everybody laughed, and Leif joined in good-naturedly.

It was so good to see the wolf back to his old self, much more like the fae he was before his mom died. The only reason he emerged from the horrible dark pit he fell into was sitting right beside him, the fae with the bright orange hair and wide-open smile. Since the mating bond, Leif skillfully struck a balance between being a strong leader and a playful wolf. Both were important elements of being a good alpha. And although we were teasing him—and he took it good-naturedly—he could be a powerful and dominant fae when the situation required it. I'd seen him silence a hulking wolf with a look.

"So, I guess you can't just ask Sanctus for the Stone," Neela said.

"No. But I asked his rival, Erevan Reissan, about it. He hasn't even heard of the Stone of Veritas."

"Maybe he was lying," Alara said. Everybody stared at her,

and she reddened and whined slightly. "Oh, right, I guess not."

Leif growled at us and licked his mate's arm, and we all looked away quickly. The mating bond was still solidifying between them, and we didn't want to get in its way. It was a volatile and dangerous thing when put under pressure.

"So what are you going to do next?" Neela asked. "You need to find the Stone. And quickly. The Shadow Walkers are attacking more boldly every day. Every fae in Verda City knows about them. Some are keeping their faelings home from school."

Taking in the lively atmosphere, I glanced around the room. Some fiddlers played a jaunty tune in the corner, but the music was barely audible above the loud conversations and laughter. "I know. I will keep searching in the Court until I find it," I said.

"What if it isn't in the Court?" Leif asked. "It could be anywhere in the realm."

"No. An object so priceless would be kept close to the prince."

"Maybe Sanctus doesn't even know about it. You should ask him," Neela said.

I looked at my spiky-haired friend. Two years ago, she was wondering around the mortal world stealing to survive, and now she was expected to rule in the fae realm. There was a lot she didn't understand, and politics was right at the top of the list.

"I can't just ask him," I said.

She downed the rest of her beer and then wiped her mouth. "Why not? He'll have to tell the truth about it."

I looked around for help, but everyone was just staring at me. I supposed I was the expert on all things Fen, having been here for the past week. "Only if he chooses to answer the question.

You can just avoid speaking, and the truth stays inside you."

"Nope," Leif interrupted, "not here. Truth refuses to stay inside me. It wants to splatter itself all over the rest of you, like I want to splatter myself over Alara." He turned to me solemnly. "Sorry, babe. I know you're jealous."

"Great Gaia, I'm not jealous of you, wolf boy," I spluttered. "I do not want to have sex with you. But I used to. Damn." I cupped a hand over my mouth. Ronan leaped to his feet and came around me, stepping between me and Alara in case he needed to keep her off me. I batted him aside. "I am not jealous of you and Leif," I said directly to Alara, staring into her orange eyes. "I'm just jealous of your great relationship. Fuck!"

When he was certain Alara wouldn't go feral, Ronan returned to his seat on my other side. I caught a glimpse of bare chest before he pulled his black cloak tight. Ronan went full smirk. "What were you saying about being able to keep the truth inside you?" He knew me well enough to know I wouldn't ordinarily confess to any level of jealousy, especially about my friends' good relationships.

"Oh, shut up," I said, folding my arms. This realm was really doing a number on me. But I wouldn't allow it. Deliberately, I unfolded my arms, straightened my posture, and breathed deeply. "I will continue to search the Court for a while longer, and if that fails, I will search elsewhere."

As the conversation died down, all my friends' eyes were on me, like that wasn't good enough. But I didn't see what else I could do.

Neela slammed a shot of Fae Fizz and muttered something into her wrist tattoo. Then she landed her sky-blue gaze on me. "And ask the prince about the Stone," she insisted.

I glowered at her. "Unlikely." But my scowl soon disappeared. There was a real sense of festival and celebration in the bar, and it was contagious. It seeped into my skin, making me wriggle, affecting everybody else too.

Leif smacked a kiss on Alara's cheek, then raised his glass to announce a toast. "Speaking of sex," he shouted.

"Which we weren't," I noted.

"Let's go start the Wild Hunt."

We all clinked glasses, and Leif and Alara broke into howls, which a few other shifters around the bar joined in.

I felt it through my bones and into my very essence. The Wild Hunt was about to begin.

Gabrelle

Fae poured out of the tavern and along the cobblestones to the village outskirts. Around the next bend, the path opened out to the vast Green Valley, surrounded by mountains and forested in tall trees, shrouded in mist. A mythical and magical place.

The heirs and I paused as the valley opened out before and below us, and Leif gripped my arm. "Can you feel it? Can you feel the sex?"

Weirdly, I could. The air was filled with sensuality but tinged with violence. My blood pumped hot through my veins.

Leif removed his cloak and revealed lightweight silver armor engraved with fur and fangs. He grinned wolfishly, looking every inch a feral hunter.

Fae divided into two groups during the Wild Hunt. Predators and prey. It used to be that males were predators and females prey, but the old traditions had evolved, and now every fae could decide which role they wanted to play. The only rule was that you had to clearly indicate your chosen role and couldn't switch during the Hunt.

Leif, in his glinting silver armor, was clearly a hunter. He growled when Alara removed her long, flowing cloak and revealed her costume of thin strips of fur pulled tight across her body, barely covering her nipples and pussy. For somebody who claimed to dislike being naked, I had certainly seen a lot of her vagina. The fur marked her as prey. Leif was pawing at the grass, not bothering to hide his possessive passion for his mate. Gaia forbid anybody get between them tonight.

Neela surprised me by also revealing a prey costume, a furry bikini top and a leather miniskirt that made her look curvier than she really was.

"You've come as prey, Neela?" I asked, raising an eyebrow. "That's disappointing. I took you for the master in your relationship."

Ronan and Neela were evenly matched in strength of mind, and I thought she had the slight edge. She shrugged, "He insisted on hunting this year. Next year, it's my turn. It's all about give and take."

Ronan wore black leather hunting pants, no shirt, and a mask of the finest filigree metal shaped like old-fashioned armor. He looked like he was about to indulge in some serious dungeon fetish sex.

"Cute," I said with a smirk, and he flashed me a menacing grin that made me think there was more to their sex life than I imagined.

"What are you wearing underneath that cloak?" Neela asked me. "I bet you look hot as fuck."

"Of course," I replied, then let my soft red cloak fall to the grass. I wore a version of hunting leathers but heavily altered. It was a blood-red leather corset top with half-cups that exposed most of my breasts and black lace panties that would come off easily. The thigh-high black hunting boots completed the look, marking me as a hunter. I had learned the hard way that the heir to the house of beauty should not turn up to the Wild Hunt dressed as prey.

Even so, I drew stares. The nearest fae stepped closer, and my friends had to group around me to keep them away.

"Shit, babe, are you sure you should be here?" Leif asked.

"I'm a hunter, Leif. I can handle myself." I had my bow and arrow slung across my back, and I was prepared to use them. "Besides, none of the prey can hunt me. And none of the hunters can either. It's basically the only rule of the Hunt."

That was true, but several nearby predators were hastily changing their costumes, ripping off their weapons and looking for fur trim so they could become prey, hoping to become mine.

But I had only one fae in mind.

Thorne Sanctus was the crown prince, and there was no current monarch, so he was the Hunt's Leader. He roared loudly, getting everybody's attention. He was shirtless, exposing a better body than I expected, which he usually kept hidden beneath layers of poor fashion choices. His brown leather pants were snug, revealing muscular legs and a large cock already at half-mast. His cheeks were painted in boar blood, and his blue-black hair shone wild beneath the crescent moon. He looked strong, like a mythical fae warrior, and his voice boomed. "I declare the Wild Hunt open."

A horn blasted, and the prey fled down the hill toward the misted forest at the valley's base, the start of the frenzied chase. Some were mounted on horseback, others used their inner magic to propel themselves forward, but most ran on supple leather boots, sprinting with wild abandon.

Erevan, wearing a black shirt and leather pants, appeared at my side, holding a sword. "I'm glad you're here," he said.

"I'm glad you're here, too."

He looked me up and down slowly, taking in my thigh-high

boots, skimpy panties, and blood-red corset. "I expected you in fur and feathers," he growled, unable to drag his gaze from my breasts.

I arched an eyebrow and forced his gaze upward with a finger under his chin. "I am a hunter to the core, Erevan, But I admit, I hoped you'd be dressed as prey."

The butterscotch-haired male stared at me a moment longer, looking eerily like Leif. Then he dropped his sword, stripped off his leather pants, pulled off his black shirt and tore it to strips, then tied the rags around his waist, barely covering his enormous cock. He glanced at the ground, then ducked down and retrieved a fallen feather, which he tucked behind his ear. "I am," he said with a wink, sprinting down into the valley and the mist.

A second horn blasted, marking the release of the hunters. Leif howled, and several other wolves joined in as we sprinted down the hill. My heart thudded, merging with the pounding of hooves and beating of wings. As soon as I dived into the mist, the sounds intensified, a cacophony of echoing laughter and shrieks.

The chase was on. My feet carried me quickly through the trees, and I pushed myself to move faster, searching for Erevan. He'd masked himself with the mist, but I knew he was out there. I could feel him.

As I ran, the thrill of the hunt coursed through me. Everything felt heightened—sight, sound, smell—every sense felt alive and powerful. The scent of wildflowers filled the air, and distant calls and howls echoed through the fog-bound trees.

I leaped over logs and ducked beneath branches as I searched for Erevan, following my hunter's instincts, my breath coming in ragged gasps. Eventually, I came across a clearing filled with bright wildflowers. In the center was a small pond, its surface shimmering in the silver light of the crescent moon. Erevan had stopped at its edge, his chest rising and falling heavily as he leaned down to sip water.

I froze in my tracks, not wanting to spook him away before I could capture him. He might want to have sex with me, but there was deep fae pride in evading capture, so he would try his hardest.

Closing my eyes, I summoned Stealth and cloaked myself in its magic, then I stalked across the clearing, trying to make no noise. Erevan's heaving chest drew my eye. As much as I sometimes despised beauty, I was drawn to it like a moth to moonlight. Inexorably. It was in my blood.

And Erevan was beautiful. Firm, sculpted muscles rippled across his broad chest and back as he bent. His hair was deep, lustrous butterscotch, and his skin glowed like copper in the moonlight. I felt the urge to reach out and touch him, to feel the warmth of his body against mine.

I stole up behind him, my feet making no sound on the soft grass. He whirled around, sniffing the air. He could sense my presence, but he couldn't see me.

"Who's there?"

"Somebody who wants to claim you," I said, watching his reaction to my words. The feather had disappeared from behind his ear, and the ragged strips of cloth around his waist hid little. His cock jumped, and the muscles of his belly tensed.

"You'll have to catch me first," he said huskily.

I darted to his other side, so my voice came from a different direction. "Oh, I will," I promised.

He took off, running faster than I could have imagined. His feet barely seemed to touch the ground. He barreled into a massive sticky web that must belong to the most enormous spider in existence, but it didn't even slow his sprint. It must be an illusion.

"I certainly hope it is," I muttered as I plunged into the sticky mess and was relieved when I brushed right through it.

The chase was not limited to the physical realm. It ventured into the ethereal plane, where we navigated through illusions, trickery, and tests of perception and intuition. Like the spider web.

But I took nothing for granted because the Wild Hunt was risky, with treacherous terrain and territorial creatures I didn't want to piss off.

The web illusion cleared, and I saw a muscled fae thrusting himself into a female. I was taken aback, thinking it was Erevan, then I realized it was Leif fucking Alara. A male with a broken leg was whimpering in the bushes beside them.

"What the hell happened here?" I asked.

Leif locked eyes with me for a moment mid-thrust before Alara growled, and he looked away instantly. "That dude tried to catch me," Alara explained, pointing at the broken-legged fae. "And Leif stopped him."

"I see."

I looked around, trying to figure out which way Erevan would have gone. He was an Ascended Water fae, so he would be drawn to water. Perhaps he'd doubled back to that pond. I retraced my steps, leaped over logs, and avoided other snarling hunters, trying to navigate through the swirling mist.

He was at the pond, chest heaving and wearing tattered black material as a belt.

Another hunter appeared from behind a tree, stalking Erevan. I didn't have time to play with my food any longer, so I whipped an arrow out of my bow and fired, piercing the black tattered rags at Erevan's waist and pinning him to a sapling.

I stepped forward. "He's mine," I claimed loudly, and with my arrow poking out of his clothes, it was hard to deny.

The other hunter stalked away, and Erevan looked at me, his lips twitching in a tiny smile of admiration. I crossed the clearing, not bothering to hide my footsteps swishing through the grass.

He tensed as I slipped my arm around his waist and drew him close, the fingers of my other hand pressing into the firm muscles of his chest. I could feel his heart pounding against my arm, and he let out a low, pained groan.

"You can't escape me now," I whispered.

Erevan's head fell back, and he let out a long, shuddering sigh. "I don't want to," he murmured.

Gabrelle

I had Erevan at my mercy, his skin streaked in blood and dirt, his chest bare. Already, his cock was hard just from my presence, pushing up the tattered black rags on his waist.

"I didn't think you'd catch me," Erevan said breathily. "But I'm glad you did."

My arrow still pinned him to the sapling. I stepped behind the young tree behind him so he couldn't see me. But I could see him, his skin copper, his musky scent growing stronger every second.

I leaned forward and stood on tiptoes to whisper into his ear, still keeping a sliver of hot air between our bodies. "I was always going to catch you, Erevan. I always get what I want."

He shivered, and I could feel his muscles tense beneath my fingertips as I brushed them across his skin. His breathing was heavy, and I knew he was lost in the moment, even more than I was. The sensation of power was intoxicating, and my pussy grew hot and wet. My lips moved to his earlobe, and I felt him shudder beneath me as I sucked and licked.

I let out a low chuckle before slowly trailing my lips down the side of his neck. His body quaked with anticipation as I alternated between biting his earlobe and gentle kisses. He moaned softly each time my tongue swept along the back of his neck, sending waves of pleasure through him.

Reaching around from behind him, I trailed my hands across the expanse of his chest before coming to rest on either side of him, my fingers gently brushing the soft hairs just above his belly button. My thumbs found their way to either side of his navel, tracing tiny circles around it in a slow rhythm as my body pressed against him from behind, the sapling caught between us.

I gave myself a moment of relief, pressing my aching nipples and pussy hard against his ass and back, then I put distance between us again.

"No touching," I said as I moved around to stand before him and saw his lips parted in desire, his hooded eyes watching my every move. My hand trailed down his torso, feeling each ridge of muscle. His breathing grew deeper, and he strained against the arrow, desperate to be closer. I inched forward again until my breath was hot on his ear.

"You can't escape me, Erevan. I can feel your pulse racing, ready and willing for whatever pleasure I have in store for you."

He moaned in response, pulling himself against the arrow impaling his clothes.

Smirking, I leaned around him and took hold of the arrow with both hands. With one hard yank, I released him from the sapling's grasp. He stumbled forward a pace before regaining his balance and turning around to face me.

His eyes were bright with anticipation as they met mine, a mixture of fear and lust that sent heat coursing through my blood. His skin was flushed hot. "Where did you learn how to hunt?" he asked. The heat in his eyes was intoxicating.

"Never underestimate a princess." With an evil smile, I grabbed one of his wrists and twisted his arm behind his back, holding it painfully behind him. He shifted to relieve the pressure, but I shook my head and inched closer until my lips brushed his. Moving quickly, I roughly crushed his mouth against mine, my tongue parting his lips and darting inside. He moaned against my kiss, and I released his wrist, my hand snaking down to his ass. I squeezed it hard, and he groaned into my open mouth.

"You're the sexiest, most beautiful fae I've ever seen," he said, reaching out and grabbing my hips. "I'm gonna make you come harder than you ever have."

I let the compliment wash over me. It didn't get me hot because I'd heard it a thousand times, but the pressure of his fingers digging into my hips did, and so did his promise.

Mist rolled out of the surrounding forest and over us, kissing my exposed flesh and making me shiver. It brought wild, disorienting howls and calls, so I kept one hand firmly on my captured prize to keep myself anchored. The mist rolled away, and a naked female stumbled past, her knees and elbows grazed and bleeding. Her eyes were wide, and she was sobbing, but it wasn't clear if she was crying from terror or arousal. Both were common in the Wild Hunt.

Not from me, though. I never cried during or after sex—that was for the weak-willed, and I was a tower of strength.

I stepped away from Erevan, and his hands fell from my hips. My gaze tracked down his body, and his jaw clenched as he looked down at himself. The ragged fabric tied around his waist was utterly torn, exposing his hardened cock.

I ducked down and pushed my face against his crotch, breathing deeply. "This is going to be fun," I told him. "If you give me the pleasure you promised, I'll spare your life."

I had no intention of killing him, I was only bluffing. But it wasn't unheard of for predators to get carried away and kill their quarry during the Wild Hunt, so he might believe me. The threat added to my excitement, and from his sharp intake of breath, he felt the same.

I closed my eyes and savored the musky scent of his cock. It had been growing harder the entire time I'd been torturing him, and now I could see it throbbing. I listened to his breathing and let it guide my lips as they found their way around the thick shaft.

He groaned softly, and the sound sent a shiver through me, his pleasure rolling through me like the mist. I wanted to feel his cock hardening in my mouth, so I increased the pressure of my lips, forcing my tongue out and around him. Then I gently nibbled the base of his cock, a bite that turned into a kiss.

"Oh, shit," he moaned. "Fuck, your mouth feels so good."

I slid my hand behind his back and into his ass crack, my nimble fingers teasing his tight asshole. His cock twitched as I brushed my thumb across his anus. His body tensed for a second, but then he relaxed as my tongue swirled around his cock again. I ran my tongue down the length of his shaft to his balls, sucking each in turn.

They were slightly heavy and rough to the touch, and he hissed each time I licked them. As I sucked on the right one, my thumb pressed against his asshole. His muscles tensed. I stopped immediately, not wanting him to explode without me.

I stepped away from Erevan and held out my hand to him. "You can touch me now," I instructed. I'd had enough of these games of predator and prey—now, I just needed him deep inside me.

His hands found my hips, my ass, the length of my back, and he pressed his hard cock into my belly and claimed my mouth with his.

I lost myself in the kiss. He was hot, sexy, and I needed release. Needed him.

I pressed against him and leaned into his ear. "I want you to fuck me," I whispered. "Hard."

He moaned, and I felt his hands slide beneath me, holding me up off the ground. He turned me and tossed me against the nearest tree. He stepped toward me and ripped open my blood-red leather corset, exposing my breasts. He cupped them in his hands and squeezed them together. He kissed my neck and shoulder, then sucked on my nipples, tracing lines of fire along my skin.

He moved from one breast to the next, alternating between them and then sucking on them in tandem. I moaned and ran my hands through his butterscotch hair. His body pressed against mine, his hard cock pressing into my belly.

He sucked my nipples until they were hard, pulled his mouth away, and grabbed the back of my head. He kissed me fiercely. I moaned into his mouth, my body aching to feel more of him. I squeezed his cock, the hard shaft throbbed in my hand, and I was ready.

He broke away from the kiss and looked me in the eye. "I'm going to fuck you so hard," he growled. "And I'm going to make you come so many times you're going to beg me to stop."

"Do it," I moaned.

He grabbed me by the hips and pushed me against the tree. I wrapped my legs around his waist, and he held me steady as his lips found mine.

I pulled him closer, deepening the kiss and feeling his hips grind into me, his cock rubbing against my pubic bone. "Oh, fuck," I groaned. "Your dick feels good."

"I bet your pussy does, too," he growled, pushing aside the crotch of my black panties and pressing the head of his cock to my opening. "I'm going to stretch your tight little pussy like it's never been stretched before, Gabrelle."

His words turned me on more, and I rocked against him, needing to feel the head of his cock inside me.

He thrust his hips, and his cock sank into me, stretching me to my limits. I groaned, and he growled.

"You're gonna come so hard around my cock," he told me. His voice was low, and he breathed heavily into my neck. His hips moved again, and he fucked me hard and fast, his cock slamming into my pussy.

"Yes," I moaned, feeling the pressure building inside me, my muscles tightening and my thighs shaking.

"Oh, yes," I moaned again, and the pressure released. I came hard, my pussy clamped down on his cock, and my muscles spasmed.

He didn't stop fucking me, my orgasm driving him wild, and he fucked me harder and faster. I pulled him closer, wrapped my arms around his neck, our bodies pressed together.

"Oh, fuck, Gabrelle," he moaned against my mouth. "I'm going to come."

I pushed my hips against him, wanting to feel his hot cum rush into me. His cock throbbed inside me, and he finally exploded in a shuddering orgasm.

He held me a few more moments, sagging bonelessly until I wriggled to be free, and he put me down. My boots hit the soft grass, and I surveyed him. "Is that it?" I asked with a half-grin. "What happened to making me come more times than I ever have?"

I wasn't really pissed. That was a good orgasm and precisely the distraction I needed. A hot man, a willing subject, a good release.

"Oh, babe," he said, reminding me of Leif again, his hair flopping in his face. "You're so fucking hot, I couldn't hold myself back. Just give me a few minutes, okay? Next time, I promise. Next time."

The reminder of my buddy Leif took me out of the moment. I shrugged and relaced my blood-red corset, pulling it tight and finishing it with a quick-release bow. "Maybe." I took out the spare lacing from my corset to tie a noose around Erevan's neck, which I then knotted around his wrists. He was my prize, and I was going to display him.

Gabrelle

I stepped out of the shadows of the deep forest and climbed the hill toward the blazing bonfire, leading Erevan by the blood-red rope around his wrists and neck. I had been hunting for hours, and it would soon be morning. Anticipation lay thick in the air. I had done it. I had succeeded in the Wild Hunt and was coming home victorious.

The hill was alive with activity. Everywhere fae were celebrating, talking, and dancing, the victors with massive grins. Most of the champions were predators, although some feathered prey sneaked back into the light uncaptured, brimming with pride.

It had been too long since I'd attended such a gathering. Usually, the parties I attended were only for High Fae, nobles with an interest in politics and ruling. But this celebration was wild and inclusive and joyous. I watched one lesser fae lead a Fen courtier out of the mist, secured with a rope around his erect cock. Anything could happen at the Wild Hunt.

At the center of the flattened top of the hillock was a huge bonfire, and fae were gathered around it with food and drink while raucous musicians played wildly nearby. I led Erevan to the bonfire and let him pull me up a log to sit on.

"Go and get me some food," I ordered him.

He smirked and held out his bound hands. "That might be difficult," he remarked mildly.

I enjoyed the repartee, but I kept my smile hidden. No point undermining my reputation as an ice princess. When I unbound his hands, he bowed, then wandered over to the massive trestle tables to fetch me my rewards. Despite being covered in mud and scratches and with only a tattered belt for an outfit, he didn't look defeated. If anything, my butterscotch-haired warrior seemed as proud as punch at having been captured by the heir of House Allura.

Scanning the crowd, I caught sight of Crown Prince Thorne Sanctus watching me, scowling, as usual. The boar blood streaking his cheeks was mixed with dirt, and the female tied up beside him had put up a good fight, judging by the long red scratch down his bare chest. He saw who I had conquered and must know I was becoming close with his political enemy. Was that fear that shimmered in his blue-black eyes, dancing in the reflected firelight?

I wouldn't give him the satisfaction of caring, so I averted my gaze. I watched a victorious lesser fae command her captured courtier to bring her a drink, and I smiled. Ordinarily, I benefited from the fae hierarchy, but it was still fun to see it overturned occasionally.

Ronan picked his way through the growing crowd toward me, towing Neela with a black leather rope. Both of them were smirking hard enough to burst.

"How was your first Hunt, Neela?"

"Fucking rockstar," she said. "Like, so good. Is this even legal? Holy shit. I used my Grower magic to make a vine fuck Ronan while a winged faerie rode it, and he—"

"Okay," Ronan interrupted, placing a hand over his lover's

mouth. "I don't think she needs all the details."

"No," I agreed, "I definitely don't."

We swapped war stories and compared scratches and bruises, and when Erevan returned with my food, I ate greedily.

More fae slinked out of the misty forest to join us while others finished feasting and began dancing. The music was wild and raw, the drums thumping through my body and reverberating into the log beneath my butt. It was intoxicating. Absolute debauchery. And I loved it.

I got up to stretch my legs and explore the celebration. I watched the musicians for a long time, caught in the sway and beat, fascinated by their skill. I'd spent a long time learning the faeboe, but my songs were always complicated and classical, bringing none of the raw joy these fae did.

Propelled by the beat, I wandered through the throng of fae, further away from the bonfire and into the shadows, weaving around others in a dance of my own.

I felt a presence watching me. A chill ran down my spine, and my heartrate picked up. I stopped in my tracks and slowly turned around. There stood Thorne, looking at me with an expression of anger so intense that it almost had a physical presence. The boar blood streaking his cheeks and the fresh scratch on his bare chest smelled coppery and bitter. His blue-black gaze locked onto mine, and he took one step closer to me, his face set in a hard line.

"What are you doing here?" he demanded coldly.

I cocked out a hip, letting the line of my leg and body speak for itself, making full use of my assets. "I am free to attend the Wild Hunt, like anybody else." I tried to hide my fear, but it prickled beneath my skin. "You asked me to stay until after the Hunt."

Thorne snorted and stepped even closer, blocking out the light from the bonfire. It glowed around him, casting him in an angelic aura that couldn't be further from the truth. "It's not safe for you here."

I laughed, more out of disbelief than amusement. "If you think I'm scared of you," I replied with a smirk, "you're right." Fuck, I hadn't meant to admit that. Damn realm magic.

He sneered and leaned down to my level, seeming larger than I remembered as he blocked out the low crescent moon. His voice was low and menacing. "You don't have the slightest idea what I'm capable of," he warned me. "Leave now before you find out."

For a moment, I stared up at him in disbelief. How dare he? I was a princess. I had conquered the Wild Hunt without a scratch. He had no right to threaten me like this.

Anger boiled inside me, and my fingernails dug into my palms. "I will not be intimidated by a fae whose power lies solely in his lineage and wealth."

He snorted dismissively. "That's the same place your power comes from, trickster."

"No," I corrected him. "Mine also comes from within." I tapped into my Lure magic and threaded the power through my next words. "Leave me alone." The command wouldn't last for long—the magic would expire in a few minutes or hours, depending on the strength of his mind. But at least he would leave me in peace for now.

I could see him struggling to resist my Lure, and I enjoyed watching him squirm, seeing the anger and defeat in his eyes.

But before he left, he spoke. "You commanded me to leave you alone, so I cannot leave you surrounded by all these fae." He scooped me into his arms, holding me like a bride, and raced down the hill while I jigged and bounced in his arms, screaming. My calls blended into the howls and hurrahs of the wild celebration and didn't attract any notice from the other fae.

Thorne plunged into the mist at the base of the hill, then into the dark forest. In the early pre-dawn hours, the shadows were as deep as space beneath the thick canopy.

He sprinted far into the forest, and the mist was so disorienting in the growing morning light that I quickly lost all sense of place. When I finally found the presence of mind to use Lure, I screeched, "Put me down!"

That screech echoed in the white world, bouncing off unseen trees and sounding in my ears like a wild fae. Where was my inner ice princess when I needed her? And why did this prick always loosen my control and bring out my worst?

At my Lured command, Thorne tossed me onto the ground, and I tumbled over and over, banging my limbs and scratching my exposed arms and legs.

"How dare you?" I demanded, trying to find my inner queenliness, but it was hard while stumbling to my feet and bleeding.

"You told me to put you down." His voice was disembodied, coming from somewhere nearby, but I couldn't see him. "And you told me to leave you alone," he said, then his footsteps retreated into the distance.

Dammit. I didn't have a clue where I was. But I knew what lurked in the forest, and I wouldn't survive long here alone.

I took a deep breath and slowly surveyed my surroundings. I was completely lost in the thick mist that blanketed the forest. My palms were clammy, and I tried to remember which direction we had come from. In the forest, everything looked the same, and even though I could hear faint voices and laughter from up on the hill, everything around me felt disturbingly still and quiet.

I took another look around, desperation scrabbling at me. The trees were tall, their branches reaching out like dark claws trying to snag me as I walked past. The ground was wet and slippery beneath my feet, making it difficult to keep my balance as I stumbled through the fog.

Suddenly, I heard a twig snap behind me. It sounded too close for comfort, so I spun around, hoping to catch whoever it was off guard. But there was nothing there except more white mist and trees fading into the distance.

I kept walking, forcing myself not to look back until I suddenly felt a presence bearing down on me.

I whirled around and gasped, my heart racing. It was Thorne, his face contorted in rage, and every muscle in his bare chest coiled as he lunged at me. I scrambled backward, barely evading him. He kept coming at me, snarling and snatching like a wild animal. I clenched my fists and prepared to fight him off, summoning my magic to protect myself.

My Lure spell had worn off by now, but I hadn't been exaggerating when I said, 'My power also comes from within.' With courage fueled by those words, I summoned a jolting spell and flung it against Thorne with all my might.

He stumbled backward, caught off guard by my strength. At that moment, we were equal adversaries, fae locked in a battle of life or death. He was stronger, but I was better trained.

I frantically searched the ground for something to use as a weapon. My bow and arrow were leaning against a log by the bonfire; otherwise, he'd be dead by now. My hand alighted on a jagged branch just as Thorne lunged toward me.

I dodged aside and jabbed at him with my makeshift weapon while screaming for help from whatever god might be listening. I'd even take Mortia's help now.

Thorne's momentum carried him forward and knocked us both off balance as we tumbled into one of the many mud puddles dotting the forest floor. We fought fiercely in the muck, each trying desperately to gain purchase. His bigger size was an advantage in the slippery mud, and he maneuvered himself on top of me, pinning me down with his weight so I could barely breathe.

"Are you really going to kill me?" I asked. "Not a very princely move. But, then again, you're not a very princely fae, are you? You left that stuff to your sister."

He growled like a feral beast and pinned my hands above my head in the mud. "I told you to leave while you had the chance. And yes. I'm really going to kill you."

Fear lanced through me, dumping adrenaline into my bloodstream. A threat in Fen held more weight than a threat anywhere else in existence. He wasn't bluffing. He wasn't lying. Thorne intended to kill me.

In one lousy chess move, I'd thrown myself into a fight I had little chance of surviving.

Thorne

Gabrelle Allura was pinned beneath me in the mud, with mist swirling around us and dark trees looming overhead. My chest pressed against her blood-red leather corset, and her breasts squeezed out the top. My leather-clad legs were spread on either side of her, but I was careful not to leave her room to move—those thigh-high black hunting boots would do a lot of damage.

I pressed her wrists into the squishy ground above her head. We were close enough that her passionfruit scent mingled with the smell of the mud. She spat a lock of dusty pink hair out of her mouth and tried to tempt me with a smile. "You can't kill me, Thorne, yo—"

"Don't call me that," I growled. She had no right to use my first name. She'd asked permission, and I'd denied it, yet she was poking the bear. I was already filled with cold rage, and she was making it worse.

"Please don't interrupt," she said calmly as though she was holding court. "As I was saying, you can't kill me because your courtiers will be disgusted with you. There's no way they'll support you onto the throne if you murder me in cold blood."

Cold blood was an excellent way to describe the liquid flowing through my veins, ice fucking cold.

"What a shame you will disappear during the Wild Hunt," I said, matching her warm we're-having-a-tea-party tone despite the ice in my veins. "But, of course, several fae succumb to the forest every year. To an over-excited hunter or to one of the native beasts. Or just to the creeping mist."

A tendril of fog curled around my forearms, right beside her face, as though listening to my threat.

"What a pity," I continued, "that a visiting princess will be among this Hunt's victims."

I barely recognized the words spilling from my gritted teeth. I barely recognized the fae I was becoming. I had never killed anybody with my bare hands—sure, I'd ordered executions when the realm's fate required it, but never through personal rage.

But this female brought out the worst in me. She was a liar and a thief, and every syllable out of her mouth was pure venom. Usually about Arrow's death. Or my mother's. Or my lack of training in ruling. Every word she spoke was an arrow tipped with poison she'd designed to torment me.

Well, she wouldn't torment me any longer. She wriggled beneath me, her breathing ragged as her lungs battled to overcome my weight.

Time to end this.

I brought my knees up, either side of her waist, to give me more room to maneuver. I grabbed both her wrists in one hand and shifted to press my other against her throat.

The little firebrand took advantage of my movement and squirmed, mustering all her strength in one last desperate effort to break free. I loosened my hold for a split second, and the trickster princess wriggled out from beneath me in a flash of movement, her black panty-clad ass scrambling away.

She sprinted into the fog, immediately disappearing. Her footsteps grew muffled, seeming to come from all sides, and then disappeared.

"Fuck." I got to my feet and surveyed the scene. The mud was trampled, and the mist hovered and watched, reprimanding me for my failure. I brushed off the clumps of dirt clinging to my brown leather pants and wiped off my bare chest, then headed into the mist toward the bonfire.

Soon, the celebrations would end, and the second hunting round would begin. But I would be long gone before then. I'd done my part as crown prince, opening the Wild Hunt and then chasing down a female dressed as a bunny rabbit with massive white boobs that jiggled gorgeously as I fucked her from behind.

I'd done my part, played politics, and showed my face. Now I could leave.

My heart was heavy as I made my way along the dark path, my mind as foggy as the woods. Memories of my mother and sister floated to the surface of my consciousness, two faces I'd never see again. The only two faces I'd ever cared about.

Arrow died in a Shadow Walker attack on Verdan soil. And yet, every time the Verdan princess opened her mouth, she threw Arrow at me like a weapon when she should be on her knees, begging my forgiveness for the part her own realm played in my sister's death.

Arrow was a good sister and an even better diplomat. She diligently learned the names of ascending family members of all foreign royalty so she could personally congratulate each and every one. She didn't care about egos, she didn't even hold foreigners' lying ways against them, she just wanted to forge cultural connections and ensure the safety of our realm.

And as a result, she was at an Ascension celebration in Verda when the Shadow Walkers attacked. She had been turned into a walking husk of herself and then put down like a true dog. Her head removed, her body salted, and her remains burned.

For weeks afterward, my mother barely spoke. Her eyes were red from crying, and she seemed to be in a trance, unable to process what had happened. I tried my best to comfort her, but nothing helped—not stories about Arrow's courage, hot cups of kraco, or anything else I could think of. I wanted so badly for us both to have some sense of closure, but it felt impossible when there was no body left for us to grieve over.

At least I'd still had Mom. My father was no more than a counterpart in a contract, somebody my mother had agreed to procreate with to produce strong offspring worthy of ruling, and he was never a part of my life. I didn't even know if he was alive. It didn't matter; he was just a DNA donor.

My mother was everything. She could teach me what I needed to know to become a good ruler—we should have had hundreds of years left together.

But then she, too, died in a Shadow Walker attack.

My chest tightened as I remembered sobbing into my mother's dress as she lay lifeless on her bed, cold to the touch yet still smelling faintly of her favorite jasmine perfume.

The Shadow Walker attacks never would have happened if some greedy Verdan sailor hadn't brought the Walkers from the Shadow Isles on his barge. There was nothing the Realm of Verda could do to atone for how they'd destroyed my family.

And Gabrelle Allura just kept kicking my wounds, sticking her dainty little foot into the gash and pounding at my bleeding, broken organs until I couldn't take it any longer.

I finally emerged from the mist and skirted the bonfire at a distance, not wanting to attract any attention. After walking for an hour, I made it back to the Court of Fen and sneaked down the secret staircase in the alleyway that led directly to my chambers.

Needing to feel clean, I beelined for the shower, turned on the hot water, and scrubbed myself in the glorious steam.

The steam was thick and enveloped me in a cocoon of warmth. As the heat trailed down my legs, I thought of Gabrelle Allura again. I hated how beautiful she was, detested every inch of her flawless brown skin and those soft, plum lips that yearned to be kissed.

I hated her long, curving hair in the most exquisite shade of dusty pink and those pink eyes that switched between defiant and seductive, as perfectly deceitful as the rest of her. I could almost feel her curves pressed tight against my body, her slender frame writhing with pleasure under mine.

I imagined what it would be like to have Gabrelle here in my shower with me, the two of us cuddled under the spray, water dripping down our bodies as we explored one another without inhibition.

I remembered the feel of her body pressed beneath mine in the mud, the brutal intensity of her face. Her dismissive laugh echoed in my head, and my cock hardened in response. Images of her blood-red corset and full breasts pressed against my chest played like a movie reel.

My hands moved from my neck and chest, lower and lower, until they found their way to my cock.

My strokes quickened as I imagined her writhing beneath me, her nails digging into my back as she silently begged for more. Knowing that nobody would be able to hear us if we'd fucked in the forest mist made it even more alluring, like a forbidden secret only for us.

The hot water ran over my body as I pleasured myself with Gabrelle's body on repeat in my mind.

I imagined her tight pussy pressed against mine as we moved together in perfect harmony, her breasts bouncing with each thrust. Her moans filled the room and gave me goosebumps of pleasure. Every part of her body was on fire and begged for more attention from me.

My breathing quickened as I closed my eyes and allowed myself to be fully immersed in this fantasy world with Gabrelle Allura as queen. She looked up at me with big pink eyes full of passion and desire.

I increased the pressure and intensity, taking pleasure in every sensation that washed over me, each stroke more exquisite than the last until I couldn't take it anymore. With a shuddering gasp, I sprayed cum all over the shower tiles.

Gabrelle

The days and nights of the Wild Hunt blurred together, and I enjoyed hunting several different males and one female—just for the variety. After I returned to the Court, I slept for days, not even caring about the dreariness of my room.

Waking up, feeling refreshed, I felt a burst of excitement. The entire city of Isslia had closed down for the Wild Hunt, and to celebrate the beginning of a new year, the Court was holding a ball.

Finally, all the luggage I'd brought would be handy. There were numerous options: gowns made of light and delicate fabrics in shades of ivory, navy blue, and emerald green. Each was beautiful, but tonight I wanted to turn heads.

Finally deciding on a white gown with intricate gold embroidery stitched along the bodice, sleeves, and skirt hemline, I called for my Dresser to help me before remembering she wasn't with me. Nor were any of my other serving fae or friends. And Prince Prick certainly hadn't provided me with any help.

No matter, I could do it myself. Taking the dress out of its protective covering with reverence, I inspected it before slipping it over my head. The fabric felt like a gentle caress against my skin as it hugged my curves and draped gracefully to the floor. I paired it with a long cape of midnight blue velvet lined with ivory satin. Its hood framed my face in an elegant way that would draw attention to me without being too ostentatious.

To complete the look and drive home the point that I was a damn princess and should be treated with respect, I added a diamond tiara encrusted with rubies that made my eyes sparkle.

The throne room had been converted into a grand ballroom. The bluestone pillars and the mosaic of snowflakes on the ceiling looked less austere when paired with warm glowing torches, light string music, and hundreds of well-dressed fae. Even the raised ice throne on the central dais looked less imposing.

I'd nailed my outfit. Back home, the hooded velvet cape would have been too much, but Fen was a more formal realm, and here, even the tiara worked.

Heads turned as I passed. As the heir to the throne of beauty in the Realm of Greed and Excess meant I was always in the spotlight. Sometimes it bothered me. Sometimes I outright hated it. But tonight, I planned to use it.

Sneaking my way around the Court to find the Stone of Veritas hadn't worked, so I had to change tactics. I would go back to my roots and flirt my way to success.

Mother would be so proud. That thought was almost enough to stop me, but there was more at stake than just my identity, more than just the question of whether I was a beauty queen like my mother or a stealth master like my father.

I had to find the Stone. It was the only weapon against the Shadow Walkers. Once it was found, I could go back to my identity crisis. I still had months before my Ascension to figure it all out.

GABRELLE

Music swelled from the corner, where a small orchestra played classical music. Just strings and faeboe—perhaps I could become a musician when all this was over. No, who was I kidding? I loved court life usually...but less so when I was being hunted by the crown prince.

A male in a crisp blue suit that complemented his hair and eyes asked me to dance, and I willingly agreed. He moved elegantly and fawned all over me, but when I asked about the Stone of Veritas, he told me he'd never heard of it. I moved on to another dance partner, then another, swapping leather cologne for rose perfume and tailored suits for beautiful gowns, but not discovering anything about the Stone of Veritas.

A voice boomed from behind me. "May I have this dance, Gabrelle?"

I whirled around. Sanctus. "How can I refuse?" I said sweetly, accepting his hand. "I mean, really, is there a way I can refuse? Because if there is, I'd love to."

He ignored me and pulled me close, and the orchestra began a slow melody that had us moving languidly around the floor.

"You dance well," he said.

I looked up at him, not bothering to bat my lashes or smile. "Why did you ask me to dance? Is this an apology?"

"No," he said. "Absolutely not. Where are the other heirs, your friends?" He spoke that last word like he barely knew how to pronounce it. How many friends did Prince Prick have? None that I could see.

The other heirs had returned to Verda as soon the Wild Hunt was over, and I knew at least one would visit Caprice next week for their Ascension rite.

But that was none of Sanctus's business, and I refused to be distracted by his questions. "If it isn't an apology, do you still intend to kill me?"

He chuckled darkly, pulling me close to whisper in my ear. "Absolutely, little trickster. Unless you leave the realm willingly." His breath was hot and minty, leaving the skin of my arms in gooseflesh. Threats had a way of doing that to me.

I twirled out to arm's length, then spiraled close again. "What if I told somebody?" I asked. "What would you do then? If one of these courtiers flat-out asked you for the truth, demanded to know if you tried to murder me on the Hunt? You'd be screwed."

He shook his head as though I were a foolish faeling while directing me gracefully between the other dancing couples. "There are other ways of answering a question than with the whole truth. In fact, fae hear their own version of the truth, regardless of what they're told. I could simply say that I thought you were slightly unhinged, which I do, and they would take that as a denial."

I scoffed, catching his minty scent and noticing the darker undertones. "Indeed. For somebody obsessed with honesty, you're the best liar I've ever met."

Thorne pressed his hand into the small of my back, guiding me smoothly. "I never lie," he growled, his ferocity taking me by surprise. "I live in Fen, the realm of truth, verity, and honesty. Things you know little about."

"Hmm," I said, twirling under his raised arm. "The Realm of Verity and Lies. You've perfected the art of deceit, Thorne. For you, it isn't about the words you say, it's about the ones you don't. And, if you do speak, one has to listen very carefully to all the silences to figure out what's actually happening."

"Don't be ludicrous. You have no idea what you're talking about."

GABRELLE

I plastered an innocent look on my face, concealing the storm of emotions swirling within me. "What? Me? The princess of trickery, as you keep calling me. Are you suggesting I don't know anything about truth and lies?" In fact, with my father's Stealth running through my blood, and my mother's Lure, I knew more about deception than anybody. Annoyingly, my frustration toward Thorne was tingled with admiration because his straightforwardness contrasted with my own carefully crafted deceptions.

He laughed darkly and spun me around. "Oh, you are exactly what it says on the box. A deceptive, cold bitch."

I maintained my façade of calm, though beneath the surface, a pang of hurt and defiance stung. "Why, thank you, prince," I said coquettishly with a false smile.

I'd worked hard on learning to master my emotions, and being an ice-cold bitch was part of the price. No, it was the prize. So this male's insults washed off me. If he'd called me a beauty queen or a superficial seductress, I might have been offended.

He held me close and muttered rude nothings in my ear while I smiled like a mannequin. Anybody watching would assume we were having a perfectly polite conversation—apart from the scowl engraved on Thorne's face.

At least Thorne Sanctus was exactly the fae he was. He was upfront and frank, not nearly as calculating as me. Everything about me was an act—either Lure or Stealth, temptation or disguise, beauty or lies. No part of me was real. But everything about Thorne was real. I couldn't help admiring that. I didn't have to like the prick—in fact, it was really hard to work up enthusiasm for someone who wanted you dead—but I still admired him.

He was one hundred percent Thorne Sanctus, Crown Prince Prick.

As soon as the song ended, I nodded at the prince. "So long, Thorne. I hope I never have to dance with you again." I walked off with a genuine smile on my lips—I quite liked this honesty stuff.

I tried dancing with some more fae, but I had no luck flirting out the whereabouts of the Stone of Veritas. Either everybody was far too guarded and protective of their secrets, or they had none. Disappointment and frustration warred within me until I couldn't take it any longer.

I curtsied at my latest partner and left the ballroom. If I had any hope of finding the Stone, it would not be here, and now was an excellent opportunity to explore. I'd spent hours upon hours scouring the Court with no luck, but I couldn't give up.

Maybe Thorne didn't have the damn Stone. But if he didn't, who did? Who even knew about its existence? Nobody that I'd spoken to about it. The more questions that came up, the more desperate and anxious I felt.

My feet clattered against the lifeless stone floor, echoing as I made my way down the deserted corridors of the Court. The chilling darkness closed in, suffocating me, its weight squeezing my chest and seeping into my bones.

My mind went all over the place, scattered and unfocused. I was completely alone and vulnerable as hell. If someone jumped me here, not even the gods would hear my screams.

Damn, Gabrelle, keep it together.

Every creak, every whisper of movement magnified in the deep stillness, sending shivers of terror cascading down my spine. My pulse quickened, urging me to run faster as though an unseen danger lurked just behind me, ready to strike. In this dim labyrinth, the walls seemed to twist and writhe, creating menacing silhouettes that stalked my every step. The once familiar Court now felt like a sinister trap, each corner a potential hiding place for my impending doom.

If I was killed in this gloomy tunnel, all hope of finding the Stone would be lost. The Shadow Walkers would rule uncontested over Arathay. I spun toward a sound as something stirred in a nearby alcove. Somebody was there.

Then Erevan was behind me, holding me, calming me down and comforting me. "What's wrong, Gabrelle? You're so spooked. Is everything okay?"

I turned and looked at him, my heart still pounding. "Why are you here?" I demanded.

"I saw you leave the ball, and you looked distressed, so I followed you." His face was soft with concern. "Is that okay?"

My strength fled, and I burrowed my head into his warm shoulder. "Thorne's trying to kill me, and I need to find the Stone of Veritas before he does." Erevan's arms were strong and protective, tightening around me at those words.

"That useless prick will never lay a finger on you if I have anything to do with it," he said. "I promise. I will do whatever I can to protect you."

I sagged against him, feeling suddenly exhausted.

"And," Erevan continued. "I'll help you find that Stone, whatever it is. I promise."

A promise in a realm where every word is a promise. I smiled, feeling safe for the first time in days.

Thorne

I kept my eye on Gabrelle Allura for the rest of the evening. She danced with several fae, batting her too-long eyelashes and flashing that sneaky smile. What was she up to, and why was she still hanging around?

It would be political suicide to ask her to leave. But after I tried to kill her at the Wild Hunt, I figured she'd scurry back to her den of greed and lust. But there she was, strutting around like nothing happened. She took it all in her stride as though she was used to living on the edge of danger. Her grace and poise were remarkable, especially since I'd threatened her again only minutes before.

An unwilling admiration and respect for Gabrelle Allura settled through me. She hadn't backed down from me, even when faced with death. Where did she find that well of courage and resilience, that strength of will? It was not an easy feat, yet here she was, still dancing and enjoying the evening despite being threatened by the Crown Prince of the Realm.

Gabrelle spun around the room, seemingly unaffected by my presence or anything else around her. The female had nerves of steel. Her carefree attitude made me envious; here I was, a bundle of nerves, constantly on edge.

A hand landed lightly on my shoulder, and Mannia Lanserne,

a seasoned politician and courtier, extended an invitation for a dance.

"Yes, I will dance with you," I replied.

Mannia Lanserne was an influential politician and senior courtier, and I needed to win her to my side if I wanted a battle-free coronation.

We twirled across the floor, discussing matters of trade and the upcoming coronation, our conversation blending seamlessly with the music and laughter that filled the ballroom. I asked for her support in my bid to become king, but she gave me no promises, just a vaguely worded resolution to "support the rightful ruler."

Perhaps Gabrelle was right, and we Fen fae were the best liars in Arathay. She told me I'd perfected the art of deceit, and maybe she was right. Perhaps we weren't that different from the fae of Verda. Or, even worse, perhaps the difference was that we hid our dishonesty behind a facade of truth, adding an extra layer of deception to our lies.

Lost in my thoughts about Gabrelle, I barely registered Mannia Lanserne's words as we swayed in a circle on the dance floor. "Are you paying attention?" Mannia snapped.

I realized we'd been swaying back and forth in one spot while my thoughts were locked on Gabrelle. "No, I was thinking of somebody else," I admitted.

The green-haired courtier frowned at me and released me from her grip. "Then you had better go and talk to whomever you cannot shake from your thoughts."

Dammit. I had just pissed off a powerful courtier—Gabrelle was affecting my political aspirations just by lurking in my mind.

I glanced across at the trickster princess. Her dusty pink

hair was glowing in the soft lighting, and the subtle gold embroidery in her gown marked her as special. Her tiara was less subtle. Way less subtle. She was bashing me over the head, reminding me she was a princess.

Well, she was still out of her own realm and interfering in my business, hurting my prospects of continuing my family's legacy as monarchs of the kingdom.

The princess smiled prettily at her dance partner and excused herself, then slinked through the crowd. Her dress clung to her hips and belly, and when she moved, reflecting every sparkle in the room. She really was beauty personified, a perfect collection of curves and grace. Pity about the personality.

I beckoned over a senior serving fae, one of many who watched my movements in case I needed something. He was by my side in an instant. "Can I help you, Your Highness?"

"Follow Princess Allura. Report back to me on her movements. Do not let her see you."

"Yes, Prince Sanctus." He watched me for a moment longer, waiting for further instructions.

"Go!" I barked, and he scurried after the graceful princess.

I couldn't allow myself to lose sight of the fact that she was still a trickster princess. But perhaps my own biases about the Realm of Verda were clouding my judgment.

When I was younger, I had heard stories of the Realm of Verda's glories and excesses, tales of pleasure-seekers and those who sought to make a quick buck, and a reputation for corruption and deception. But those stories were always told with a tinge of envy from my elders, whispers about how the fae of Verda got away with anything they wanted because their royal families had more money than decency.

The stories were likely exaggerated, but it was hard to forget them—and even harder not to be prejudiced against Verdan fae.

But perhaps that was just a bias or misconception? After all, no kingdom would ever be completely perfect or untainted by corruption—even my realm. Gabrelle was eager to point that out.

Maybe Princess Allura represented more than I had given her credit for? After all, she seemed able to balance her diplomatic responsibilities and her personal interests, an impressive feat in its own right. The very fact she was still here showed resilience and persistence. Her fae-reading skills were certainly remarkable—she seemed to know exactly how to get fae to do what she wanted without them being aware of it. Perhaps I should credit her with strong social skills rather than writing it off as a masterclass in deception.

I sighed. I stepped out of the way as a couple whirled past me, their heads close together in earnest conversation. Balls in Fen were always a mix of pleasure and politics, and no dance was complete without a pointed discussion.

The music became more upbeat, signaling a change in the evening, the transition from business to pleasure. But I wasn't here for fun, so that was my cue to leave.

As though reading my mind, Staven Jeffers waddled to my side and leaned close. "It would be politically wise for you to stay longer."

"Politics is over for the evening, Staven," I said with a dismissive wave.

My advisor's wrinkles weighed him down, and his voice was wispy, but his words were heavy. "Politics is never over, Thorne."

He was right, of course. But with my mind on Gabrelle

and my thoughts whirling, I was doing more harm here than good—my dance with Mannia Lanserne was proof of that. Honestly, I didn't care much about sitting on the throne. I was only here to honor my mother's legacy.

"I am leaving anyway," I said, speaking the truth, but not all of it. Dammit, that beautiful princess was infecting my thoughts, her weaselly words burrowing into my brain. I could see the deceit in myself now, more clearly than ever.

"Take the back door," Staven instructed me, speaking plainly.

I moved out of the way of a whirling green gown attached to a smiling female and nodded. "Good idea."

With Mother and Arrow gone, Staven was the closest thing I had to family. My closest advisor. My closest friend. And he was about a million years old, so he had wisdom etched into his wrinkles, and I would be foolish to ignore his advice.

I followed his instructions, leaving the ballroom and passing by the ice throne on my way. Its beauty was still breathtakingly impressive, even after years of admiring it. Would I ever earn the right to sit on it? Did I even really want to?

After winding through the curving hallways of the Court and taking the lesser-known routes, I eventually reached the stairwell that opened into a quiet alleyway, hidden away from prying eyes.

The cold air hit me as soon as I stepped outside, sending shivers down my back. The quiet of the night was a welcome relief from all the chatter and swish of ball gowns in the ballroom. The stars winked at me from above, and in that moment, I felt truly alone.

Isslia was an ancient city full of secrets, and I felt its energy pulse through me as I made my way down the cobbled streets.

Its low bluestone buildings were enchanting in their own right, steeped in history and stories so intricate they seemed mythical. As I walked further away from the palace walls into more residential areas, I noticed signs of life: small gatherings of fae sitting outside their homes, huddled around small fires, their laughter and chatter carrying through the chill night air.

I made my way through the alleys, footsteps echoing against the stone walls. Every now and then, a stray cat darted out from a shadowy corner, scurrying away at my approach. The bustle of the Court felt like a distant memory, replaced by the peaceful sound of my breathing and the distant chatter of the fae residents.

As I walked in random paths, trying to clear my head, my thoughts kept drifting back to Princess Allura. There was something about her that intrigued me, despite her manipulative nature. Perhaps it was her resilience, or maybe it was the way she carried herself with such confidence. Whatever it was, I couldn't deny her pull on me.

I shook my head, trying to clear my thoughts. I had more important things to worry about, like the future of my realm and my family's legacy. I needed to focus on the future, not on some trickster princess, so it was more important than ever that she leave. With or without her consent.

Thorne

The following morning, I awoke feeling empty and flat, like a crushed cardboard box. The ball had been a colossal failure; only a handful of courtiers pledged their support. Meanwhile, I'd been obsessing over Gabrelle Fucking Allura and how the hell to get rid of her.

Killing her hadn't worked, nor had threatening her. She just held her head even higher on that elegant neck and smiled more damn winningly.

Even worse, she'd managed to invade my evening walk, the precious time I set aside to decompress and figure shit out. Suddenly, my preconceived notions about Verda came crashing down. Maybe it wasn't the cesspool of debauchery I'd always thought. Maybe it was no more messed up than Fen.

Mother was dead. Arrow was dead. The whole damn world was falling apart, and it all started with me. I needed a break. Bad.

I had to escape Isslia and go to my favorite place in Fen—the Wizen Woods. As a faeling, I'd spent countless hours in that tiny shed, seeking solace from the chaos of the Court.

As I walked through the woods, the rustling orange leaves beneath my feet shattered the silence, and I kicked up twigs and small stones with every step. Finally, the shed appeared, just as I remembered it. The wood had faded to a silvery gray, full of knotholes and cracks. The roof sported a vibrant green, sprinkled with a spray of moss. Stepping inside, I found the interior surprisingly well-maintained, as if someone had been dusting and sweeping regularly, though I knew that couldn't be true.

I slid down the wall with a sigh and sat on the floor, breathing deeply. The floorboards creaked and settled beneath me, and a faint, musty smell of age and dampness laced the air. Outside this place, I felt like I was suffocating—the stuffiness of the Court was weighing heavily on me. But in the shed, I could finally breathe.

But when I closed my eyes, a prickling sensation told me I was being watched. I opened them again, expecting to find someone, but the shed stood empty. Still, that eerie feeling lingered, refusing to let go.

A figure appeared in the doorway as if on cue, blocking the sunlight filtering through the green forest. It was Gabrelle Allura, dressed in tight brown hunting leathers, her bow and arrow held casually in her hands. She tilted her head, wearing that sly expression that screamed she knew more than I did.

"Hello," she said. "I wondered where you'd wandered off to."

I shot up to my feet, refusing to give her the advantage of height. "You followed me?" Outrage dripped from my words.

"You know," she purred, her voice dripping with mischief, "you can run from Court all you want, but that won't stop me chasing you."

"But how?"

She inspected her arrow, a graceful movement that oozed indifference. "It wasn't that hard, Thorne. You kept looking over your shoulder like a nervous chipmunk, practically broadcasting your intention to sneak away. And then you scurried between shadows like a first-rate sneak fail. Word of advice, Thorne, from one trickster heir to another: If you're going to sneak, don't scurry. It attracts attention and ruins the whole stealth thing."

She had a point. So did that make me a better fae than her because I was worse at sneaking around? Or did it just make me incompetent? "One trickster heir to another," I grumbled, playing back her irritating words.

She shrugged. "If the shoe fits."

I wasn't in the mood for a fight, so I let it slide. "Alright, then, why?" I asked. "Why did you follow me? Because you were dying to hang out with me in this crappy old shed?"

Gabrelle looked around, taking in the worn-down shed. It was about ten feet by twenty feet, with walls made of aging wood and glass that hadn't been touched in years. It was clean but barely functional.

"No," she said, chewing her lip. "I wasn't expecting this."

"What were you expecting? A secret lair full of the realm's deepest mysteries?"

She paused as if my joke had hit close to home. "Something like that."

I laughed and sank back down the wall, exhaustion seeping into my bones. All the mind games and battles of wits were draining me. I had come here to escape all that for a few hours, and I wasn't about to let this nosy princess ruin it. I rested my head in my hands and closed my eyes. Not very princely, but I didn't give a damn about appearances.

"So, you're not going to attack me?" she asked warily.

"No."

"Promise?"

I sighed. "Every word is a promise in Fen. I won't attack you in this shed."

She stood by the door, shifting her weight and making the floorboard creak. "And you won't push me out the door and stab me or something?"

I shook my head, my forehead swishing against my palms. "No. I won't attack you today. I promise. Okay? Now stop talking, please, I'm trying not to think."

Sounds by the door made me curious, and I lifted my head to peek. Gabrelle had set her bow by the door and removed the quiver of arrows from her back, placing it beside the wooden weapon. Then, she gracefully sat down, crossing her legs.

In her hunting leathers, she looked like a warrior. Still beautiful, but more noble, somehow, than when she wore a gown. But I still didn't trust a word out of her mouth.

She was watching me, curious. "Did you say you were trying *not* to think?"

"Yes. And all this talking is making it difficult."

She shrugged. "I'm not here to make your life easier. What are you trying not to think about?"

The word *you* sprung into my mind, but instead, I said, "Everything," which was also true. Here, in my childhood playground, it felt easier to talk. The world shrank to this narrow space, and the weight of my responsibilities back home seemed to evaporate. I didn't have to be a prince here. I could just be Thorne, the faeling who had played hide-and-seek with Arrow, inventing pretend games and dreaming grand adventures.

"What is this place?" Gabrelle asked, her voice pitched low.

"An old hunter's shed. It was my refuge when I was young.

I came here to get away from Mother or when I needed some time alone. Other times Arrow would come, and we played together."

Gabrelle looked around at the walls full of memories. She pointed to a spot between two boards of wood, where a few basic drawings were still visible after all these years. "You did those?"

"Yeah," I said softly, feeling oddly vulnerable. "I used to come here and draw pictures while trying to think up new adventure stories for me and my sister."

I waited for a barbed comment, some jibe about Arrow being dead and me being unprepared for the role of king. Every time my sister came up in conversation, Gabrelle used it as a chance to shoot me down.

But not this time. She just looked around, her intense pink gaze taking everything in. "How does pretending work? You can't say, 'We're pirates sailing in a blue boat' because the realm's magic won't allow the lie."

Gabrelle didn't seem to be goading me. She seemed genuinely curious.

But the thought of everything I'd lost made my voice harsher than intended. "Don't be an idiot. You just said, 'We're pirates sailing in a blue boat.' Being truthful isn't the same thing as lacking in imagination." I didn't say it, but I had often wondered if the realm magic affected my creativity, dampening it somehow. But the trickster didn't need to know that.

The silence that descended was heavier than before as if something had shifted but gone unsaid. It felt like Gabrelle wanted to ask more about my sister, whether I missed her or was still grieving. I waited for her to voice the question, wanting to talk about Arrow but dreading it at the same time. But Gabrelle just kept looking around the shed, and the moment passed with the question left unasked.

I took a deep breath and said, "I'm going now." I climbed to my feet. I didn't feel any more energetic or lighter than before I came—perhaps the shed had lost its touch now that Arrow was gone. Maybe my sister's death had stolen whatever magic resided in this place.

Or maybe it was just this interfering princess who turned everything she touched to rot.

I waved a hand around the near-empty shed. "Feel free to search the boards for hidden treasure or expensive faeboes, or whatever it is you're looking for."

To my surprise, a chuckle escaped Gabrelle's lips. "If only it was that simple."

I locked eyes with her, refusing to back down. "You are intelligent."

"Yes," she replied, meeting my gaze from where she sat cross-legged on the floor. Her eyebrows knitted together for a moment as she tried to figure out where my line of questioning was coming from.

"You are cunning."

"Thank you," she said flippantly, deciding to take it as a compliment.

"Good with fae."

"Of course."

"So just tell me why you're really here—enough with the bullshit about passing on condolences for my mother. Whatever it is, maybe I can help you, so you can hurry up and leave Fen."

She parted her lips and, in one graceful movement, got to her feet. She stared me up and down as if assessing my trustworthiness—which was hilarious, coming from her.

"If I tell you, will you help me?" she asked, her pink gaze piercing and intense.

"Didn't I just say so?" I demanded, a note of frustration creeping into my voice.

Her eyes narrowed. "No, actually, you said *maybe* you could help me. Then you tried to wriggle out of it by saying, 'Didn't I just say so?' which was technically a question instead of a lie. But still misleading. So no, I definitely can't trust you, and I definitely won't tell you what I'm here for. Other than to pass on my condolences." She snatched up her bow and arrow and, with one hand on the doorknob, she turned over her shoulder. "Condolences," she spat, then she stalked away.

Gabrelle

I couldn't hold Erevan off any longer, so I promised to go with him to dinner the next evening. We met in the central plaza of the Court, and when he saw me in my figure-hugging purple jumpsuit, his eyes almost exploded. "Good Gaia, Gabrelle. You look devastating."

He pulled my hand to his lips, and I smiled. Compliments about my beauty always put me at ease, making me feel right at home in these conversations.

Erevan took me to a restaurant in the middle of Isslia. The room was stark and almost colorless, a bareness that made it seem cold and uninviting. Its walls were simple white stone, its floors plain flagstones, and its seating was straight-backed and uncomfortable.

"I've been in cozier places," I said dryly after we'd been ushered to a seat. My back was against a mirrored wall, and he sat to my right.

Erevan smiled, his eyes twinkling. "I wanted to show you that things aren't always as they seem here in Fen."

His clothes were immaculately pressed and perfectly tailored, accentuating his broad shoulders, strong arms, and well-defined waist. His butterscotch eyes twinkled as he smiled, and the fabric of his shirt seemed to glow in the stark light of the restaurant.

His expression was flirty and interested, and it made me feel comfortable. I was at home in this situation. I'd had this evening a thousand times before with a thousand similar males, always on my own terms.

I smiled silkily. "Oh, yes? You've made me curious. What runs beneath the surface?"

Erevan leaned in closer, his eyes locked onto mine. "Secrets, Gabrelle. Deep, dark secrets. The kind that keep you up at night, wondering what's really going on behind closed doors."

A shiver ran the length of my spine. There was something almost sinister about the way he spoke, as if he wasn't the fae I thought, wasn't just like all the other males I'd spent a thousand evenings flirting with. "And what about you, Erevan? What secrets do you keep hidden away?"

He chuckled, a low, throaty sound that piqued my interest. "Oh, I have plenty. But they're not nearly as interesting as the ones I could tell about this city and its citizens."

A waiter brought us wine, a cold-climate white from the mountains of Ourea that was pleasantly dry on my palette but not as good as a Dionysus.

After the waiter left, I ran a lazy finger around the rim of my wine glass. "Tell me more about Isslia's secrets," I murmured.

Erevan leaned in, his breath warm against my ear. "Well, for starters, this restaurant is run by a bunch of smugglers. It's their cover for all sorts of illegal activities."

Now, that was interesting. I swirled my wine. "Illegal activities? And here I was thinking that fae from Fen were all uptight bastards."

He grinned. "They smuggle in exotic stuff from other realms, things that are forbidden here in Fen. Like Loweena leaves from Verda or Unseelie jewelry from the Realm of Dust. They've got it all."

"Unseelie jewelry?" I asked. That was notoriously hard to find, even back home, and completely outlawed in the uptight utopia of Fen.

Erevan sipped his wine. "They're very careful not to get caught."

I shrugged. "They'd better be. They're ruled by a king with a swing-happy executioner."

Erevan grumbled, "Thorne isn't king. He's just babysitting until the real ruler gets crowned."

Interesting. I knew Erevan was a political rival but didn't realize he had serious designs on the throne. I cast a seductive smile and tilted my chin to soften the question, to hide how much I wanted the answer. "And, let me guess, the rightful king is you?"

He glanced at me, his butterscotch eyes warming the stark light in their reflection. "Maybe not the rightful king, but I'm the right king."

He took a long gulp of wine, and I sipped on mine while I considered his words. He obviously believed them—otherwise, he couldn't have spoken them—but were they true? Would Erevan make a better ruler than Thorne? I liked him a lot more, but being likable wasn't exactly a prerequisite for ruling.

A waiter came and took our orders. Annoyingly, Erevan ordered for me, but I just smiled, and as soon as the serving fae left, I asked, "Why are you the right king?"

Leaning back in his chair, Erevan narrowed his eyes slightly, contemplating his response. "Because I get the fae of Fen. I understand their needs, their desires, and their fears. And I know how to lead them to a better future."

He paused, his gaze intense. "Thorne, on the other hand, is too caught up in preserving tradition and upholding his family's legacy. He's not willing to take risks or make bold decisions. He's just not the leader Fen needs right now."

I took another sip of wine, savoring the crisp, icy taste. "So, what kind of leader would you be, Erevan?"

He smiled, a slow, seductive curve of his lips. "A visionary one. Someone who isn't afraid of the future."

I chewed my lip, thinking. "Thorne has a steel rod up his ass, but his family has ruled for centuries. It's in his blood." As a crown princess, I didn't want to start a trend of usurping the rightful rulers—even if they were dicks.

Erevan scoffed. "You've met his family, right?"

"Of course. I paid my respects to Queen Sanctus when I last visited Isslia. And Arrow attends many of the same Ascension events as I do, in all the different realms."

"Attended, you mean. Before she died."

I tilted my head. "Obviously." Being corrected was a pet peeve of mine, especially on such a pedantic point. But this conversation was more interesting than I expected, so I persevered. "What of it?"

He slowly tapped the table with a finger as though tapping out a beat with his thoughts. "You say the Sanctus family is bred to rule. And Arrow considered herself an excellent diplomat. But she wasn't."

I waited for him to say more, but he just stared at me as though he'd proved his point, his finger tapping away on the table. "Was that a question?" I finally asked.

"Come on, tell me. What did you and the other Verdan heirs think of Arrow?"

I opened my mouth to say something diplomatic and measured, but instead, I said, "We all thought she was a bitch. Honesty is one thing, but she took it too far—there's no need to be such an asshole."

Erevan burst out laughing. I joined in, although in a more measured way, and the tension from our conversation melted away. Erevan made an enjoyable companion. Charming, intelligent, and surprisingly insightful. Maybe he would make a good king after all.

"You said you met Arrow Sanctus at Ascension events throughout Arathay?" he asked. "Perhaps I should start attending them to build connections in other realms."

I cast my face neutral. "That would be a wise diplomatic move. I'm surprised you haven't already thought of it."

Irritation skittered across his face, but he quickly hid it. "I couldn't make such a bold move on the throne while Queen Sanctus still ruled. But, with her unfit son in charge, things are different." He gave me a hungry once-over. "Perhaps I'll attend your Ascension in Verda. I believe it is in a little over two months."

I smiled. "Well, well, looks like someone's paying attention."

"Of course." He snapped his fingers, and a serving fae refilled our wine glasses. "I assume you will ascend into Lure," he said silkily, devouring me with his gaze. "Your beauty combined with that power would make you an unstoppable force."

Trying to suppress the truth bubbling within me, fueled by Gaia's realm magic, I took a gulp of wine to keep it at bay. Honestly, I hadn't made up my mind about my ascension yet. My mother had Lure, and my father had Stealth, and both intrigued me. But being like my mother was the last thing I wanted, so I was leaning toward choosing Stealth.

"Well, lucky for me, I still have ten weeks to decide," I said truthfully, but I added a playful smile to make it sound less like I was confessing my indecisiveness.

As our food arrived, Erevan launched into a discussion about his plans for Fen's future. He spoke passionately about his ideas for change, progress, and building a better tomorrow. Grabbing his wine glass, he motioned for me to do the same. "To a better future," he said, clinking his glass against mine.

While I didn't want to encourage coups against rightful leaders, I couldn't deny that collaborating with Fen would be more effective under Erevan's rule than Thorne's. I smiled, buying some time to come up with the proper response, but Erevan didn't let up. "Speaking of a better future, I have some news that might interest you."

His voice was low and serious now, and I leaned forward in anticipation. This evening was becoming very fruitful. Erevan took a sip of wine before speaking. "My sources have located the Stone of Veritas."

My pulse jumped. Had he really found it? After weeks of searching in vain, had Erevan managed to track it down? "Where is it?" I asked languidly, but my white knuckles twisting my napkin gave away my urgency.

Erevan leaned closer and dropped his voice even lower. "It's hidden in the catacombs beneath Essylia Castle."

The geography of the realms was hammered into us heirs from a young age, and the name Essylia Castle was familiar. "That's the old seat of power in Fen? Where the kings and queens used to live, thousands of years ago."

He nodded. "I'm impressed. It's a ruin now, on the northern coast of Fen. The terrain is treacherous, and there are a bunch of pissed-off magical creatures between here and there. I don't know why you want the Stone, but if I were you, I'd think twice about going after it."

Lost in thought, I absentmindedly chewed my lip. I couldn't let Erevan know how crucial the Stone was to me—I didn't trust him not to try and snatch it for himself. But I was prepared to face any number of wild creatures to get my hands on it. I'd rather encounter a pteroclaw or a croconad than be zombified by a Shadow Walker.

"That lip thing you do is very distracting."

"Is it?" Of course I knew it was, but in this case, it wasn't deliberate.

Erevan cocked his head, his eyes smoldering. "So, I suppose you won't tell me why you want that Stone?"

I bit my lip again. It was deliberate this time. "No. Not even if you torture it out of me," I said slowly, using my mouth to full effect, well aware of how he stared at it.

Amusement danced in Erevan's eyes as he leaned across the table, his lips almost touching mine. "Is that a challenge, princess?" he whispered. "Because you know I'm up for it."

I grinned. "Not a challenge, just a fact."

Erevan's warm breath ghosted over my lips. "Well, I suppose I can't fault a fae for her secrets."

"Not when you're a master of secrets yourself," I answered breathily, heat racing from my mouth all over my skin.

I tipped forward, closing the distance between us, and our lips met in a fiery kiss. His tongue slipped into my mouth, and I moaned softly, deliberately, running my hands through his hair. I had to keep him on my side.

When we finally pulled away, breathless and panting, Erevan rested his forehead against mine. "You drive me crazy," he muttered.

I smirked. "That's the idea."

He chuckled, but then his expression turned serious again. "Are you still going after the Stone?"

"Yes," I whispered.

"I don't want you to."

I smiled and leaned back, opening some space between us. "Too bad."

"At least let me come with you."

The company would be nice. The protection would be even better, but I couldn't fully trust him. With his political motives and desire for the throne, he might seize the Stone for his own gain.

"No," I said. "I must go alone. But..." I stood up slowly so he could take in every inch of my tight purple jumpsuit. "I could use some company tonight."

Thorne

My boots clacking against the marble floor echoed around the chamber as I strode, creating a rhythm that built to a crescendo with every pass. The silk tapestries rustled in the cool breeze from the window.

The meeting with Blostte and Summers was a disaster. Their demands were unreasonable, and I couldn't meet them without selling out my own values. They would only support me onto the throne if I relaxed import restrictions, allowing their businesses to grow. Corrupt fucking assholes.

As I turned the corner, I caught a glimpse of my reflection in one of the mirrors that lined the walls. My eyes were sunken and bloodshot, pitiless black holes, and I looked exhausted.

The truth was, I was tired—not just physically but mentally and emotionally drained. Being in a position of power was never easy, but it was even harder when your position was as tenuous as mine. The coronation was in two weeks, and I still hadn't guaranteed the courtiers' support. They all saw this interregnum period as an opportunity to lobby for their own self-interests, playing me off against my rivals for who would give them a better deal.

But no way was I backing down. My mother ruled with an iron fist, not negotiating with corrupt courtiers, and she taught

Arrow to do the same. Now it was on my shoulders to follow through.

The skills required to gain the throne were different from those required to rule well. Diplomacy versus strength, promises versus action, lies versus truth.

It was like walking a tightrope, trying to keep that delicate balance every day. And now, with Blostte and Summers breathing down my neck, I was about to tip over the edge.

I sank into one of the chairs by the window, letting out a long, dramatic sigh. The view was ethereal, starlight twinkling off the bluestone walls of the Court, a circle of radiance and perfect order. At this time of the evening, the world was settling to rest.

As I contemplated the weight of my responsibilities, a soft footfall sounded behind me. Staven Jeffers shuffled into the room, dragging his wrinkles with him. "Your Highness, you requested updates on the movements of Princess Gabrelle..."

"What is it this time?" I demanded.

"She has accompanied Erevan Reissan to dinner at a restaurant called the Smooth Shellfish."

Dammit. Why did that trickster princess keep causing me trouble? "Are they alone?" I barked.

"Yes, Your Highness."

"Keep me informed. I would like to know where they go next."

"Yes, Your Highness." Staven nodded, and his wispy hair floated around his head. He turned and shuffled out of the room, closing the door behind him.

That news really pissed me off. No point in changing for bed because I had no hope of sleeping while my enemies were conspiring against me. The closer Allura became to Reissan, the worse my position became.

My fingers drummed out a tune on the armrest of the suede chair as I considered the possibilities. I had no proof of treason. Perhaps Gabrelle and Erevan were not discussing the affairs of the kingdom. Perhaps they had a different agenda. They hooked up during the Wild Hunt when emotions and chaos peaked...Was their relationship more than just a political alliance?

Heat spiked through my blood at that prospect. But surely, it was nothing more than anger at two powerful fae working against me. Surely, the hot anger had nothing to do with imagining them together?

My feelings toward Gabrelle were becoming complicated. It was impossible to deny my own biases against the Realm of Verda. Still, I couldn't determine whether those biases influenced my hatred of the trickster princess or justified it.

She'd surprised me at the shed in the Wizen Woods. Not only by turning up in the first place but by her restraint and respect. She hadn't tormented me about Arrow, like usual, but had been quiet and considered as we discussed her.

Dammit, this upcoming coronation was screwing with my head. I didn't even know my own feelings anymore.

A soft knock broke the silence. Staven Jeffers limped into the room, his wrinkles threatening to consume him. "Your Highness," he said with a bow of his white head. "Princess Gabrelle has returned to her bedroom, and Erevan is with her."

My anger boiled over at this news. What was Gabrelle thinking? She was playing with fire—and she had no idea how dangerous it could be. Was she really so naive?

But then, I remembered that she had grown up in Verda—a world filled with creatures far more devious and cunning than any fae in my court. Maybe naivety wasn't the issue here; maybe she knew exactly what she was doing. Either way, I wasn't going to let this go unchecked. Not again.

I nodded solemnly at Staven Jeffers before dismissing him.

I rose from my seat slowly, my mind still racing with questions. What were they doing in there? Was their relationship more than just political?

Gathering my thoughts carefully, I started toward the bedchamber. If something was going on between them, I would find out what it was. It was my prerogative as king to investigate potential treason.

The last time I'd confronted her, she'd wriggled out from under me during the Wild Hunt and fled. But this time, there would be no turning away. This time, Gabrelle wouldn't escape.

I had put the princess in our worst guest room, little more than a musty closet on the fifth floor. Annoyingly, she hadn't voiced a word of complaint—I'd hoped to illustrate how superficial she was by forcing her to complain about her lodgings, but she hadn't made a peep.

By the time I arrived outside her door, Erevan had already left. Her door swung open, and I jumped into a shadow and watched her sneak out alone. She wore her hunting clothes, dark brown leather pants that hugged her hips more than strictly necessary, and a form-fitting brown leather tunic that practically made love to her breasts.

I had already noticed her paying attention to the layout of the Court as if she was making a mental map of it, and now she put it to use. She ducked up a staircase hidden from view by a heavy tapestry depicting a fox hunt, one that was no doubt commissioned centuries ago when such activities were more common at Court.

She somehow managed to avoid all of the guards, so they wouldn't try to stop her from leaving.

I watched her step out into the night air, her bow slung on one side and a pack on the other. She paused for a moment to take it all in, then her chest rose and fell before she strode into the city as if drawn by some invisible force.

I tailed her, making sure to keep a safe distance. She moved with purpose through the winding streets that always reminded me of ice rivers, her dusty pink hair the only color in the world.

Where was she heading? Wherever it was, it would reveal her true purpose for being in Fen, and I had to find it out. She made her way steadily north in as straight a line as the winding streets allowed. Thank Gaia, I hadn't changed into my pajamas and still wore a long-sleeved shirt, long black pants, and boots. Not quite as practical as Gabrelle's hunting leathers, but it would do.

I followed her at a distance and stuck to the building's shadows wherever I could, keeping my feet silent on the paving stones. Finally, we reached the city outskirts, where the bluestone buildings met the dense green forest. Gabrelle paused for a moment, looking up at the wild wood. Surely, she didn't intend to go in there? Everybody in Fen knew the dangers that lurked in the forests, the desperate beasts and the ever-shifting swamps.

But she did. She hunched down her shoulders and strode into the forest without a backward glance.

"Fuck," I murmured. What the hell should I do now? This was my best chance at uncovering her treason—or whatever the hell she was doing—but the city ended here for a reason. Because everything beyond was deadly.

"Fuck," I said again, then walked to the forest's edge and stepped inside. The starlight immediately dimmed, struggling to penetrate the thick canopy. It smelled of mud filled with rotting leaves, like mangroves on steroids, and I tried to breathe in sips to avoid the stench.

I could barely see Gabrelle ahead, just a blur in the darkness. I had to be careful not to get too close so she didn't hear me coming. But it was difficult, especially in the low light. I followed Gabrelle's faint path through the woods, using my ears more than my eyes. I heard her steps, soft and sure as if she'd been born in these forests.

I heard a sudden movement and saw a glint of steel in the dark, then something cold and sharp pressed against my throat.

Gabrelle stood behind me, her dagger pressed to my neck. "Why are you following me?" she hissed, her glowing eyes full of anger.

I held up my hands in surrender, my heart racing. I wouldn't put it past this female to slice me open. "I could ask you the same thing," I said, trying to keep my voice steady. "What are you doing out here, trickster?"

She didn't answer, her grip on the dagger tightening. The blade pricked my skin, and warm blood trickled down my neck, but I refused to back down.

"I need to know what you're up to," I said, trying to stay calm. "You and Erevan. Are you plotting against me?"

Gabrelle's eyes narrowed. "Erevan and I are just friends," she said, her voice cold. "And even if we weren't, it's none of your business."

"It is my business," I said, my voice rising. "I'm the king of this realm, Gabrelle. If you're plotting against me, it's treason!"

Gabrelle laughed bitterly, the sound echoing through the forest. "Treason?" she said. "I have no fucking interest in your realm or your politics, okay? Zero."

The pressure at my throat eased, and the dangerous princess stepped away, letting me breathe and think. "You're not working with Erevan to take my throne?"

Her pink eyes blazed from her dark face. "No. I am not working with Erevan to take your throne. You're an asshole, but, like I always tell Neela, you don't need to be likable to be a good queen. Or, in your case, king."

She was telling the truth. She had to be. I sagged in relief, and with one final sneer, she walked away. She had only gone a few steps when I trotted to catch her up. "So, what are you doing here?"

"Traveling," she barked.

"I can see that."

"Then why ask?"

I sighed. "Where the hell are you headed?"

She stopped so fast I almost walked into her back. Without turning around, she asked, "If I tell you, will you promise not to stop me?"

Oh, shit, that was a tough question. I knew this female well enough to know she would leave me for dead—maybe literally—if I didn't agree. If I didn't make the promise, I would never find out what she was up to.

"Does it affect my realm?" I asked, needing more information before I made a decision.

Gabrelle turned around slowly. "It affects every realm. If I don't find what I'm looking for, we will all fall sooner or later."

The words came easily, flowing from me like destiny. "In

that case, I promise. If you tell me what you're looking for, I won't stop you from finding it."

She surveyed me intensely, and amidst all the mud, I caught a whiff of passionfruit. She opened her mouth to speak.

Gabrelle

The prince's blue-black hair shimmered like nighttime in the dim light, making it hard to see where he ended and the forest began.

He wanted to know where I was going and what I was looking for. And I wanted to tell him. Thorne was different from every other fae I'd ever met. Every. Single. One. Including my best friends. They all fawned over my beauty, and even though the other heirs had learned to resist it, they still mentioned it constantly. It was tiring. And after an evening in Erevan's company, with him admiring me every second sentence, the difference was refreshing.

Thorne had never, not once, admired my beauty. I mean, he despised me, so it wasn't all good, but I liked having my physical appearance ignored.

So, despite my better judgment, I told him. "I'm looking for a relic called the Stone of Veritas. It is the only thing that can kill a Shadow Walker. Once I find it, we will use it to take back Verda."

Neela had suggested I tell Thorne the truth, and I'd delayed doing so. I might be curious about why he wasn't drawn to my beauty and what his true values were, but I didn't trust him. A barrel of snakes was more trustworthy than Prince Sanctus.

But he'd promised not to stop me from finding the Stone, and he couldn't wriggle out of that.

"To take back Verda?" he muttered. "You said you were looking for something to help all of Arathay."

"Yes," I said slowly, like I was talking to an idiot. "When the Shadow Walkers have consumed every fae in the Realm of Verda, they will keep moving west, spreading across Arathay like a plague. It's just a short trip from Verda across the northeast corner of Brume to your very own Realm of Fen. I'm quite sure the Walkers don't recognize our borders because they exist beyond Gaia's will. If they aren't defeated, they will come here sooner rather than later. So get out of my way so I can go find the Stone of Veritas."

I turned on my heel and left him gaping, looking more like a shuttlefish than a prince. I stumbled over a low branch and grazed my shin, but I had enough poise not to show my pain.

When he was almost out of hearing range, I heard Thorne start jogging through the bushes, coming after me.

"I don't need your help," I called over my shoulder. "Or your warnings. Or your scorn."

He caught me up, barely breathing hard. "I'm coming with you," he growled.

"No, you're not."

He grabbed my shoulder and spun me around. "Listen, if this Stone is as important as you say it is—"

"Look, bud—"

"No, no, I believe you. I'm just saying that given this Stone is so important, you need help. Erevan Reissan clearly isn't going to help you, so I will. You have a better chance of surviving with me. In fact, if we can go back to the palace and gather some troops, we'll do even better. We could have Fliers takes us straight there."

My hands flew to my hips. My emotions were so much looser than usual, and it was hard to even keep my body under control. Usually, my every move was planned and orchestrated, but now my limbs were going rogue. "No! We're going to Essylia Castle. If too many fae come with us, it will set off every booby trap within fifty miles."

I watched in satisfaction as the blood drained from Thorne's face. His carved jaw turned pure white, standing stark against the dark forest. "Essylia Castle was abandoned for a reason, you know. It's cursed."

"I know that," I snapped. "And I also know it's the only place where the Stone of Veritas can be found. So we don't have a choice."

Thorne stared at me, his eyes boring into mine. "Alright then," he said, finally. "But I'm still coming with you."

"Fine," I muttered in agreement. "But don't get in my way."

We set off at a brisk pace, crunching over the dry leaves. The forest was dark and foreboding and seemed to close in around us as we walked. Every sound made me jump, and I found myself constantly looking over my shoulder.

Honestly, Thorne's constant presence behind me was starting to ease my nerves. I didn't bother glancing back, but damn, I could practically feel his eyes boring into me. "How did you know I was behind you," he asked.

I called over my shoulder without slowing down. "Like I told you, you're terrible at sneaking. Honestly, I gave you a quick lesson on skulking the other day, and you still suck at it. I guess you're a slow learner."

His voice sounded amused. "I guess so."

We continued walking through the forest, our footsteps

becoming softer as the ground became wetter and swampier.

The trees grew sparser, more like maypoles than bushes, and the air was thick with the stench of mud.

Out of nowhere, a piercing screech tore through the forest, shattering the tranquility of our surroundings. My body froze in terror, and before I could react, Thorne instinctively shoved me behind him, shielding me from harm even though he was unarmed.

My heart thudding against my ribs, I peered around his shoulder and saw an enormous beast looming in a clearing ahead of us. It had huge wings tucked against its sides and wickedly sharp claws that looked like they could tear us to shreds in seconds.

Fuck. A pteroclaw. I plucked an arrow from my quiver and readied my bow, sighting the creature along my arrow's shaft. I stepped out from behind Thorne. I couldn't hide behind him because, despite my pounding heart and shaking limbs, at least I had a weapon. He only had his fists.

The beast roared again before swooping down toward us with its talons outstretched. The wind rushed past us as it came closer and closer. Its eyes were black coals, its mouth wide open, showing rows of razor-sharp teeth.

It screeched again, and I felt like my ears would burst. Thorne moved to my side, his muscles tense and his eyes focused on the pteroclaw. He didn't have a weapon and knew he couldn't take the creature on with his bare hands, but he refused to leave me to face it alone.

I drew my bow back, aiming for its heart. The pteroclaw was getting closer, its claws almost touching the ground.

"Wait!" Thorne yelled, grabbing my arm and yanking it aside. "Don't shoot it."

"Why not?" I hissed, my eyes still locked on the beast.

"It's not attacking us," he said, his voice low and measured. "Look at it. It's not making any aggressive moves."

I hesitated, but then I saw what he meant. The pteroclaw had stopped before us, still crouched low to the ground but no longer in attack mode. Instead, it was staring at us with its beady, coal eyes.

My fingers loosened on the bowstring. Thorne was right. The pteroclaw wasn't attacking us. But seriously, why the hell was it just staring? And what was it doing in these parts? Pteroclaws were known to stick to the northern coast of Fen, clawing their way through fish, not lurking around these southerly swamps.

The pteroclaw tilted its head to one side as if it was sizing us up. Then, with a sudden burst of movement, it leaped into the air and flew off into the distance.

I lowered my bow, my heart still pounding in my chest. "What was that all about?"

Thorne shook his head. "I don't know, but we should keep moving. We don't want to be here if that thing decides to come back."

He had a point. We set off again, moving as quickly as we could through the increasingly swampy forest. The ground was slick, and I squished into mud as deep as my knees more times than I could count. The going was slow, and I let Thorne take the lead because he seemed better at finding the firmer ground.

I watched Thorne in awe as he gracefully maneuvered through the swampy mess. Seriously, the guy had the agility of a cat, always finding a steady path while I stumbled and squished around. His muscles moved like liquid beneath his snug shirt. Mesmerizing. Usually, I was the elegant one, but I'd met my match.

He paused for a moment, looking up at the sky before turning back to look at me. I straightened my spine and tried to look refined, but there was definitely mud on my cheeks and sweat in my hair. Why the hell did I care what he thought of me anyway? Force of habit, I supposed.

Thorne gestured for me to follow him, leading me through an area that looked impassable until he pointed out a small path along the bank of the swamp—one that I never would have found alone.

As we continued, I had time to consider Thorne. When we'd first met, he'd been rude. Prince Prick. From careful questioning and deduction, I'd figured out that he hated everybody from the Realm of Verda. A touch of jealousy, perhaps, and anger that Arrow had died on our soil. So he'd been a bastard to me and put me in the worst room in the Court.

Could I fault him for that? How often had I wished I could lock away a fawning admirer just because they irritated me? Perhaps he was just like me but with stronger convictions, somebody who acted on those impulses instead of hiding them behind a mask of indifference.

He navigated the obstacles we encountered with unwavering confidence and strength, never hesitating, always so sure of himself.

After a few long hours of hiking, I was already glad to have Thorne with me. He knew these swamplands better than I ever could, and his clever navigation had saved me hours of trudging through thigh-deep mud.

So why did uneasiness snake through me every time I looked at him?

Gabrelle

After the third time I stumbled and faceplanted in the stinky mud, Thorne called a halt. "We make camp here," he said, sounding like he'd reached his limit.

I opened my mouth to disagree but was exhausted, and the words wouldn't come. Honestly, it felt good for somebody else to take charge for once. As a princess, nobody ranked higher than me in Verda except for the ruling kings and queens, and I avoided them whenever possible. The other heirs were my friends but were also my competition, so I rarely let them take control of any situation when I could do so myself.

But here, in the middle of this Gaia-forsaken swamp, I could allow myself to release the reins. For one night, at least.

Thorne set about gathering firewood, and I watched with admiration as he worked. He was strong, and his movements were graceful, even when bent in half over a fallen log to snap it into pieces. I passed him the kindling I had collected while daydreaming, and soon enough, we had enough wood for a small campfire.

We laid out some dry rushes on a raised patch of land, and Thorne settled down to sleep.

Exhaustion dragged at my limbs, but I couldn't sleep in this state.

"Efflanio levitas," I murmured and concentrated, removing the worst of the muck from my body. Mud flicked off in little spurts, reuniting with the ground.

Thorne lay with his hands behind his head and his legs crossed at the ankles, completely at ease. "Why are you doing that?" he asked, and I didn't detect any malice in his voice, so I answered.

"I'm the heir of House Allura. I can't go to bed looking like I've been half-digested by a pteroclaw."

He chewed his lip. In the firelight, it looked sexy, so fucking sexy, and I kept staring at his mouth as he spoke. "Nobody's here, nobody can see you. I promise I won't tell." His mouth was so full and luscious, and for a moment, I wondered why the hell I hadn't ever kissed him. Why hadn't I even considered it? His jawline was perfect, a cut line that curved around those kissable lips.

"Oh," I tried to keep my composure. "I, er...I guess it's just who I am. The beauty queen."

He kept staring at me as I hoovered up the mud, making me aware of my every movement. His gaze was suddenly as heavy as the world, and I loved the feel of it on my legs as I cleaned them off.

"I thought you hated being called that," he said, still watching me.

That jolted me out of my lust. "What? How could you possibly know that?"

He smiled slowly, those perfect lips parting and revealing straight white teeth. I could dive into that mouth and live a happy life inside it. "I'm not just a self-obsessed prick," he said languidly, tossing back words I'd used to describe him. "I pay attention. I notice how you react to things. Like how you tolerate Erevan because he pays you compliments, just like you're used to, and he makes you feel comfortable."

My mouth fell open, and I stared at him as he continued listing insights I thought I had kept hidden from the world.

"And," he continued, "how you spent hours every day mapping out the Court, searching every nook and cranny for... well, now I know you were looking for the Stone."

My limbs were numb, and my whole face was frozen. "But how...what did...how do you know all that?"

I could almost feel all the power flow from me to him in this conversation. He was definitely winning.

And sexy. So damn sexy. When did he get so attractive? Those mesmerizing lips moved again. "Like I said, I pay attention. Especially to you."

Dammit, this male was intoxicating. Why was he saying these things? His compliments were worth a thousand compliments from any other fae because they were so hard won. And because he had to be speaking the truth.

"Especially me?" I asked, sounding like a hopeful little girl with a big crush. I hated my small, quivering voice and the flush in my cheeks, but I couldn't stop them.

"Of course," he said. "Because I thought you were an enemy to the throne."

"Oh." That stopped my foolish thoughts about hooking up with this sexy prince. "Of course. That makes sense."

He smiled, only this time, it looked slightly cruel on his stern face. "Why? Did you think there was another reason I was paying you such close attention?"

I immediately started to deny it, but Gaia's realm magic twisted my words. "Yes." Fuck. I hadn't meant to say that. My control was worsening the longer I spent in this stupid truth-telling realm—shouldn't it be getting better?

Thorne raised an eyebrow, and my heart rate skyrocketed as I waited for his response. "And what reason might that be?" he asked, his voice low and dangerous.

I felt trapped, cornered like a wild animal. I didn't want to admit it, but I couldn't lie either. "I suppose," I said, barely above a whisper. "Maybe because you found me compelling."

Thorne's eyes darkened, and I couldn't tell if it was with anger or something else entirely. "Is that so?" he said, and I could hear the smugness in his tone.

I felt exposed and vulnerable and wished I could disappear into the mud. "Yes," I said, my voice barely audible.

Thorne leaned forward, his eyes locked on mine. "Well, Princess Allura," he purred, low and seductive. "I think you'll find that I can be very...compelling." He leaned in closer, his piercing gaze locked onto mine.

I swallowed hard, my heart pounding. It wasn't supposed to go like this. I was supposed to be in command, smiling and flirting and playing him like the faeboe, but instead, I was averting my eyes, whispering like a timid mouse, and my heart was about to fucking burst.

I couldn't tell him all that, not when he was so close, and his eyes were so intense. "It doesn't matter," I said weakly, trying to push him away. "Let's get some sleep."

But Thorne wasn't going to let it go. He grabbed my wrist and pulled me toward him, his face just inches from mine. "Tell me," he demanded. "Do you want to..."

His question petered out as some blue returned to his dark eyes, and he seemed to pull himself back from the edge of something. As he did, my shoulders straightened, and I managed to pull myself together, finding some of that inner strength I usually had on tap.

"Do I want to what?" I asked, sure he'd been about to ask me to kiss him. That put me on more certain ground, back where I belonged.

He released my wrist and pulled back. The firelight flickered off one side of his body, shimmering off the scar on his face, making him flash between approachable and terrifying. "Why do you do that?" he asked.

"Do what?" I asked, looking into the dancing flames.

"Why do you hide behind a shield of ice? Is the world so scary that you can't face it without a barrier?"

Just like that, in a few short sentences, he brought my world crashing down again. "What? How did...?" I stared at him, saw those blue-black eyes piercing me, his whole body angled toward me, and my control started to slip again. "They call me the ice princess," I said. "When they're not calling me the beauty queen."

His voice was quiet, lined with earnest intensity. "And do you like that?"

"Well, it's better than trickster," I said, and he snorted a laugh. "But, yes, I worked hard to earn the nickname ice princess. It means that nothing in the world can affect me. I am apart from it all," I said proudly, raising my chin and straightening my back.

The fire crackled beside us, and a frog croaked nearby. But, despite myself, I was waiting for Thorne's reply. This fae treated me so differently from anyone I'd ever met, and it was disorienting, like I'd been walking along a straight, paved path, and suddenly I was standing in the middle of a field, completely lost. Or, in this case, a swamp.

I almost got whiplash as I turned to look at him when he

finally spoke. "Yeah, a barrier between you and the world. Maybe that's not a good thing. Is there anybody you let through? Mentium or Flora, or any of them?"

"Partly," I confessed. "They're my best friends, and I could rely on them for anything, but...but I guess I hide my true self, even from them."

Thorne leaned closer, his eyes locked onto mine. "Why?" he asked softly. "Why do you keep yourself hidden? What are you afraid of?"

I hesitated, my mind racing as I tried to come up with an answer. I should just shut up and go to sleep, but the words tumbled out. "I don't know," I said. "Maybe I'm afraid of being vulnerable. Or maybe I'm afraid of being judged or not measuring up to expectations."

Thorne's expression softened as he reached to take my hand but then thought better of it and pulled away. "I understand that," he said. "I've felt that way myself. But sometimes, you have to take a risk. You have to be willing to let others see you for who you really are."

I looked down at his hand in his lap, wishing it were intertwined with mine, and warmth spread through my body. "And what if they don't like what they see?" I asked, barely above a whisper.

"Then they're not worth your time," Thorne replied firmly. "You shouldn't have to change yourself to make others like you. You should be loved for who you are, flaws and all."

His words hit a chord deep within me, and tears pricked at the corner of my eyes. Thorne had a way of getting to me, breaking through my defenses and making me feel things I didn't want to. But maybe it was time to take a risk, to let down my guard and let someone in. Maybe I didn't have to be the ice princess or the beauty queen, maybe I could just be me.

I turned to face him, our faces mere inches apart. He smelled of mint, and his lips drew my gaze again like perfect fucking magnets.

"Thank you," I murmured. "For understanding."

Thorne's lips curved, and I forced my gaze to his eyes, which crinkled at the edges. "Anytime, Princess. Anytime."

And as we sat there in comfortable silence, I felt a shift in our relationship. We went from being enemies to something more, something deeper. And as much as I tried to deny it, I was drawn to him, to his intensity and his vulnerability.

And his perfect damn mouth.

Thorne

After our long night of trudging through mud, we slept until late morning, despite the terrible, non-existent mattress.

"And you thought the room I gave you at Court was bad," I joked, earning a beautiful smile from the muddy princess.

I woke with a raging hard-on after dreaming about Gabrelle all night, and I had to roll away from her until it went down, pretending to be slow to wake.

It didn't long to break camp—we just kicked out the smoldering embers of the fire, and we were done.

Gabrelle chucked me a hard bread roll from her pack. "Breakfast," she said. "I presume you didn't bring anything to contribute?"

"Er, no." I held up the roll. "Thanks."

"Consider it thanks for your extreme hospitality," she said playfully, and I laughed.

Bantering with Gabrelle felt strange after all the tension between us. After all those hours I'd spent detesting her because she came from the Realm of Verda. But since I'd examined my biases, it was like a fog had lifted, and I could see her clearly. She wasn't just beautiful, and she certainly wasn't shallow. She had depths I was only just discovering.

As we set off along the raised path between the swamps, she

caught me staring at her and arched an eyebrow playfully. "Did you have something to say?" she asked cheekily.

"Nope, I don't want to say anything. I don't even want you to look at me." I kept imagining her naked and writhing beneath me, like how she'd wriggled in the mud of Green Valley during the Wild Hunt. Only in my imagination, I wasn't trying to kill her. My cock was hardening even as we squelched through the mud—which is why I didn't want her to look at me.

She strode past me, taking the lead. "Good Gaia, I don't know if I'll ever get used to your brutal honesty," she muttered, misinterpreting my words.

As the day dragged on, my stomach growled harder and louder. I found some rowenuts growing on a bush, and we ate our fill while resting. Finding water was no difficulty because little springs of fresh water bubbled up in pockets at frequent intervals.

But as dusk fell, I noticed Gabrelle limping slightly. "What's wrong with you?" I asked, frowning.

She stopped and turned around to look at me. Mud splattered her clothes, and several droplets marred her perfect face—which only made her more beautiful. "Well, let me see." She began counting off her flaws on her fingers. "According to you, I'm superficial, arrogant, weak, foolish, unfeeling, uns—"

"Shut up. Look, I'm sorry I said those things. They're not true."

She tilted her head, and I swear that action alone was enough to get my cock's attention. "Oh, really?"

I ran a hand through my hair. "Look, I thought they were true, obviously, but...I was wrong."

She held her pose like a warrior statue, the picture of fiery determination. She wasn't going to let me off easy. "Yes," she said. "You were."

This trickster princess had so much more depth than I ever realized. Our conversation last night proved that—she tried to be what others needed her to be and sometimes lost herself in the process. "You're selfless," I admitted as the truth revealed itself to me. I'd had her so wrong. Just look at what she was going through to help Arathay.

She finally broke her severe pose, smirking. "I wouldn't go that far, Thorne. Or should I call you Prince Sanctus?" she asked with a grin.

I laughed. "Thorne will be fine. And I'll keep calling you the trickster."

She narrowed her eyes. "Prince Prick it is."

"Er, I prefer Thorne."

The last rays of sunlight that filtered through the canopy at an angle twinkled off her dusty pink eyes. "Of course you do. Well, too bad, Prince Prick."

She turned and kept walking, her strides still long and strong even after all these hours of hiking. But that slight limp hadn't gone away.

"What's wrong with your leg? You're limping."

"It's nothing," she called over her shoulder. "Just a blister."

"The strongest army can be felled by blisters," I retorted. "Let me take a look."

"You're not a Healer," she muttered, although she found a dry spot to sit down, then peeled off her left boot and sock, revealing a nasty, oozing blister that looked painful.

"No, you know very well I'm a Binder." At my Ascension rite, I had made Arrow promise to kill me. She did, of course, being a fae of her word, so I ascended into Binding, which meant I could enforce and bind individuals to their spoken promises. I could create unbreakable oaths, ensuring that anyone who made a pledge in my presence must fulfill it.

"Mmm, well, if I ever need to enter into any contracts, I'll come ask for your help," she said, wincing as I poked at her injury.

I pulled out a couple of different plants from my pocket. I crushed the broad, shiny leaf and handed it to Gabrelle. "For the pain," I told her.

She arched an eyebrow. "A Brayson leaf? Did you just happen to have this on you when you followed me out of the Court?"

"No, but I kept my eyes open today and picked a few useful things."

She accepted the medicine and munched on it, and I saw the pain relief work through her body, as the tension in her shoulders dissipated and her jaw relaxed. "Thank you. What's the other one? I don't recognize it."

"A thistlebud flower. I'll pack it against the wound, and it will stop infection and promote healing." I worked carefully, laying the light purple plant across the oozing flesh, then wrapping it tightly in a strip of fabric I tore from my sleeve.

"You're quite useful after all," Gabrelle said, joking, but the hint of admiration in her voice sent warmth through my body. Gaia help me, I wanted to impress this female.

I reluctantly released her foot, memorizing the feel of her silken skin and the tingle of her touch.

We kept hiking, but as night fell, my wariness crept up. The rotting smell of the mangroves seemed to get stronger as the light fled, and a chorus of frogs erupted around us, making me start. The sky turned a deep navy blue, and stars appeared like sprinkled powder, turning the mangroves into lunging shadows.

"We should think about camping soon," I said.

Gabrelle shook her head. "No. I want to make it to the castle tonight."

The thought of entering the cursed castle at night made my skin crawl, and I jumped at a loud frog croak near my boot. "We should wait until morning. We don't want to set off more boobytraps than we have to, and we won't be able to see much at night. Plus, we'll be refreshed in the morning. We'll think more clearly."

Gabrelle stopped and turned to me again. She looked weary, like she needed a good sleep and a comforting cuddle. I would happily provide both. "Okay," she said. "I guess you're right."

We searched the area for a dry spot to sleep and start a campfire, eventually finding an open patch of ground sheltered by mangrove trees. I scavenged for firewood while Gabrelle looked for kindling and tinder, and soon we had a roaring blaze in front of us. With the stars twinkling above and the sound of the ocean waves now audible above the croaking frogs, it was easy to forget our mission and just be two fae.

We shared some rowenuts we had collected earlier, their crunch satisfying our hunger, and we quenched our thirst with water from a nearby spring. I was intensely aware of every one of Gabrelle's movements, where she was looking, trying to gauge if her blister was causing her pain. Trying to gauge if she was thinking about me as much as I was thinking about her.

I couldn't hold it in any longer. I opened my mouth to speak.

Thorne

"Why did you break into my rooms at Court?" I asked, leaning back on my elbows to escape the intense heat of the roaring campfire. I found a comfortable spot in the dirt, wriggling my butt into an ass-sized hollow.

Gabrelle glanced at me, her mud-spattered face showing her surprise. "I was looking for the Stone of Veritas. I thought that must be obvious by now."

Unlike last night, Gabrelle hadn't spent an hour cleaning herself off with magic. I'd like to think my advice about not conforming to expectations affected her, but she was likely too tired after two days of trekking and crappy sleep.

In the stillness of the night, the chorus of frogs sang, their croaks echoing through the dense undergrowth. I leaned back on my elbows to get my face further from the hot fire. "Did you think the Stone was in my prized faeboe?"

She laughed, a full-bodied sound that was so different from the tinkling chimes I'd heard from her before. This was raw and real, and it made me grin. "No," she said, "I just liked the faeboe and wanted to take a closer look."

I barked a laugh. "That is so much less mysterious than I thought!" I sipped water from a hollowed-out rock shaped like a cup. "I didn't realize you were musical."

Gabrelle had her legs crossed and was leaning back on her arms, like I was. The position thrust her breasts forward, and it was very distracting. "Oh, really? I thought your spies would have reported that Erevan gifted me a faeboe."

"He did?" Jealousy stabbed me momentarily, but I forced it aside. Gabrelle was a grown fae, and she could do whatever—and whoever—she pleased. But it didn't mean I had to like it.

"Yes. Just a regular faeboe. It's nice enough, but nothing compared to yours. Where'd you get it?"

The truth was that my music room gave me more comfort than anywhere else in Arathay. It was my haven, my refuge, the place where I could truly relax. "I'm drawn to musical instruments," I said, stumbling over the words, trying to explain the depths of my musical compulsion. "I saw that magnificent faeboe in Fenwick and needed to own it."

She hummed in agreement. "I understand. I'm a bit the same way myself. The whole world goes blurry when I'm playing, and it's just me and my music. Then, when I emerge, I feel whole again."

"Like you can face the world again?"

"Exactly." The fire made her eyes and hair glow, turning them from dusty pink to deep purple. She parted her full lips, which were almost black in this light, and began to sing.

Her melodic voice filled the air. She had a beautiful tone that carried far in the night sky, and I could have listened to it all night while staring at her.

But I needed to join in, I hadn't sung in months, and my voice was slightly rusty when I started, but it soon warmed, my baritone complementing her alto as if we had been singing together for years.

When the song was over, my heart felt lighter, and a gentle smile filled Gabrelle's face. I wanted to know more about her. I wanted to know everything.

"Do your parents sing?" I asked.

She shuddered. "Mother? Certainly not. She thinks singers and entertainers are lesser fae who perform for us. She thinks royalty has no business entertaining others." That aligned with everything I'd thought about Queen Allura, but I'd recently had to re-think all my prejudices.

"And your father, Hyde Allura?" I asked.

Her slight smile vanished. "He is the Queen's Consort and takes that role very seriously. I suspect he was musical in his youth, but now he's focused on supporting Mother to keep the realm in order." She looked away from me, her gaze distant as she continued. "I have no siblings or cousins, nobody else to take up the mantle of royalty." She looked up at me then, her eyes filled with sadness. "Do you feel it too? The pressure to follow in your parents' footsteps?"

"My mother wasn't into music," I said, watching the red heat glow and pulse inside a burning log. "But she always encouraged me." Using the past tense to refer to Mother still hurt, and a hard lump formed in my throat. "But she wanted me to use music to focus on the past and our family history. She always talked about the Fen rulers of old and how we needed to live up to their legacy to ensure a prosperous future for our citizens."

This particular topic was heavy with history between me and Gabrelle because I used to think she delighted in tormenting me with Arrow's death. But now I wanted to share with her, even though it left me vulnerable.

"And now that you have to rule," she began delicately. "Do

you feel even more pressure?"

I considered that. Everything I did and thought since Mother's death was related to continuing the family legacy. It was a wheelbarrow I pushed everywhere, filled with the need to rule as a Sanctus would rule, win the courtiers' approval and support as a Sanctus should, and be a king my ancestors would be proud of.

"Yes," I confessed. I had never said the words aloud before, had barely dared to think them, yet I was telling Princess Allura from the Realm of Verda my inner secrets. "I feel nothing but pressure from my mother's legacy, and with Arrow gone, it is all down to me. Nobody else can carry the family name forward. The realm depends on me. Me alone."

The weight of my words hung in the air, and we sat in silence for a moment, the gravity of our vulnerabilities seeping into the space between us.

Gabrelle shifted closer and laid a warm hand on the bare skin of my arm, where I'd torn the sleeve off earlier. A rush of warmth spread through my body, accompanied by the gentle scent of passionfruit that clung to her skin. "You aren't alone, Thorne." My bicep jumped when she touched it, and her lips quirked in response. She was so damn sexy, and just the warmth of her palm on my skin had heat flowing through my body.

I cleared my throat. "Growing up in royal circles, I was constantly reminded of my family's role in leading the realm. It used to make me proud, and it still does. But with Arrow gone, it also adds more pressure." Gaia, it felt good to say the words out loud, like letting the syllables loose through the swamplands would reduce their effect on me.

Gabrelle's hot hand didn't leave my bicep, and my awareness

was almost entirely on it. The campfire crackled, and she moved her hand slowly down my arm in a soft caress. My cock jumped to attention, and my breathing shortened. I didn't want to move an inch in case I broke the spell.

As our conversation settled, a charged silence replaced it, and the air seemed to thicken with desire. Gabrelle leaned in closer, her lips grazing my ear, her touch sending shivers down to my toes.

The noise of a twig snapping pierced the silence, seeming immensely loud in the quiet night like it had been sent from Gaia to break us apart. Gabrelle's eyes widened, and she gasped. Her hand flew away from me, and she was on her feet in a blink of an eye, peering into the darkness beyond our campfire.

The forest seemed to hold its breath as a chill ran down my spine like an unseen presence loomed nearby.

"What is it?" I asked as I got up, my heart thumping hard against my chest.

The moonless night engulfed us in an eerie cloak of darkness, with only the crackling campfire offering a flickering light. Every rustle of leaves or distant hoot of an owl set my senses on edge.

"The Shadow Walkers," Gabrelle said in a hushed voice that barely contained her fear.

"No," I said. "They've never been spotted this far north or west."

Gabrelle shook her head, every muscle in her body tense. She immediately cast a faelight in the palm of her hand, expanding it to ensure it covered us both. "They're moving, Thorne," she said, her voice tight. "They might be this far across the land already, we don't know. Nobody believed in them for ages in Verda, and some fae still think they're a myth. But I'm not taking a chance. We have to stay awake so we can keep a light burning."

I peered into the darkness, unable to see anything but the piercing black. "We have the fire. That will keep them away."

"Not if it goes out," she snapped. "You sleep, I'll keep a lookout."

I shook my head, adamant. "No. I'll keep the first lookout while you sleep." Gabrelle opened her mouth to protest, but I cut her off. "We both need our rest if we're going to make it to Essylia Castle in one piece. We can take turns watching the fire and casting faelight on our backs."

Gabrelle finally nodded her agreement and curled next to me on the ground by the campfire. I sat beside her, feeling strangely safe with the fire on our fronts and my faelight on our backs. Casting the spell took a little energy and would add to my fatigue tomorrow, but it was worth it to put Gabrelle at ease. She was so close that I could feel the warmth radiating off her body.

I felt my heart open and let my feelings for her swell within me. I wanted her to know how much I admired her strength and courage, and I wanted her to know that if she needed anything, I was there for her. "Gabrelle, I want you to know I'm here for you. Whatever happens in the castle tomorrow, I'm right there with you."

Gabrelle smiled sleepily and nuzzled against me for extra warmth. "Thank you," she said softly.

Gabrelle

When I woke, the sun was well over the horizon, casting long shadows across the marshlands. I sat bolt upright, thrumming with adrenaline. Thorne hadn't woken me for my shift on watch. He lay beside me like a corpse, and my fear ratcheted up a notch. I shoved his shoulder, hard. *Wake up, please. Come on!*

He stretched like a cat in the sun and blinked open his eyes, smiling when he saw me. "Good morning."

"Why didn't you wake me?" I demanded, scowling. "We had a deal. You take the first shift, and I take the second. I thought you were a fae of your word!"

His blue-black hair was disheveled, and mud spattered his clothing, and I'd just hurled the worst insult I could think of for an uptight male like him...but he just smiled lazily and put his hands behind his head. "You looked so innocent sleeping there, I couldn't bear to disturb you."

"You seriously went to sleep and left us vulnerable to the Shadow Walkers? Are you kidding me? We're damn lucky to be breathing right now!"

He kept smiling up at me as though I were praising his strategic genius. "No, trickster. I waited until dawn before I took a little nap." He yawned widely, showing his nice teeth.

"I'm a bit tired now."

I scowled to cover my surprise at how generous he had been in letting me sleep. Gaia knew I needed the Zs. "Well, I don't want to wait any longer, so get up and get moving."

From the corner of my eye, I watched his precise movements, so graceful and deliberate. He reminded me of a shark in the way he moved smoothly through the world, then suddenly snapped in an unexpected direction.

He was already on his feet, sweeping his gaze over the horizon. "Let's move out, then."

Each step made the ground squelch beneath our feet, the boggy mud threatening to suck us in with every move. We had to navigate cautiously, or we'd find ourselves knee-deep in this disgusting muck. The whole damn thing felt like an endless struggle, the heaviness of the air weighing us down with every painstaking trudge.

Finally, we crested a hill, and I sighed in relief as the ground grew drier and more solid, granting us a reprieve from the marshlands' grasp.

We had reached the northern coast of Fen. To the right, angry waves thundered and slammed against a cliff far below, and straight ahead was a valley with an ancient crumbling castle perched atop a rocky outcrop. Elyssia Castle.

Its broken turrets reached for the sky like claws. It was eerie and yet somehow breathtakingly beautiful all at once. Thorne let out a low whistle, and I caught my breath. Magic surrounded the castle like a protective cloak. The walls were dotted with trees whose leaves rustled in some unknown breeze, and ivy crept up its sides like fingers.

Thorne gestured for me to go first as we descended into the valley. He followed close behind, his eyes alert for any signs of danger.

Suddenly, a loud screech pierced the air. A chill spiderwebbed my skin, and a group of creatures soared in the sky with wings glowing like fire in the sunlight.

I stumbled, Thorne's quick hands steadying me before I tumbled down the hill.

"Pteroclaws," he breathed.

They swooped lower and lower, directly overhead.

"They're hunting us," I said. "I should never have let that one live the other day. It's brought friends."

The pteroclaws opened their beaks and let out an ear-splitting shriek that echoed through the valley and set my head ringing. I froze, my eyes locked on the flock.

"Should we run, or—"

The flock descended with lightning speed, talons outstretched and claws spread wide. Thorne yanked me out of the way just in time as claws swiped near my head.

Their wings beat furiously as they attacked, blowing my hair across my face. Terrifying screeches echoed off the valley walls, and the creatures swarmed us in a tornado of feathers and claws.

I pulled out my bow. "Catch me," I yelled at Thorne. Then, without waiting for an answer, I looked up at the sky and let myself fall back while I released an arrow right into the eye of the nearest pteroclaw. Thorne caught me, holding me at a sharp angle to the ground so I could aim skyward while the injured bird squealed and cartwheeled away.

The other pteroclaws split apart, and I quickly shot off two more arrows. One slammed into a creature's wing, while the second pierced another's heart. One bird tumbled into the long grass, and the wounded flock fled, leaving us in a cloud of feathers and dust.

We stood there for a moment, staring up into the sky at their retreating forms. Thorne smiled down at me. "You never cease to surprise me."

The expression on his face filled me with sunlight, completely ruining the smirk I was going for. "You shouldn't be surprised when a warrior princess defeats a pack of pigeons."

He scoffed. "Those were no pigeons."

I slung my bow back over my shoulder and picked my way over to the fallen pteroclaw to retrieve the arrow—I had a feeling I'd need it. I'd lost two in the fight, so I only had eight remaining in my quiver, and I couldn't afford to lose any of them.

When I reached the bird, I firmly grasped the arrow shaft and pulled it out of the feathered corpse. The pteroclaw's eyes had glazed over, and its wings were still wide, as if in flight. I ran my fingers over its soft feathers. How could something as dainty as a feather carry something as heavy as a pteroclaw?

When I turned away, Thorne was watching me with an expression of admiration mixed with something else that made my heart flutter.

How could someone as uptight as Thorne hold so much open generosity? He'd shown me his vulnerabilities last night and the enormous pressure he was under. Previously, I'd never realized how lucky I was to have the other heirs by my side. We trained together, fought together, and we would rule together. But seeing Thorne's loneliness, I finally understood the value of their support. While he had no one.

He broke the silence. "They were the castle's first defense."

"We should have killed the lookout yesterday."

I looked up at him and saw his dark gaze clouded with regret.

"I'm sorry I stayed your hand."

My hand went instantly to his arm. "It wasn't your fault. You gave advice, and I decided whether to follow it. That's how a team works."

The corded muscle of his forearm relaxed. "Are you saying we're a team, trickster princess?" he smirked.

I squeezed his arm, enjoying the firmness and warmth. "Just for today," I said, quirking a smile.

Elyssia Castle was just down the hill, perched on the outcrop over the crashing ocean. We set out, leaving a field of feathers behind us. I kept an eye on the sky and the ground for any signs of danger while my pulse kept a fast rhythm. The long grass swished against my knees as I considered what other boobytraps lay in store in this ancient, crumbling castle.

Passing through an ancient arched gateway, we entered a vast courtyard filled with standing stones from different eras. Right at the center of the square, a breathtaking grand round fountain with multiple tiers stood, its water long gone, leaving behind an eerie emptiness that permeated the air.

Thorne's hand gently pressed against the small of my back, a wordless comfort reminding me that he stood by my side. I took a deep breath and stepped closer to him, feeling his warmth radiate through my body.

The castle was even more imposing up close, with dark stones and sharp turrets looming over us. As we crossed the courtyard, careful not to step on any loose rocks that might set off hidden traps, I couldn't shake the feeling of being watched. The hairs on my neck stood up, and I scanned the area for any signs of danger. But nothing was out of place, just the eerie silence that hung over the castle like a shroud.

Thorne must have felt it, too, because his grip on my back

tightened. "Stay close," he whispered, his voice sending shivers over my skin.

"Obviously," I muttered.

As we approached the castle entrance, a gaping black hole with the door long rotted away, a sense of foreboding washed over me. Stepping into the dark foyer, our footsteps echoed off the worn stone walls, sending an unsettling echo throughout the air. The air was thick with the smell of dust and decay, and a wave of nausea rushed over me, but I forced it aside. I didn't have time for weakness.

The castle looked worse than my wildest nightmares. The stone walls crumbled, and the wooden doors swung precariously on their hinges or were completely gone.

We cautiously ventured down a hallway adorned with stone statues of warriors frozen in various battle poses. My gaze lingered on each meticulously carved figure, their stony expressions etched with a hint of ancient valor. I knew better than to get close—legend said these statues were enchanted to come to life and attack intruders—but their lifelike expressions still pulled me in, and I longed to touch one.

"We come in peace," I murmured to them in case they were planning something.

Thorne chuckled. "Do you always address the furniture?"

"Shh," I hissed. "This place is cursed. I'm happy to be polite to the decor if my life depends on it."

He laughed louder then, and I shushed him again. "Polite when your life's on the line," he chuckled. "Ain't that the truth."

At the end of the hall was a large lion statue standing majestically amidst the debris. Its curved mane cascaded down its back like waves in an ocean, and its tail swept across the floor in a graceful arc. As we got closer, it seemed almost alive, as if it were about to pounce at any moment. We stopped just outside its reach, and Thorne stepped around me to get a better look at it. His fingers glided over the lion's face before he whispered something under his breath. Instantly, the lion's head began to move, turning from side to side as if surveying us.

"Now, who's talking to the furniture?" I mumbled.

As the lion's head moved, surveying us with an almost lifelike gaze, we carefully steered clear of its reach, proceeding cautiously down the next corridor.

"Don't touch anything," I hissed. "Anything could be cursed, so—"

It happened in an instant. Thorne completely ignored my excellent advice and ran his fingers along an old tapestry. The hanging rug sprang to life instantly, ensnaring him in its tight embrace. Panic surged through me as the fabric wrapped around him, concealing him from sight.

"Thorne! Get out of there. Thorne!" Without a moment's thought, my bow was in my arms in firing position, and I had nocked an arrow.

The tapestry abruptly released its grip, falling back into place with an unsettling silence. My heart raced, and I searched the corridor for any trace of the prince, but he had vanished, leaving only the eerie stillness that clung to the air.

Gabrelle

In the blink of an eye, Thorne disappeared, leaving me alone in the echoing corridor. One moment he was there, reaching out to pat the tapestry like an idiot, the next, he was gone.

"Thorne!" I called his name again and again until my throat grew hoarse, acting like a damn fool and awakening every last curse in the castle.

As soon as I figured out that yelling might get me killed, I shut my mouth, but my heart wouldn't quieten. It was pumping like I was in Gaia's physical trial for the Verdan heirs.

Damn. I glanced around, trying to figure out a solution. But my mind couldn't get past the fact that Thorne was gone. There was only one thing to be done. I reached out to touch the tapestry so it would take me wherever it had taken him...but the damn carpet did nothing. It was ordinary, pliable wool.

I threw it aside in disgust, cursing under my breath. I would have to find him myself. I strode along the corridor and into the first room I came to. Taking half a step onto the rug, I felt the ground give way underfoot, and I pulled back just in time before I plunged into the spike-covered pit beneath the carpet.

"Fuck this place," I muttered. So much for being polite to the furniture.

I carefully stepped away from the treacherous rug, my

frustration at the castle growing with each near-miss. Back in the hallway, I paused for a moment, studying the walls. Something wasn't quite right...they seemed to be shifting ever so slightly. Almost like they were alive. The stone beneath my feet rearranged itself every few steps so that I was walking in circles no matter which direction I was going, like I was being herded somewhere. This castle was a living maze—the Weavers had done an excellent job of cursing it when the kings and queens of old abandoned it.

My heart was thumping in my chest as I continued, pushing past cobweb-covered portraits and heavy wooden doors that opened on their own accord as if inviting me inside.

With my next footstep, I heard a faint click, then I was falling, leaving my stomach somewhere above me as wind rushed past me and my hair flew up. I was spiraling down a stone chute, the walls flying past me, then, with a squeal, I dropped out and landed on my ass on the stone. That would leave a bruise.

I got to my feet, rubbing my butt, and summoned light on the palm of my hand. These were the catacombs. A shiver ran through me—the air was much colder here, and the sense of being surrounded by skeletons added to the chill. There was a strange beauty to it, though, a feeling of being suspended in time, surrounded by ancient secrets and mysteries. I wandered along, resisting the urge to run my fingers along the cold stone walls lined with crumbling tombs. Small crevices and alcoves gave way to still more passageways.

I tried not to breathe in the stale, musty air and ignore the underlying scent of decay and mold that clung to the ancient tombs like fog.

But I had to keep going. I followed my instincts and the faint imaginings of fading voices that echoed through the tunnels.

As I moved deeper into the catacombs, the tombs became larger and more elaborate, adorned with intricate carvings of dragons and crowns. The deeper I went, the colder it got, and the more certain I was that I had made a mistake trusting my gut and recklessly entering the castle.

But then, out of nowhere, Thorne appeared. He stood in a small alcove with ancient symbols etched into the stone walls. His eyes lit up when he saw me—it felt like years since I'd last seen him—and he threw his arms around me.

"You're alright," I said, melting into his hug. His warmth seeped into my shivering bones, and his minty scent wrapped me up. Relief sagged through me, hot and heavy.

"Yes," he murmured into my hair.

"I told you not to touch the tapestry," I scolded, but my words had no venom. I permitted myself to relax into his embrace for a moment—there would be time to be Princess Allura later.

"Yeah," he said. "Remind me to pay more attention to what you say in future."

I smiled into his chest. "Gladly."

We stepped back, and Thorne gestured to a rock altar in the center of the alcove behind him, surrounded by tall pillars cloaked in shadows. And there it was: the Stone of Veritas. A pale gem that glowed blue with an otherworldly light, pulsing with energy so strong that I could feel it singing through my veins.

I stepped forward tentatively, my heart thudding as I reached out and grasped the stone. It felt surprisingly warm against my skin, like a living thing beating with ancient wisdom and knowledge.

As soon as I touched it, the air crackled with energy, and

faint whispers on the edge of hearing filled my ears. A rock barrier slammed across the passageway, blocking our exit, and the soft whispers grew louder and louder until I had to cover my ears against their words. "You have taken the Stone of Veritas."

"Yes, we have. Shut up," Thorne said, his hands over his ears.

A figure materialized before us, tall and shadowy with features that morphed as I tried it focus on them. It held the Stone, which I was suddenly no longer holding. "If you want to leave with the Stone of Veritas, you must speak one difficult truth. The Gem of Truth will only leave with a fae who possesses an honest heart."

My heart was pounding, and my bow was already in my arms with an arrow nocked, aiming at the shadowy figure.

Thorne put a warm hand on my shoulder. "You cannot shoot the Truth Warden."

I squared my shoulders and lined up the shot. "Wanna bet?" I loosed my arrow, piercing the shadowy figure's heart, but the missile passed straight through and clattered against the rock wall behind.

I glanced at Thorne, who was smirking at me. "Maybe you should listen to me too, occasionally."

"Hmm," I muttered.

The Truth Warden didn't seem bothered by my attempt on its life. Probably because it didn't have a life. It just repeated in precisely the same tone as before, "If you want to leave with the Stone of Veritas, you must speak one difficult truth. The Gem of Truth will only leave with a fae who possesses an honest heart."

One difficult truth. Okay, that didn't sound too hard. I gave it a second's thought, chewing my lip, then declared, "I don't like you," to the Truth Warden. "That's a truth, and I bet it's difficult for you to hear."

"It is not," the Warden said. "You must tell your truth to each other, not to me. I am but a memory of Weavers past, and although it can be difficult to be honest to your memories, it is harder to be honest to others."

This Warden didn't seem about to attack us, and since he was just a memory, I didn't think he could. I walked around him to collect my arrow, "Excuse me," then returned it to my quiver and slung my bow back over my shoulder.

"Polite to furniture and anthropomorphic memories," Thorne noted with a smirk.

"Yes, well, this particular memory holds our lives in its hands, so a little politeness seems in order."

Thorne sat on the ground and leaned against the alcove wall.

"What are you doing?"

"We'll be here for a while. I might as well get comfortable."

"What do you mean?"

"We'll be here until we reveal a difficult truth to each other. Until then, the Truth Warden won't let us leave."

I cocked out a hip. "But what if I'd come alone? Who would I have told my truth to?"

The figure of the Warden shimmered. "You would have perished."

My hands flew to my hips. "Look, buddy, if you're just a bunch of memories, how can you answer my questions?"

The Warden shimmered in a nonexistent breeze. "Certain questions, including this one, are banal. Responses are pre-prepared."

"Banal," I snarled. "Rude."

Looking around the cramped alcove, I tried to take in my situation. I was stuck in this stone tomb until I could tell Thorne one difficult truth, and he could tell me one too. The wall carvings were ornate and beautiful, and we could both cast faelight to keep it lit. Plus, we had water and, I hoped, plenty of oxygen.

But if I'd come alone, I would have become just another dead body in the catacombs.

I shivered, slipped off my pack, rested my bow and quiver against the wall, and sat beside Thorne, close enough that my crossed knee touched his thigh. The stone was cold beneath my bruised butt, so I shifted uncomfortably.

"Why weren't you polite to me when I held your life in my hands?" Thorne asked.

I looked up at him and saw that his blue-black gaze was earnest. "You never had my life in your hands."

"I could have executed you in the castle."

I scoffed. "You could have tried. In fact, you did try."

Silence. Long, heavy silence. "I did, didn't I? I'm sorry."

As pleased as I was for the apology, my first reaction was to glance around and see if the Warden had shifted the stone gate blocking our exit. But apparently, Thorne's apology didn't count as a difficult truth.

"I forgive you," I said. "I can hold my own, so I wasn't too worried."

Thorne's voice was quiet. "You can, can't you. You're a very impressive fae."

Again, my head whirled around to check the stone gate. "So are you," I ventured, hoping that would be truthful enough to release us.

The figure of the Warden had disappeared, but I could sense

it near us, listening.

"Stop worrying about the difficult truth," Thorne said. He saw me shivering and pulled me closer with an arm around my shoulder, keeping me warm. "Either it will come, or it won't."

"I didn't peg you as the philosophical type," I said, nuzzling against his chest. I curled into him and tucked my hands against his side, soaking up every bit of heat I could.

He chuckled. "Only when it comes to magical stones that could save the future of our land." His hand ran down my arm. "Plus, I don't mind being trapped here. With you, Gabrelle."

My name on his lips was an aphrodisiac, and my nipples pointed into peaks, and my pussy pulsed in desire. "Because I'm beautiful?" I asked, already hearing a note of breathlessness in my voice.

"No," he growled, turning to face me, his breath warming my cheek. "Because you're remarkable and strong and persistent and generous and intelligent."

My skin flushed as he slid closer, so my crossed knee slid over his thigh. He kissed my cheek first, a warm touch that sent shivers down my spine. His breath was warm on my skin, sending an ache deep into my stomach.

He kissed me then. His lips were warm and soft against mine, and I wanted to drown in his kiss. He tasted of sweet honey and mint, and I wanted more. My heart pounded wildly, and all I could think about was tasting more of him.

Gabrelle

Thorne's hands roamed my body, sending tingles down to my toes and desire curling through my belly. He cupped the back of my neck, making a place for himself at the base of my throat. His fingers brushed across my leather vest just below my breasts, taunting me with a touch that made me feverish.

Nothing mattered except his touch on me. Not the hunt for the Stone. Not the dark, lifeless catacombs around us. Not the shadowy Truth Warden who observed us from the mists of the past.

Just Thorne. His hands, his lips, his hulking presence. His hand moved lower, tracing over my collarbone and down. He slowly unlaced the front of my jerkin, his knuckles pressing lightly against my skin, making me ache for a firmer touch. Finally, the jerkin lay open, and Thorne pressed his hot hand over the thin fabric of my shirt, cupping my breast.

The prince groaned as he squeezed my breasts, his hungry black eyes trailing over my body.

He touched my neck, pulled me toward him, and kissed me hard. His tongue forced my lips open as he reached one arm behind me and cupped my ass with his free hand.

"Fuck," I growled as he squeezed my ass, hard. "That's not very polite."

His breath was hot, and he snarled into my ear. "I'm not feeling very polite, little trickster."

I arched my back into him, panting. Desire coursed through me, unlike anything I'd ever felt. Not because I felt sexy or beautiful. Because I felt known.

He pulled me over so I was straddling him, my ass resting on his outstretched thighs. With strong hands, he cupped my breasts through the fabric. Then he pressed his thumb and forefinger on each nipple until they were erect and throbbing.

"Take your shirt off," he commanded.

I did as he said. It was amazing to relinquish control to somebody I trusted and follow his orders. In every other sexual encounter in my life, I'd been in total control. I'd granted the sex like a favor, allowed my partner to undress, suckle, and adore me, and permitted him to grant me an orgasm.

But this was entirely different. I was at Thorne's mercy. My hatred had flicked into powerful, drugging lust. If he abandoned me and cast me aside right now, I would weep.

He gazed at my full breasts, then trailed hungry kisses over them, holding me up so my knees barely touched the ground so he could get full access. My back arched, and I moaned, a primordial cry that came directly from my soul as he took my nipple into his mouth and sucked, hard.

The cold air rippled over my exposed skin, but I didn't care. I was hot now, full of warmth and need, and I didn't care about the freezing temperature or the hard stone. All I cared about was pressing myself harder against Thorne.

I pawed at his shirt, roving my hands over his strong shoulders, then lower, over his chest, tugging his shirt up over his head. A gasp escaped me as I took him in. The scar on his face stood out, red and angry in his arousal. His lips were full, and his blue-black eyes were hungry. His jaw was cut, and his neck was corded and tan. But his chest was something else. Carved by Gaia herself, a perfect specimen of masculinity, with toned planes over rippling muscle.

"You're beautiful," I breathed, and he smiled up at me.

"Nobody's ever accused me of that before," he said, leaning in to kiss me, but I pushed him back with a palm on his muscled pec so I could examine him a moment longer.

"Beautiful," I repeated, suddenly understanding why beauty held such power.

He yanked me closer and pressed his lips against mine, and I devoured him, nibbling and licking and moving my lips against his in perfect synchrony, like I was born to do it. He gripped the back of my head like it was keeping him alive, and I responded with another desperate moan.

His hands gripped my hips. His touch ignited a fire that raced along my nerves and made me want to chase him. He made me feel like a priceless treasure he wanted to discover again and again, as though I were something worth spending his whole life searching for.

He moved gently, stroking my stomach and hips. His hands moved lower until they reached between us, cupping me between my legs through my leather pants.

The fabric was thick, too thick, but I could still feel the motion of his thumb, rubbing slow circles over my clit with a firm pressure that sent sparks of pleasure coursing through me. I moaned into his mouth as he alternated between soft caresses and harder strokes, sending waves of pleasure through me that left me panting.

"Are we really going to do this here?" I panted. "In a crypt?"

"Yes," he growled. "And if anybody tries to stop us, I'll

fucking kill them." He kissed me full on the lips, his hand on my lower back dragging me closer. "That's my difficult truth," he said.

I didn't even glance at the stone barrier. I didn't want to escape right now. I only wanted to stay here pressed against Thorne.

In one powerful movement, he went from sitting to standing, taking me with him, and placed me gently on my feet.

Was he stopping this? Because I'd said that stupid thing about us being in a crypt? I would fucking weep. I would get down on my knees and beg him to keep going like I had zero dignity. Who fucking cared about dignity? I wanted and needed him, and I would do anything to get him.

But he wasn't ending this—the look in his eyes was pure need. "Take off your pants," he said hoarsely, and I did. I wriggled out of my tight leathers while his gaze never left me.

"Good girl," he growled.

This was the most obedient I'd ever been, and it felt wonderful. Only because I trusted him. Because he was different than anyone I'd ever met. Right now, I'd do anything for him.

As soon as I stood before him in just my bra and panties, he bent down and laid our clothes as a makeshift mattress that would keep the worst of the cold off our skin. Then he picked me up, much stronger than I expected, and laid me on my back like an offering to Mortia.

We had cast globes of faelight and left them flickering above us, casting warm shadows through the chamber. Thorne's blue-black hair reflected like the night sky, and I gazed up at his perfect chest and warrior scar, needing him closer. His cock was tenting his pants, huge and inviting, and I wanted to feel it pressing against my thigh, against my belly, in my mouth, and filling my pussy. "Come to me," I said when I couldn't take it anymore.

He growled and lowered himself over me like he was doing a pushup, then kissed my lips. I grabbed his neck and shoulder, pulling him closer, wanting to feel his weight against the length of my body. As I pulled myself up, our chests rubbed against each other in sweet friction as we continued to devour each other's mouths hungrily, but then he did a pushup, resisting my tug, and I fell back to the makeshift mattress.

He kissed down my neck, over the crest of my breasts and down the shallow of my belly. "Fuck," I murmured as he reached my panties and ripped them off me with a tearing of material, exposing me completely.

"Fuck," he murmured this time, staring at my pussy.

Then he slid one finger inside me, then another. His fingers teased me, plunging inside and out in a gentle rhythm until I was panting with desire for him.

The feel of him was overwhelming, and I clung to him, amazed at how right it felt. My skin felt alive in his embrace, my breath quickened, and my heart raced. I felt like I could fly, like I belonged in his arms forever.

He cursed and plunged his face deep into my pussy as he pulled my hips toward him to taste me for the first time. His tongue flicked up and down like a flame over my sensitive flesh. His lips lathed softly over every part of me before probing deeper with his tongue, pushing me further and further into blissful abandon. In seconds I could feel my muscles contracting in waves of pleasure, and heat rose within me until I was a writhing mass of ecstasy.

Finally, I could take no more and released a guttural cry as wave after wave of hot pleasure coursed through me.

Sobbing with emotional release, I sprung off the floor and into his lap, making him cradle me as I cried, literal fucking tears dropping off my jaw.

"Shh," he said, patting my hair and letting me tuck my head into his neck.

My response was crazy. Who cried after sex? I mean, I knew some weak-willed freaks did, but never me. No, I was always in control of my sexual partners and my emotions. But not this time. A switch had flicked inside me, opening the floodgates, allowing me to be free.

As I sobbed into Thorne's warm, beautiful neck, I released myself completely to him, body and soul. He patted me, held me, and whispered calming words until my shuddering subsided, leaving me with a sense of pure bliss.

Thorne looked at me, smirking. "Was it really that bad, little trickster?"

I laughed, a joyous bubbling of emotion, and looked up into his blue-black eyes, those mysterious pools I wanted to know more about. I became aware of his hard cock between us, pressing into my thigh, still eager and ready, jumping against my flesh.

"No," I said silkily, noticing heat building inside me again. "But I bet I can do better."

Thorne

Gabrelle was cradled on my chest, her dusty pink eyes still wet. She looked up at me with an emotion I'd never seen on her before—a deep, intense longing.

I felt emotionally connected to her, more than I would ever have thought possible. Like she was fused with me now. Not because she'd just orgasmed on my tongue, hard and sobbing, but because we'd had each other's backs through battle and more. I trusted her, and I read the same in her eyes.

My cock was already hard and pressing into her thigh. As her eyes turned lustful again, my heart thundered with anticipation.

She ran her hands down my arms and over my chest, her delicate fingers tracing the contours of my body. My muscles tensed as she teased my neck and lips with her soft lips, her breath hot on my skin.

Her bra was the only piece of clothing left on her body, and I reached around behind her and popped it open, and her breast jiggled as they released, drawing a long moan from my throat. She was so beautiful. Not because of her perfect dark skin, smooth curves, or gorgeous face. But because she was strong and brave and loving and generous, and that made her beauty into sexual power that I was unable to stay away from.

I bent forward and kissed her breasts, licking and tasting her, my whole body alive and quivering with desire. Her breasts pushed into my mouth faster and faster with each breath she took as I coaxed her back to ecstasy. I wanted her back up on the clifftop I had her teetering on earlier, subject to my whims.

Her hand dipped down from my chest, across my stomach, reached between us, and grabbed my cock. Her eyes grew wide as she worked her fingers through the fabric of my pants and felt the heat of me. I locked my gaze on her face, monitoring her every reaction and thought as she worked me with those expert fingers. She wanted this just as much as I did. That was clear.

I couldn't wait a moment longer, so I pressed in and kissed her hungrily, one hand on her neck and the other on her hips.

She stopped holding my cock and ran a finger down the scar on my face, trailing over my long-healed injury. My hands cupped her face for a moment and then slid down to cup her ass, pulling her hips toward me. She was still sideways on my lap, so I surged forward and lay her back on the pile of discarded clothing, now completely naked, a feast just for me.

She watched carefully as I stood and unbuckled my belt, letting it clink to the stone floor, then pulled down my pants and kicked them away. I kneeled at her feet and looked up the length of her body, the shapely toned legs, her throbbing wet pussy that smelled and tasted divine, her taut belly and magnificent round breasts, and her face that smiled down at me gently.

"I want this more than anything," I said reverently. "I want you more than anything."

She gave me a wicked smile. "Then take me, prince."

I crawled up her body, one knee on either side, letting my

throbbing cock slide up the inside of her legs, indenting her flesh and tormenting my aching length.

Her breathing grew louder, panting in time with me, and her whole body quivered and moved with every intake of air, making me harder and hotter.

I reached her throat and plunged, my tongue tracing small circles on her skin, making her moan louder and louder until I couldn't hold back and I pressed the tip of my cock against her wetness and pushed inside, entering the Princess of Verda's body, Gabrelle's body, my aching cock finally sliding into her tight, wet pussy. She clung to me, digging her nails into my back and crying out.

I could die and be happy to have such an infinite moment etched in my mind. I thrust into her again, and she clung to me as I drove deeper again and again.

I was pulled into her as if she were a massive black hole and I was an insignificant speck of dust. Each time my cock sank into her burning hot, wet pussy, I grew closer and closer to the edge.

I thrust into her, unable to get deep enough or hard enough, needing more of the feeling, needing more of her. I ground my hips against hers, my teeth clenched as I fought the urge to come too soon as my cock worked inside her.

She had to orgasm first. I claimed her with my lips and ground my hips against hers, fucking her hard while she screamed my name. I watched her face as she came, her eyes dripping with lust. Her skin turned darker, then tinted with red as her body trembled. She threw back her head and moaned loudly, like an opera singer making love to a packed audience. Each moan fed my desire. Her orgasm washed over me in a wave, pulling me up and tensing my muscles at the same time.

My cock swelled inside her tight, velvety tunnel as cum jetted out from the tip, filling her.

When it was over, we lay in a tangled heap of limbs and sweat, our breathing slowing as our hearts returned to normal. We would have to dress soon because the chamber was so cold, but we had a few moments to lie together, naked and entwined, belly to belly on the thin pile of clothes.

Gabrelle's head rested on my bicep. A few short weeks ago, I thought she was superficial and dishonest, but she was the opposite. She had an inner strength and integrity I could only aspire to, and those tears she'd shed after her first orgasm were the most honest and authentic things I'd ever seen.

I pulled her tight, feeling a connection beyond words. Loosening my grip so I could look into her eyes, I spoke the words I never thought possible. "I love you, Gabrelle."

The sentence echoed around the small chamber, bouncing off the engraved walls and in the tiny spaces between our bodies. It didn't matter if she didn't love me back, I just needed to tell her the truth. I tried to read an answer in her face to ensure I hadn't spooked her. Her cheeks shone under the faelight globes, and her lips quirked. "I love you too, Thorne."

With a click and the smell of smoke, the Truth Warden materialized by the stone barrier, holding the Stone of Veritas in his palm. He looked down at us in our nakedness. I scrambled to my feet and tugged on my pants, but Gabrelle just climbed gracefully to standing and stood with her hip cocked in magnificent disregard for being nude. Honesty personified.

"Two difficult truths have been shared," he declared.

I spluttered. "Really? The truth was that I love her?"

Gabrelle was graceful as usual, with not a splutter in sight. "The truth is different for each fae who seeks the Stone," she said.

I looked at her in awe, composed even though she stood completely naked. So right. "How do you know that?"

She threw me a cheeky glance and raised a shoulder. "It seems pretty obvious to me." She turned to the Warden. "Can we leave now? With the Stone, I mean. I'm not going without that."

The ghostly figure bowed his head and disappeared. The rock gate rumbled upward, opening up the space to the hallways and our exit, and the Stone of Veritas appeared in Gabrelle's hand.

"Now what?" I asked, barely able to concentrate on what was happening while the beauty princess was naked before me.

"Now we try to get out of here without dying," she said.

I looked her up and down. "I think you should get dressed first?"

She narrowed her eyes at me. "Just because I love you doesn't mean you get to order me around."

I grinned and closed the space between us with a stride. I kissed her on the lips, long and hard, breathing in her passionfruit aroma. "Sucked in, you love me," I teased. "And I'd prefer it if you didn't get dressed, to be honest. Let's go and see if we can avoid any more traps."

Sadly, she pulled on her leather pants and thin travel shirt, then laced her leather jerkin. She still looked hot as fuck, though. She gave me a curt nod. "Let's go."

Gabrelle

The corridors were dimly lit by the glow of our faelight as we passed by tomb after tomb. We raced down the twisting corridors of the catacombs, dark shadows dancing around us as if reaching out to touch us as we passed. Our boots slapped against the stone floor as we jogged, blending with the occasional creaks and groans deep within the maze.

I veered around a glinting metal trap, still running, and finally, I saw a sparkle of daylight from an opening ahead.

As I sprinted up some stone stairs and emerged into full sun, Thorne raced behind me and then beside me. I shielded my eyes, taking a moment to catch my breath and appreciate the newfound freedom. Then I ran across the courtyard, under the stone archway, and through the long grass to the top of the hill. I stopped, panting, with one eye on the sky, looking for pteroclaws. The ocean was loud out here, pounding against the cliffs on our left. I hadn't noticed before, but if I peered across the water, I could see the shimmering veil that marked the edge of our world and the start of the mortal one.

Thorne pulled me into a kiss, and I melted against his chest and almost started weeping again. It was too much. My emotions were wild and scattered like seeds in the wind, and I felt like I was drowning in them.

GABRELLE

I didn't know how to control my emotions anymore. I used to be the ice princess, the one who never showed a flicker of emotion, but here I was with Thorne, and my feelings were a raging storm that I couldn't contain. My heart raced, almost panicking, as he embraced me and kissed me, and my entire body was alight in flames as if each cell was individually screaming out for more.

My logical mind told me to push him away before things escalated any further, but the feeling of his arms around me left me paralyzed and unable to move. In that moment, all I wanted was for the two of us to stay together in our little world where nothing mattered except us.

But deep down inside, fear slowly started consuming my thoughts until finally, it overwhelmed everything else, and I abruptly pulled away from him. Time seemed to slow as panic began rising within me like floodwaters breaching a dam wall. "We should keep going."

"Are you okay? Are you hurt?" Concern clouded Thorne's blue-black eyes, and I turned my back on him. "I'm fine. Let's keep moving."

But I wasn't fine. My feelings were too strong for me to contain. I plunged down the other side of the hill, heading southeast, back into the swampy mangroves. Thorne didn't push it, he just followed, and we soon fell into a rhythm of walking, plowing through mud and across grassy tufts, mostly in silence.

I patted the Stone of Veritas in my pocket to reassure myself why I had come here. I tried to concentrate on the path ahead, but my emotions kept swelling and receding like the tide. Thorne was unlocking something inside of me that I had kept safe and hidden for years. Suddenly, I was vulnerable and exposed. All my feelings ran hot and deep, so intense that they left me trembling.

My control used to be supreme, effortless, but now everything was slipping away. Whenever Thorne looked at me or put his hand on mine, my heart raced faster than the wind whipping across the cliffside.

After hours of trudging, long after the sun had set, we reached a dry patch of grass in the middle of the swamp that would make do for a camp. Thorne grabbed some fallen branches and any dry wood he could and lit a small fire. The light was comforting and warm against my skin, and some of my turmoil melted away.

Thorne lay beside the fire, then he held out his hand for me. I took it without hesitation, and he drew me closer until I was nestled against his chest. He kissed me softly on the forehead, and in that moment, all my worries melted away. Here, with him by my side, I felt safe.

We talked long into the night, with our twin faelights hovering behind us to ward off any Shadow Walkers.

I watched him as he spoke, marveling at how easy it was for him to talk without worrying about repercussions or judgment from others. His thick blue-black hair glowed under the firelight, and his scar was barely visible.

I had never talked so openly but wanted to tell Thorne everything, even things I hadn't told the other heirs. My thoughts turned to my upcoming Ascension rite, and I asked Thorne about his. He was a Binder, one who could make a promise binding and only breakable through death. He told me he could barely remember the rite, that it was all a blur, which was the same frustrating answer I got from all Ascended.

I had recently turned twenty-five, with a grand party put on by my mother, who didn't recognize the irony of an ice queen hosting a masked ball. My Ascension rite was in a few months, the first rite following my twenty-fifth birthday. To ascend into my full magic, I had to kill myself with it. If I wanted Lupin, like Leif, I would need a wolf to kill me. If I wanted to be a Grower, like Neela, I would need to kill myself with a plant—I think she used a poisonous flower.

"What will you choose to ascend to?" he asked.

"Mother has Lure," I said, and Thorne nodded. "And Father has Stealth." He already knew this, of course. All royal offspring were educated in the politics of other realms. "Everybody assumes I'll ascend to Lure, but I'm not sure if I will," I admitted.

Whenever I'd said that to the heirs, they laughed or joked around, assuming I was kidding. But I wasn't.

"Why not?" Thorne asked, his hand casually draped over my hip.

"Because my mother has Lure, and I've seen the heartless things she's done with it," I confessed.

The fire crackled, dancing with flames, and Thorne's arms held me close. A surge of love pulsed through me, alarming in its intensity.

"No magic is good or evil," he said softly. "You need to choose what's right for you. It doesn't matter what your mother has, you don't have to define yourself by her. Lure can be powerful, and it won't change who you are. You can use it for whatever purpose you want. Don't let your mother stop you from being who you are deep down. Just choose from your heart."

A frog croaked loudly from the mud, and I leaned forward to add more wood to the fire. Thorne was right. I associated Lure so strongly with my mother that I assumed it was inherently heartless and cold, like her.

But it wasn't. It could be whatever I wanted it to be.

"I'll take the first watch tonight," I said.

Thorne tried to object, but I could see the weariness creep over him. He had barely slept last night, so I convinced him to lay his head on the grass and close his eyes.

Watching over him, a powerful love seized me. I wanted to protect him from the world. He'd proven himself a worthy opponent, a reliable comrade, and an excellent lover. Now I would protect him. I strengthened my faelight and watched as his limbs relaxed and the muscles in his face loosened.

Soon he was asleep, and I kept watching him. Thorne stirred slightly in his sleep, and I smiled as he muttered something incomprehensible. My feelings for him were terrifying. I wriggled further away so we were no longer touching—I needed to get some distance to figure out what was happening.

Why was I so deeply in love? Why so sudden? I was wildly out of control, so unlike the fae I'd been for my entire life.

Agitation crept through me, inch by inch, making me squirm on the cold ground. My bruised ass from falling down that chute didn't help, either.

The longer I stared at Thorne, the less my feelings made sense. I was Gabrelle Allura, the Ice Princess of Verda, always in control of myself. Never swayed by another.

The realization hit me like a wave and had me swaying where I sat. These feelings weren't love, they were part of the curse of Elyssia Castle. It tricked me into having feelings, and it tricked Thorne into believing I was honest. Neither of those things was possible.

I stood up and stepped away from Thorne, edging out to the

far side of the fire. This weeping, emotional fae was not my true self; it was just a trick of the castle. I had to become strong again and protect myself against these feelings that were so out of character. My subjects in Verda deserved more of their future queen.

My breathing quickened as I tried to calm my racing heart. Taking deep breaths, I closed my eyes and tried to make sense of the situation. The castle had trapped us and forced confessions of love from us, manipulating us every step of the way.

I opened my eyes and looked at Thorne again, the flames flickering against his blue-black hair. He seemed so peaceful in his sleep, and I wished I could join him there for just a few moments more. But I knew that if I did, the castle's dark magic would ensnare me forever, and I might never crawl out of his arms.

Well, I refused to be under anyone's control—not even my own emotions.

There was one thing I could do to break myself from the curse. I dug through my pack and scrawled a quick note, then whispered, "Avem volare," and watched my spellbird fly away, with familiar ice solidifying in my veins.

Thorne

I dreamed of Gabrelle all night and woke with a raging hard-on that I hoped she might be able to do something about. But she just told me it was my shift to watch, then turned her back and curled in a ball, facing away from the fire.

I spent the early hours of the dark morning thinking about Gabrelle, but other tasks nudged into my mind. The Fen Ascension rite was tomorrow, and I needed to be there—as a crown prince with shaky support, I couldn't afford to miss it. As morning lightened into day, the tension of running late stiffened my limbs.

But Gabrelle was more important, and she needed the rest. So I tiptoed around camp, leaving her to sleep as I collected water and searched for rowenuts. When the sun had risen high into the sky, she finally woke, rubbing her eyes. Her face twitched as frustration set in, and she cursed under her breath.

"Time to go, trickster," I said lightly, but she just stared at me, shouldered her pack and bow, and stomped off. "Is everything okay?"

She ignored me and kept walking. We trudged through the swamp all morning, grunting at the incessant mud and growing hungry.

Her foul mood didn't improve. Was it because we'd had sex?

Amazing fucking sex. Or because she said she loved me? Or was something else entirely souring her mood? She hadn't said anything in hours and refused to answer my questions. What the hell was going on?

We stopped to drink and rest near a large tree at the edge of a clearing. She plopped down on a log and stared into the distance, seemingly oblivious to my presence, like she'd built an invisible wall between us.

Whatever it was, I wanted to make things better for her but knew enough to give her space until she felt ready to talk about it. Until then, I could only remain patient and show her kindness, even if it went unacknowledged.

So I held back my questions and followed after her with a heavy heart. Whatever it was, we would sort it out.

The day continued on, and soon the air grew chill. The sun was setting, and we still hadn't reached flat dry ground where we could camp. We trudged quickly, and an odd tingle skittered over my skin as I noticed the small animals had stopped scurrying through the undergrowth.

"Down!"

I tackled Gabrelle to the ground just as a gust of icy wind walloped us. Monochrome flakes swirled around us like snow, but not quite—they were hard and jagged, like broken glass. Soon they would grow into daggers of ice, then spears. An ice storm.

The storm rose around us in an instant, raging cold and dangerous, and although I was covering most of Gabrelle's body with mine, I saw slashes of red appear on her exposed arms.

"We need cover," I shouted. "Follow me on three."

I counted down, shouting my commands, eyeing a crevice

between two rocks that was the only protection around. On "one," I yanked Gabrelle to her feet, shoved her into the gap, and then dived onto her.

My long-sleeved shirt had a customary metal plate sewn into the front and back to protect against the famous Fen ice storms, but Gabrelle's hunting leathers were no match for the icy daggers. So I had to pin her down, despite her wriggling complaints.

A tree snapped in half from the weight of its frozen branches and thundered to the ground beside us. We huddled in the crevice as the storm raged, and Gabrelle convulsed with shivers. Suddenly, just as fast as it started, the ice storm retreated, leaving soggy leaves and crisp, cold air.

I did a push-up to put space between us, which I was sure Gabrelle wanted. Pausing for a moment, our faces mere inches apart, I waited for a sign of permission, but she closed her eyes and averted her head, waiting for me to move. I jumped to my feet and looked her over for injuries.

"Are you okay?" I asked. She was tough and refused to show any signs of pain, but that jagged red line streaked across her forearm, exposing flesh that should never see the light of day. When I stepped closer to assess the damage, she yanked her arm away.

"I'm fine." She jerked a thumb at my leg. "Worry about yourself."

I saw a gash in the back of my thigh, along with hundreds of smaller cuts. Honestly, I didn't give a fuck about my injuries, I was more worried about Gabrelle's sudden icy mood. A little blood loss was nothing.

"I'm okay." I took a tentative step, and my leg buckled.

She sighed, and her expression flashed with something

unreadable. "Let's make camp here."

The ground wasn't too boggy, although it wasn't exactly dry. But after the flash storm, the whole area would be wet. "Yep, good idea."

I ripped off the remaining sleeve of my shirt, tied it around my thigh, and started collecting wood, looking for dry pieces underneath wet ones, but Gabrelle didn't move to help. "What caused the storm?" she asked.

"Nobody knows." I discarded a wet log and kept looking. "Some fae say they come when Gaia is annoyed."

She ducked her face to hide her reaction, but I saw fear cross her face. "Gaia must be really pissed at someone," she muttered.

"It's all hogwash," I said, finally finding some dry wood. "The ice storms are random. That's why we wear metal plates sewn into our clothes."

She hummed noncommittally while I continued to search for wood.

It was already well after nightfall. When we finally built the fire, I slumped onto the ground beside it as exhaustion weighed me down. But Gabrelle took the time to clean off her clothes like she had the first night. She pulled the muck from her hair, wiped away the blood, and repaired the worst holes in her brown leather pants, making herself a pretty princess. Then we slept another night under the stars.

My pull to her was so strong that I could barely keep away from her, although I knew that was what she wanted. I was filled with love as I gazed at her, snuggling into a pile of leaves. Despite her anger and frustration, I loved how strong she was, how passionate she was about everything she did, and how all the darkness disappeared from her eyes when she smiled.

She was everything I wanted: loyal, wild, and fiercely independent. In truth, I admired her far more than she could ever imagine. Despite my best efforts to resist, Gabrelle had won my heart. We'd started as bitter enemies, but now she was the air that kept me alive, and I would never let her go.

But by the following day, I was really beginning to worry about her. She kept me at a distance, pushing away my attempts at conversation, and we trudged all day in silence.

Finally, footsore and weary from the stench of mud and the dark silence of the swamp, with the gash in the back of my thigh thudding with every heartbeat, I saw sunlight spreading across the forest canopy. The light was a relief after so long in a sticky, dank wilderness of reeds and trees that hid predators behind every leaf. Tonight, we would sleep without worrying about being eaten alive.

We stepped out into daylight on the outskirts of Isslia, blinking against the brightness. There was a freshness to the air, a crispness that replaced the oppressive smell of mud and swamp. The smell of wood smoke and cooking food drifted on the breeze from some nearby homes.

But I didn't have long to appreciate the improved surroundings. With a scrape of boots and the ringing of steel, we were instantly surrounded by fae with their weapons drawn.

Adrenaline dumped into my bloodstream. "What are you doing?" I boomed, scanning the ring of faces and suddenly wishing I'd taken greater care of my own appearance. I needed to look like the Crown Prince of Fen, not a homeless vagrant. "Do you know who I am?"

Erevan stepped forward, his head high. His shoulders were squared and broad, the stance of someone confident in his own power. His dark yellow eyes were cold and calculating, and his lips were curled up in a smirk that was almost a sneer. His voice was low and commanding, with a hint of laughter. "They know exactly who you are, Thorne. You're the last remaining son of the late queen. The first Sanctus in generations who won't rule Fen."

The swords surrounding us glinted in the low afternoon light, their edges sharp and deadly.

Erevan wasn't finished. He looked at Gabrelle. In his white-collared shirt, freshly polished shoes, and a sparkling silver sword at his side, he looked like a fitting match for Gabrelle. "And Princess Allura," he said, "future Queen of Verda." He dipped his head like the promise of a bow.

Jealousy roared through me like wildfire at how he looked at her, using her first name and sharing an intimate glance. He was more handsome than me and more accomplished in fine arts and diplomacy. Even worse, I knew they'd had sex during the Wild Hunt, and maybe since then, but surely it couldn't have been anything like the passion she and I had shared.

"Tell me, Gabrelle," Erevan continued with his snake-charmer's smile. "Did you retrieve the Stone of Veritas?"

I waited for her to deny that she'd found the Stone. Not outright, of course, Gaia's realm magic wouldn't permit that. But in courtly misleadings and flattery.

But her face was blank. "Yes," she said, and my mouth fell open. But I could hardly fault her for honesty, not when I'd spent so much time attacking her for lying.

Erevan's butterscotch eyes lit up, and he stalked closer. "May I see it?"

"Of course not," I interjected, but Gabrelle and Erevan both ignored me. Rage boiled inside me.

I watched helplessly as Erevan inched closer to Gabrelle, a

predatory gleam in his eye and awe on his face. She fished the Stone from her pocket and held it out for Erevan to see. It glowed blue and ethereal like a gem from Gaia's hair.

Erevan peered closer. "May I?"

Gabrelle didn't move or speak, so Erevan plucked the Stone from her palm, grinning like crazy. "It's beautiful."

"Give it back to her," I demanded.

The conniving fae pocketed the Stone of Veritas that Gabrelle and I had risked our lives for. "No, I don't think so."

Finally, Gabrelle stirred from her stupor. Her bow was in firing position in an instant, with an arrow on the string. "Give me back the Stone, Erevan." Her voice was diamond.

The circle of fae around us stamped their feet in unison, setting off a puff of dirt with a loud thud. Their swords glinted in the dying sun.

Erevan smirked. "This is where it gets interesting." He turned his dark yellow gaze on me, openly assessing me. "This is where we strike a bargain. If you still think you're fit to be king," he said, taking in my muddy appearance and bedraggled state as though it reflected my worth. "Then you must let me keep the Stone. If you want the Stone back, you must give me the kingdom. It is as simple as that."

Gabrelle's jaw ground so hard I could hear her teeth creaking. "That wasn't the deal, asshole. You said you'd do everything possible to help me find the Stone."

Erevan made a show of looking shocked. His eyebrows shot up, and his mouth formed an O. "And I did, my dear. I helped you find it. I didn't say anything about letting you keep it." He chuckled darkly. "You still have a lot to learn about surviving in Fen, beauty queen."

I wanted to object to him calling her that, reducing her to

nothing more than her physical appearance. But my mind was ringing as Gabrelle's and Erevan's conversation echoed through my skull.

That wasn't the deal.

"What deal?" I asked her, unable to look away. The circle of armed fae disappeared from my mind, leaving me entirely focused on Gabrelle. It was just me and her and some deal she'd made with the devil.

She finally looked at me. I'd wanted her full attention all day, and she hadn't given it to me, but now that she did, I was afraid of what she would say. She looked pristine, with barely any mud or dirt on her, her pink hair falling in gorgeous waves around her face. But her eyes were wide and wet, and they told me everything I needed to know.

Blood pounded through my ears, and my hands curled into fists. "You made a deal with Erevan? The fae who wants my throne?"

Her plum lips vibrated, a tiny movement that betrayed her emotion. "I did it to prove I wasn't in love with you."

"What the hell does that mean?"

"The curse of Elyssia Castle. It made me think I loved you."

"And made me think you were honest," I spat.

"Exactly."

Gabrelle's confession hung heavy in the air, weighing me down like a ton of bricks. I struggled to wrap my head around what she had done and how it had affected our connection. The silence between us spoke volumes, crushing the trust we had built like fragile glass.

This fae, this trickster princess, was no paragon of honesty and goodness. She was a liar who had stabbed me through the heart with her betrayal.

When I turned from her, she emitted a small, defeated squeak. But I no longer cared. She looked like her heart was breaking, but mine was turning into steel.

I blinked, and the armed fae reappeared around me, along with Reissan's sneering face. "Keep the Stone, Erevan," I said coldly. "I want my kingdom."

A cold determination settled in as I turned my back on Gabrelle, anger and hurt building a mighty wall. With each step I took, the ties between us unraveled, leaving behind the shattered remains of our trust. I pushed roughly through the circle of fae and never looked back.

Gabrelle

I watched Thorne's retreating back, feeling emptier with every step he took.

Erevan's circle of guards relaxed their stances, sheathing their swords with a ringing of steel.

Erevan stepped toward me. "Thank you for retrieving the Stone of Veritas for me. It can't have been easy."

I snapped my gaze toward him, seeing through his fake sympathy. His brows were furrowed, and his butterscotch eyes had specks of gold in the fading sunlight. "I didn't get it for you," I snapped. "You know damn well I got it for myself. I need it to kill the Shadow Walkers. Give it back." I held out my hand for the Stone he had stolen and stashed away.

Erevan moved closer, pretending sympathy, but I saw right through him. His words stung, fueling frustration within me. I demanded he return the Stone that rightfully belonged to me. However, he shook his head sadly. "No, I won't do that. You said it kills Shadow Walkers, right? I need it to protect Fen when they approach our borders. Then King Thorne will come running to me for help, and the lesser fae will see who holds the true power. Sanctus won't remain king for long."

Detached, I examined Erevan, unable to summon the anger he deserved. He appeared like a perfect courtesan, donning finely tailored clothes and moving with grace, with a face made to be looked at. But beneath the surface, he was nothing more than a scoundrel.

"You're selfish," I said. "A liar and a thief."

Erevan smirked, clearly not offended in the least. "I am what I need to be to rule. Even in the truth-telling realm, one must navigate tricky negotiations diplomatically, a skill the Sanctus family has always lacked. Being a skilled liar in the realm where Gaia forbids lying is the greatest skill of all. So yes, I'm a liar and a thief, but I'm no more selfish than you."

That sparked a flash of emotion inside me, penetrating through the fog I'd been living in these past two days. "How do you figure? You're holding the only weapon against the Shadow Walkers as a power play to steal the throne from the Sanctus line."

He tilted his head, regarding me closely. "And you want our only weapon against the Shadow Walkers under your control. It is a Fen artifact, yet you selfishly want to take it from us."

A dark chuckle bubbled from me. "No, I want to protect you. If I kill the Walkers before they reach Fen, you'll never have to deal with them. I want to save lives."

"So do I," Erevan said. "I just want to time it right."

"You want to time it to your advantage, so you can produce the weapon and clamber your way onto the throne."

He smiled like I was a student learning my lessons well. "Exactly. Well done, Gabrelle."

"It's Princess Allura to you," I said coldly.

"Well, Princess Allura, when I'm king, I'll work with you to banish the Shadow Walkers from Verda."

"That'll be too late."

"Regardless, it's a promise."

I stared at him a moment, looking into his black soul. "Your promises aren't worth shit." I turned my back and walked away, leaving his ring of parasites with one hand on their sword hilts and the other on their dicks.

Aimlessly wandering through Elyssia, my anger fizzled out, suffocated like a flame in a vacuum. I felt empty—no emotions, no dignity.

I roamed the streets, maneuvering through the bluestone buildings like a frigid river. How fitting for the ice princess herself.

I had lost myself in Elyssia Castle, swept away by my emotional response to Thorne. The feelings were too strong, too foreign, too much. So, to prove it was all part of the curse and that I wasn't losing myself completely, I betrayed him to Erevan.

Had I become callous? Was this my destiny? To betray those who loved me?

A voice inside me whispered that I was no better than my mother, a fae who would do anything to anyone to get what she wanted.

Erevan's words screamed in my mind: "You're selfish."

Yes, I was selfish. My desire to protect the fae of Verda outweighed my loyalty to Thorne, even though he had done nothing wrong. And now I was on a path of betrayal and callousness, just like my mother.

Shame sank deep into my bones. I was no better than the ice-cold bitch of a mother I'd always hated. I'd battled so long and hard against her, and now I was becoming her.

Ducking through a narrow alleyway with pale blue buildings on either side, I heard a noise behind me and screeching from above. It sounded like the pteroclaws outside Elyssia Castle.

Had they followed me? Come to take their revenge?

I turned slowly, unable to even care. My bow was still slung across my shoulder, but I left it there. My energy was gone. My ability to care, even about my safety, was gone. Every last ounce of emotion was gone, drained away, left back there in the swamp at the moment I sent the spellbird to Erevan.

I stopped and looked at the night sky, wondering how many pteroclaws had come. The vast, breathtaking sky held no power to halt the unfolding events in this realm or any other. I was truly alone, having betrayed the only fae who genuinely loved me, with no one to catch me if I fell.

My grumbling belly brought me back to earth. There was no pteroclaw, which was almost a shame—it would have distracted me from my pathetic shame.

I kept walking. Realizing how low I had sunk made me feel even emptier. Nothing mattered anymore. Love, friendship, nothing. Darkness and despair closed in from all sides, suffocating me.

Picking up my pace, I headed to the Court. I couldn't face Thorne again, so I would leave first thing in the morning. Not only would I return to Verda without the Stone of Veritas, but I would return knowing I was no better than my mother.

Thorne had ignited a brief hope inside me that I could be something other than an ice princess, a cold-hearted bitch who didn't feel anything, a perfect paragon of royalty like society expected.

But that was bullshit. I could never be anything else. I cloaked myself in Stealth and ducked down the hidden staircase, emerging from behind the tapestry on the top floor, then wound my way down to my own room, blinking through the blurry world.

Pushing open the door, the dreary room with the hard bed and the warm blanket seemed too good for me.

I'd pushed Thorne aside for the Stone. To prove to myself I didn't need him and that the Stone was the only thing that mattered. To prove to myself that I didn't love him. That I wasn't falling apart for him.

It didn't matter if my intentions were good or if I thought my actions would protect us all in the end. All that mattered was that I had betrayed Thorne. I was my mother's daughter, an ice princess with an icicle for a heart.

I collapsed onto the bed, crushed by the weight of my actions. Was Thorne thinking about me? Was he hurting as much as I was? Tears streamed down my face, dripping off my chin and leaving dark splotches on the sheets. I had always prided myself on being strong and resilient, but now I felt weak and feeble.

I knew I should get up and play the faeboe to calm myself down. Should get up and find food for my starving body. Should go and soak in a hot bath. But I did none of those things. My energy had fled, and all I could do was lie on the mattress and cry.

Gabrelle

The smell of freshly baked breakfast meringues roused me, and I woke with my nose twitching like a damn bunny. After surviving on nothing but foraged rowenuts for days, that sweet cinnamon aroma was the best thing I'd ever smelled.

My eyes flew open to see Leif and Ronan grinning down at me.

"What the hell?" I blurted out.

Leif chuckled, grinning at Ronan. "Told you she'd wake up and be normal, not all poised and shit like usual."

Ronan squinted at me, giving me another once-over. He always had a keen eye for detecting when something was amiss. "No," he countered, perching on the edge of my mattress and making me roll into his gravity. "I've woken her up plenty of times, and she's always graceful." He scanned me from head to toe, but I had no idea what he was looking for since I was just a lump under the blanket. "What's wrong, Gabrelle?" he asked in a hushed tone.

I pushed myself into a sitting position and shuffled back, leaning against the wall. I tried to shove aside the torrent of thoughts and focus on the present. "Well, for starters, I'm starving."

Leif handed me a breakfast meringue. "Yeah. I'm always

grumpy when I'm hungry."

"Or when a beta disagrees with you," I said, having only recently discovered my buddy's dominant alpha side.

"Yeah, that too," Leif said, plopping down on the other side of the mattress. As soon as his butt made contact, he shot up again. "What the fuck? Why are you sleeping on concrete?" He looked around, taking in the tiny room. "And what's with this bedroom? Are you a prisoner or something?"

I took a few bites of the meringue, which had a light crunch on the outside and was deliciously gooey and cinnamony inside. I swallowed before answering. "No, this is my guest suite."

"Nope," Leif said, shaking his head. "This place blows. Give me silk sheets or nothing at all." He looked at me. "A pretty princess like you shouldn't have to put up with this shit. You should've bounced."

The playful banter was a temporary distraction, but underneath it all, I carried a heavy burden of betrayal and uncertainty. Ronan frowned, an expression I hadn't seen on him in ages. Lately, he always looked so happy. I knew he still missed Sebarah like hell—those two had been super close, closer than the rest of us even. And in the days after Seb died, Ronan had been desperately unhappy. I'd been too dismissive of his feelings, I now realized. He'd dwelled in those emotions for months, never emerging until he met Neela. I'd just wanted him to snap out of it and get past his mourning like the rest of us.

But it wasn't that easy. I realized that, now that I'd experienced some emotions myself. Fortunately, I'd slept like the dead all night, without dreams or nightmares, but as my brain woke up, the memory of my betrayal returned, weighing on me.

Ronan's perceptive eyes scanned my face, genuine concern shining through. "Gabrelle, something's bothering you. Don't try to brush it off. We're here for you."

Leif's usual lightheartedness faltered for a moment as he met my gaze. "You don't have to put on a brave face for us, Gabrelle. We're your friends, and we'll support you no matter what."

I couldn't face a conversation about Thorne. About how I'd had mind-blowing sex with him that transcended the physical and left me weeping with emotion. How I'd fallen so deeply in love with Thorne that I no longer knew who I was. How I'd examined myself from every angle, trying to believe I didn't have to be the beauty queen or the ice princess, but in the end, I'd realized that was all I'd ever be.

I couldn't face that. Not today, while the wounds were so fresh. Maybe tomorrow or another day—the heirs would always have my back, I knew that, so maybe one day I would tell the whole story of what happened here.

But now, I would only tell part of the truth. An Erevan-style truth. An *I'll-help-you-find-the-Stone* truth, keeping out the *Then-I'll-steal-it* part.

"I found the Stone of Veritas," I said, and my friends' faces lit with joy.

"Dude!"

"Nice! How did y—"

I raised a hand to quieten them. "But Erevan Reissan took it from me."

Leif's pale face went slack, and he ran a hand through his long silver hair. I was pleased to see he had ditched his usual sweatpants and donned light gray chinos and a collared white shirt.

Ronan, of course, wore black jeans and a black T-shirt. It wasn't exactly courtly attire, but we weren't exactly guests at Court. Especially me. Not after betraying the crown prince.

"Hang on, why are you two here?"

Leif shrugged as he nibbled on his second breakfast meringue. "We got sick of waiting for you downstairs."

"I mean, why are you here in Fen? Why did you come at all?"

Ronan's brow darkened. He got up from the mattress, releasing me from his dent, and started pacing the small room. He only made it three steps before he had to swivel and walk back. "We sent you a bunch of spellbirds, but you didn't answer. So we had to come."

I glanced down at the small pile of convulsing origami paper I'd ignored last night, still twitching with the last of the magic.

"I, er..."

Leif's silver eyes widened. "Shit, dude, you really are sick. I've never seen you so graceless."

I scowled at him. "Rude."

"Sorry, babe, it's the realm magic." The wolf scooted beside me and snuggled against me, with his back on the wall and his legs splayed across my mattress. Physical affection was how wolves comforted each other, but while Leif was still in his freshly-mated honeymoon period, this level of touching was frankly dangerous.

I looked around, alarmed. "Where's Alara?"

Leif shook his head slowly, and I watched as big, fat tears welled in his silver eyes. "She's not here, babe. I don't know if I'll survive without her." He nuzzled his hairy head into my neck, and I patted his thigh, freaking out. If something happened to his mate, Leif might go completely feral and take down the entire realm in his grief. I looked up at Ronan with wide, questioning eyes.

Ronan scoffed. "You'll see her tonight, wolf boy. I'm sure you can last a few hours without her." He turned his black gaze to me. "Alara had to finish something for her dad, but she'll be here tonight."

I gave Leif one last pat on the thigh, extricated myself from his cuddle, and finally got out of bed. This day was getting weirder by the minute. My emotions were still on lockdown, and I felt like I was examining the world through a distorted lens that made no sense.

I was planning to go home today with my tail between my legs, but instead, Ronan and Leif had turned up in my bedroom. And Alara was coming tonight?

"What the hell are you all doing here?" I exclaimed.

Leif stopped whimpering and exchanged a loaded glance with Ronan. "She's really losing the plot," the wolf said.

"Who is?" I demanded.

Ronan put a hand on my shoulder. "You, princess. You're not yourself. You're acting all, I dunno, out of control."

A massive, out-of-control sigh hurled out of me, perfectly proving his point. "I'm..." My natural impulse was to lie, but I couldn't, so I said, "I'm out of control. I'm losing it. You're right."

The heirs looked at me like the world was crumbling, like I'd just announced I ate paving stones for breakfast and wanted to marry my pillow. They looked at me like everything was exactly as bad as I suspected. And I did the only thing I could. I buckled in two and sobbed.

My friends comforted me while I bucked and cried, Ronan on one side and Leif on the other, holding me and whispering soothing sounds while I crouched on the floor and cried like a baby.

I knew that over my head, they were exchanging glances, concerned about my behavior. And that only made it worse. That made me feel even stranger, even less like myself, and even more out of control.

When my tears were spent, and my eyes were red, sore, and dry, I gave them a tight smile, then went to the bathroom to shower and dress. I could hear them muttering about me as I took off my nightgown, but the pounding hot water of the shower muffled them, and I took refuge beneath it.

"I am Gabrelle Allura," I recited, trying to take strength from it. "Heir to House Allura, future Queen of Verda." But the words rang hollow, and I kept picturing Thorne's face in the moment that he figured out I'd sent the spellbird to Erevan.

When I emerged from the shower, I was cleaner on the outside but still stank of betrayal.

I dressed in a purple jumpsuit that hugged my curves and showcased my beauty, the best armor of all. Returning to the bedroom, I placed an expressionless mask on my face. Back to myself. "First, tell me why you're here, then we'll figure out a plan to get the Stone of Veritas from Reissan."

Ronan nodded firmly, and I appreciated his businesslike response. "We are here because we learned some important news you need to hear. Preferably yesterday."

Okay, I could manage this conversation. Affairs of state were well within my wheelhouse. "What news?"

Leif bounced on the spot. "You know how you planned to attend the Ascension rite in Verda in a few months?"

I threw him a superior glance. "I am not in the habit of forgetting the date of my execution."

"Suicide," Leif corrected.

For fae to unlock our full power, we had to sacrifice ourselves with that power during the first Ascension rite after turning twenty-five. Missing, delaying, or refusing it meant a lifetime without access to our inner magic.

"Don't correct me, wolf boy."

Leif didn't care about my rudeness. He bounced on his toes like he couldn't hold in the news. "Well, since you're in Fen, the Fen rules apply. You have to attend the first Ascension rite here."

I walked over to the dresser and ran a comb through my hair. "So I'll go back to Verda."

Ronan whistled, and I flicked my gaze to him. "Spill it, moody."

"Remember how I said you needed the news yesterday?" he said. I could see he was speaking slowly, trying to control his words, fighting against the impulse to spill truths like water. "Today is too late. If you're in the realm on the day of the Ascension rite, you are bound to that realm's magic."

Leif had produced a tennis ball from somewhere, and he chucked it against the wall right by my head, then caught it. "If you don't ascend today, you can never ascend," he said.

My hand paused mid-stroke as I held the comb and stared at my two friends. My lips parted, and I focused on taking slow breaths.

Cold air kissed my shoulders and arms, and I shivered. The Fen Ascension rite was today. And, because I was in Fen today, I was subject to its realm magic. That meant I had to ascend today or forfeit my inner magic forever.

Ronan and Leif stared at me. Ronan's gaze was dark and unreadable, and Leif's filled with pity—he even let out a soft whine on my behalf.

Finally, I found my voice. "But I don't know what I want to ascend to. I haven't had time to plan how to...how to end my life. I can't ascend today. I can't do it."

Leif bounded across the room and pulled me into a hug. "You have to, babe. It's now or never." The wolf's spicy leather scent enveloped me, and its familiarity was calming, but I still couldn't grasp what was happening.

I had to ascend today. I had to take my own life. I couldn't skulk home in my shame and lock Thorne into a jail cell in the back of my mind. No, I would have to confront him and confront myself. Confront Gaia. All while not even knowing who I truly was, let alone who I wanted to become.

Gabrelle

I walked through Isslia, along the streets that wound like rivers of ice through the pale blue buildings. I was leading the procession of fae, given a place of honor as a princess about to ascend.

It had only been a few hours since I found out I had to ascend today, forced to decide which power would shape my entire existence.

Today was the day I had to kill myself.

The grand building loomed at the end of a straight section of road. The building was imposing and regal, with dark stone walls and arched windows framed with wrought iron. The dark slate roof contrasted with the white and pale blue buildings throughout the rest of Isslia, marking this place as different.

In Verda, the Ascension rites always occurred in the Plains of Forgetting, a magnificent outdoor setting imbued with nature's majesty. The ceremony details were obscured by a colorful swirling fog, with spectators standing around with their hearts in their mouths to see if the candidate would emerge from the mist with new powers. Some candidates never appeared, and their dead bodies remained forever in the fog.

I'd always pictured myself with my head held high, a firm plan in my mind, stepping into the colorful fog under Gaia's watchful eye. Some little faelings dreamed of their wedding day or mating ceremony—for me, I'd imagined my Ascension, and it was always in the Plains of Forgetting.

Not inside a dingy fae-made building devoid of natural grace, without the sun on my face and my loved ones around me.

Worst of all, I still didn't have a plan. I didn't know whether to choose Lure or Stealth. There was no denying I was drawn most strongly to Lure, the ability to control others. It flowed through my veins, bubbling under the surface, always ready to leap to my command.

But Lure was my mother's power, and I'd witnessed her using it to bed fae and bend them to her will. I didn't want that for myself. I wanted to be better than that.

The memory of Thorne's words filtered through my mental fog. *No magic is good or evil*, he'd told me. *Don't let your mother stop you from being who you are. Just choose from your heart.*

But that was before I betrayed him. Before I crumpled up his love and discarded it like trash. Before I tore my own heart in two.

Despite myself, I glanced around for a glimpse of Thorne. I felt him like a tingling in the back of my neck and somehow knew he was nearby, but I couldn't see him. An impulse struck me to use my Stealth to seek him undetected, just to look at his face before I killed myself—possibly forever.

But I was leading the procession of twenty-five-year-olds, leading them to their deaths. I couldn't just shimmer out of view and disappear; I had a role to play. Just as Mother taught me, my life was a role. Beauty queen, ice princess, heir.

Stealth was just another lie. A way to obscure the truth. Perhaps it was the most fitting skill for me. Like Lure, it could be used for good or evil.

We reached the grand, broad steps leading into the Hall of Echoes. It felt so wrong to head indoors for the Ascension rite—surely the point was to be close to Gaia. But I didn't have a choice. It was now or never, and I couldn't lead Verda as a permanently Unascended fae.

I climbed the steps and entered the cold, dark hall. The imposing space was cast in a disorienting mix of darkness and light, with the shadowy walls lit by hovering globes of faelight that flickered ever so slightly in the still air. High above, a large stained-glass window cast an eerie rainbow glow on the rows upon rows of seats that lined the hall, rising in steep tiers on all four sides. The Ascension candidates filed into position on the perimeter of the central square, and the onlookers shuffled into spots in the grandstands.

As the fae took their places, I shivered. It was cold in here, and the scent of sickly-sweet incense hung heavily, almost suffocatingly, in the air.

The ominous square in the hall's center is where I would take my life. Dread filled me as I stared at the space. I still didn't have a plan on how to kill myself. How did one Lure oneself to death? Or Stealth oneself dead? If I wanted Water magic, I could just drown myself. If I wanted to be a Weaver, I'd just cast a simple squeezing spell to close off my lungs until I suffocated.

But Lure? I had no idea. I could force someone to kiss me until I died of boredom. And Stealth was no better. I could cloak myself, sneak past everyone and hide until I died of old age.

I sighed and looked around. The Hall of Echoes was an ancient chamber that predated the recorded history of Fen. It was said to have been constructed by the first fae, who sought a sacred space dedicated to the pursuit of truth and the revelation of hidden knowledge. Legends told of a wise fae known as the Truthseeker, who discovered the ethereal resonance within the hall's walls, which amplified sound and echoes with exceptional clarity. This unique property led to its purpose as a place of truth-seeking and Ascension.

I never imagined it would be the place where I would undertake the most significant experience of my life and literally determine my future. Or, if I messed it up, I could stay dead forever, my future gone.

But I couldn't keep my mind on it. Every fae who entered the Hall drew my gaze, and I was restless, searching for one face.

Leif and Ronan strutted into the Hall, looking like the confident princes they were, handsome and proficient. Ronan wore a black two-piece suit with a black shirt, and Leif wore tailored white pants and a flowing silver shirt. But I saw the stress in Ronan's black eyes and the uncertainty in Leif's tight grin. They were worried. They knew as well as I did that this was wrong—I was in the wrong place, ascending too early, surrounded by enemies.

I stood bolt upright like there was a cypress tree up my jumpsuit. I couldn't even find the sass to smile or flirt with the Unascended on either side of me. My stomach roiled, swarming with scuttling sand crabs, and every breath I took raced after the previous one.

Still, I couldn't see him. Panic gripped me as I realized I would die without setting eyes on the fae I loved? I might never return to life and might never have the chance to apologize. But he wasn't here. I couldn't see him. Where the hell was he?

The fae I loved. Emotion swirled up inside me like a tornado until I was visibly shaking. I could see a lock of my long pink hair jumping against my shoulder, but I couldn't stop it or calm my shivering.

I loved Thorne Sanctus. And I had betrayed him. He hated me, detested me, and didn't even bother turning up to watch me die.

My gut kept whirling, and I struggled to concentrate as the other Unascended took turns killing themselves. They stumbled to the central square and committed suicide in a variety of ways, poison, violence, and spells. All except one returned to life. The unfortunate male who didn't smothered himself with handfuls of dirt, squashing the black mud into every orifice in his face until he couldn't breathe. I supposed he was aiming to control Earth. But Gaia had different ideas. His body was removed by two solemn fae dressed in dark gray suits who shuffled him out a small side door.

As the highest-ranked Unascended, I would go last. I should've spent the time planning what to do and how to do it—Lure or Coerce, kissing to death or hiding to death. But instead, I spent my precious minutes looking around for Thorne Sanctus. Apparently, I would rather lay eyes on him than successfully ascend.

Suddenly, everybody's eyes were on me. The newly Ascended, who lined the perimeter, and the observers who sat in the steeply tiered seating behind them. Every single eye was on me.

I stumbled forward, my mind blank of any thought except needing to see Thorne. My feet echoed over the pale blue flagstones, and when I stopped in the center of the Hall of Echoes, there was silence.

I didn't feel elegant or composed. Didn't feel at all like myself. Didn't know how to proceed. I just stood there, looking at all the expectant faces, my hands dangling uselessly by my sides.

Then I saw him. He was dressed as befit a king, with a tailored charcoal suit and a button-up shirt of the finest pale blue that pulled across his chest as he heaved in deep breaths, practically pulsing with anger. Outrage lit his blue-black eyes. They burned with murderous intent, reminding me of when he tried to kill me in the Wild Hunt. But the venom infected his entire body this time, right down to his white knuckles curling around the railing.

Without thinking, I spoke. "Thorne Sanctus." My voice was louder and surer than I thought possible, ringing through the Hall of Echoes. This space was designed so that Ascensions in Fen were transparent and honest, with nothing hidden. Thanks to the ethereal resonance in the walls, my words were clear, and everybody could see and hear me.

Thorne's unwavering gaze met mine, yet he remained motionless, his silence echoing through the hall like a chilling breeze. So I laced my words with Lure. "Thorne Sanctus. Come to me."

Gabrelle

My control over Lure was already good, even though I hadn't Ascended, so Thorne could not resist. He shuffled along his tier, making his way past the packed fae, then picked his way down the bluestone stairs and joined me in the center of the Hall of Echoes.

Anger etched his face, and his movements were jerky; he moved like a cranky robot. He was fighting my Lure with everything he had, but it wasn't enough.

When he was ten feet away, I told him to stop.

I didn't care about my Ascension. I wasn't even thinking about it. The only thing in my brain was Thorne Sanctus. He hated me, but I needed him. I might as well take advantage of our last meeting.

"Take your shirt off," I said, weaving the command with Lure.

A collective gasp shuddered through the observers, echoing off the hard surfaces around the Hall. These fucking Fen fae were so uptight and prudish, but I'd seen most of them with their cocks and pussies out during the Wild Hunt, and I didn't see anybody gasping like a human nun then.

Thorne scowled at me, but he unbuttoned his shirt and shrugged it off, showing off his muscled shoulders, biceps, and chest. He was glorious. An expanse of firm flesh that sent a pulse of desire straight through me, piercing my brain fog with lust.

His nostrils twitched as he smelled my arousal, and I lowered my gaze to his cock.

It twitched too, and even though his face was twisted with rage and defiance, he couldn't control the physical response I had triggered. His cock swelled slowly as I continued to look at it, his arousal growing until it was finally straining against the fabric of his pants.

He gasped, then looked around desperately, searching for someone who could break the thrall I had over him. But no one could do that—not here or now—and he knew it. He closed his eyes, surrendering himself to me.

His arousal and fire rolled off him in waves, dragging me into the depths of desire. He wanted this as much as I did, maybe more. I wanted to feel his body pressed tight against mine as he moved inside me. I had to have him now, even if it was just once before he left me forever.

I stepped closer to him, so close that our bodies were nearly touching. My Lure was strong now that he was shirtless and aroused, and I could feel its power wrapping around us both like a comforting blanket.

"Stay still," I commanded, then lightly ran my hands over his chest, feeling the heat radiating from his body and watching as a flush of pleasure spread across his cheeks. His breath shuddered out of him as he leaned into my touch, an unconscious response that made my heart soar with joy that he could still respond to me despite all the pain between us.

"Kiss me," I demanded with Lure, and he gave a low growl of warning before bending forward and taking my lips with his.

He wasn't gentle and loving—I hadn't earned that. His kiss was brutal, devouring, and he bit my lips hard enough to make me jump.

The onlookers were murmuring, transfixed, as I forced the fae I loved to kiss me, and he repaid it by biting and maiming me. But I didn't even mind. I leaned into the place where our bodies joined, our lips, taking every bite as punishment for betraying him and reward for loving him.

I pulled back, stumbling away, my chest heaving. He growled again, this time from desire, and I looked into his eyes—they were hooded with lust now, filled with need.

"Kiss me gently," I commanded with Lure, and he complied. Even though I spoke quietly, my voice echoed clearly throughout the hall. Thorne stepped forward and brushed some hair from my face, placing his hand tenderly behind my neck. His lips caressed mine tenderly as he wound his arms around my waist, pulling me closer and deepening the kiss until I was lost in a haze of pleasure. It felt so real I wanted to cry. It felt like love.

But I was forcing it, forcing him. Still, I couldn't stop. I needed this—one last, twisted goodbye.

My fingers traced down his stomach until they found the waistband of his pants, and I felt a tremor go through him when I tugged them down just enough to see the tip of his erection straining against the fabric.

"Take off your pants," I commanded, and his body stiffened before he complied. His hands shook as he slowly undid the clasp and let them drop, and I could see a flash of fear in his eyes as he revealed himself to me—completely vulnerable and exposed.

He stepped out of his pants and kicked them away as if the

fabric were filled with thorns. His breath was heavy as he stood there, wearing nothing but black boxer briefs that showed off his perfect body.

I could see every inch of him now, from his broad chest down to his strong thighs, and my breath hitched at the sight of him. He was beautiful—like something out of a dream, but real enough for me to touch.

He looked up at me, desire burning in his eyes. I wanted to take him right there in the Hall for everyone to see. Hundreds of eyes watched our every move, and every one of my actions was exposed and evil. But that made it more exciting, stimulated some hidden part of me that demanded attention. I wanted them to watch. Let them see the power I had over their crown prince. Let them watch as I fucked him right here, in their precious Hall of Echoes.

I stepped closer to him again until our bodies were just inches apart and our breaths mingled in the air between us. I wanted to stay like this forever—just looking at each other and drinking in one another's presence—but that wasn't possible. Soon he'd be gone, so all I could do was try to etch every little detail into my memory so that I'd never forget him, no matter how far away he went.

I was aroused, so fucking turned on, even though this was messed up. My pussy was so wet it dripped onto my thighs, staining the soft silk of my jumpsuit. The warm musky scent filled the air, sending a hot shiver between my legs. If Thorne didn't grab my breasts soon, they would explode.

"Touch me," I whispered, and Thorne immediately put his massive hands over my aching breasts. His hands were warm through the fabric of my jumpsuit, and I pushed upward against him. His thumbs grazed over my nipples, making me shudder and thrust into his palms, yearning for more.

"Harder," I ordered, and he didn't hesitate. He pinched my nipples, sending a wave of pleasure through me as he grabbed them with a bruising hold, pushing them together and flicking them back and forth with his thumbs.

I gasped as a tug of humiliation shot through me, but I didn't want him to stop. I was being punished. I deserved this.

I pulled his head down and kissed him again, biting hard into his bottom lip until I tasted his blood. I wanted to mark him, to brand him as mine. I wanted to show the world that Thorne Sanctus was mine, and I was his. He struggled against me, but I could feel the same need burning in him.

Glancing up, I saw every eye in the room still on us. I locked eyes with one blond male who was staring back, leaning over the banister on the first tier of spectators with his ass exposed and another male railing him from behind. The blond's hair flopped in his face with every thrust, and his pale face was flushed, but he never stopped looking at the show.

Thorne naked except for his boxer briefs. Me, panting and moaning and Luring my victim. We were the show, the spectacle the blond was obsessed with, and I fucking loved it.

"Kiss my neck," I commanded, and Thorne lifted my chin so that his mouth was inches from my neck. "Kiss me," I whispered, and Thorne's lips wrapped around my neck, kissing and nibbling, and a rush of pleasure made me moan. "Please," I begged, my voice barely more than a whisper, and I didn't even know what I was asking for.

I couldn't take it anymore. I needed him inside me. My legs shook, and my head spun, and Thorne seemed to understand because he pulled me tight against him and cupped my ass. I rubbed my pussy against his perfect cock, the desire pulsing between us, and licked a trail up his neck.

The fire between us was too much to resist. None of this was real—none of it. But for a little while, he was mine. Even if it was only a few moments, I would have him. It would have to be enough.

"Take off your boxers," I commanded, stepping back to create some distance between us. I was dimly aware that I was supposed to be ascending, that forcing Thorne to undress in front of his Court and lesser fae was not part of the plan, but I didn't care. It didn't matter if I never came into my inner power; all that mattered was this moment.

Thorne bent to remove his briefs, a canvas of coiled muscle, shoulders, chest, and forearms. When he straightened, his cock throbbed between us, thick and long, reaching for me. I hadn't Lured that. That was all him.

He was naked, and I was still fully clothed, and the fae watching us were now either open-mouthed in shock at how my Ascension was going or fucking their nearest friend.

My gaze raked over Thorne. His cock almost took up my entire field of view, and I could imagine it thrusting into me as I begged or sobbed, or me riding him and commanding him. Either scenario worked for me as long as I got to wrap my pussy around his throbbing cock and fuck him until I died.

Maybe I would come into fuck powers.

I smiled at the thought, and Thorne stepped toward me. The tenderness in his gaze had me melting. "What's so funny, trickster?" he asked, and I wondered for a moment if I could win him back.

But then his blue-black eyes turned into pitiless black holes, and his jaw hardened against me. It was over. All I could do was take advantage.

"Strip me," I commanded, my voice heavy with Lure.

He swallowed hard, and the muscles in his arms tensed. I saw confusion rush through him, the desire to resist my command, and his eyes flashed with some emotion I couldn't quite place.

My voice was low with lust when I added, "Now."

Gaia, I sounded like a monster.

The distress on Thorne's face turned to lust, and then he ripped the purple fabric from my body, throwing the ruined jumpsuit to the floor. He was panting, and his eyes were wild with lust when they locked on my naked breasts, and then he lifted his head and looked me in the eye.

I looked up at him, my heart pounding as I offered him my nudity. He only had this for a little while, and I wanted him to remember every detail of me.

"Tell me you want me," I whispered, and he closed his eyes, shaking his head. "Tell me you want me," I repeated, and he groaned and opened his eyes. His stare was electric, and I closed mine. I wanted to remember the way he looked at me—possessed, turned on, and yet still full of hatred for me.

"I fucking want you, all right?" he growled, sending shivers over my cold, exposed skin.

"Then take me," I snarled. "Lick my pussy in front of all your fae. Lick me out like a good boy." His eyes flashed with pained rage, but I pushed on, "Or would you rather fuck me?"

He grabbed me, and I knew the rage was real. My mouth was so close to his that I could feel his breath on my lips as he said, "You're such a fucking bitch. You know that?"

"I don't care," I whispered, my voice low. "I want you to fuck me."

I pressed my body to his, nudging his erection into my stomach. It was hot and hard and pulsing with life, and I put my hand on it, rubbing the head against my belly.

Thorne grabbed my wrists and pushed me away from him, and I gasped and stumbled back. I looked up at him, panting, and then he was on me.

His mouth crushed mine, and I moaned into it, devouring his minty taste, needing him entirely.

He pushed me away, and his eyes were completely black and filled with need, hatred, lust, and desire, and I needed to punish him for making me feel so strongly.

"Lick me," I demanded, this time threading it with Lure.

He dropped to his knees, hard. I spread my legs wide, and he moaned. His head dropped, and he ran the tip of his tongue over my pussy. I raked my fingers through his blue-black hair and pulled him toward me. He licked me with a slow, languid stroke, and I moaned and pushed my pussy against his mouth. His tongue was hot and wet, and it felt so fucking good on my sensitive skin. I trembled, and he growled, and I dug my fingernails into his scalp.

He gripped my thighs hard enough to bruise my skin, and he buried his face between my legs, his tongue flicking over my clit and leaving me breathless.

If I didn't know better, I'd think he really liked me. Thorne could give a fae a complex.

I growled and pulled his hair, and he growled back and bit my inner thigh. I gasped and let him take me.

My entire body was tingling now, and the ball of fire in the pit of my stomach was a raging inferno.

I loved this male. I fucking loved him. "Tell me you love me," I spat out, making sure to layer the command with Lure.

He pulled his tongue out of my pussy and looked up at me, my breasts and belly between our gazes. "I love you, Gabrelle," he said, and the fact I had to Lure him to say it made tears well in my eyes.

"Good," I said, trying to keep the sobs from my voice. "Now fuck me."

Thorne

When Gabrelle first Lured me to undress, I was acutely aware of my audience. Every fae I'd ever met, those I'd grown up with, those I'd ruled over, the courtiers I was trying to impress, my friends and enemies, everyone was watching my degradation. My complete humiliation.

Ascension rites were not supposed to go like this. The visiting bitch princess was not supposed to entrap and betray the crown prince, then humiliate him in front of his fae.

No, this was well off-script. And I hated her for it. Hated Gabrelle with every atom of my body...except, apparently, my cock.

The princess of beauty was naked and aroused, her musky scent so strong it was infecting the entire Hall of Echoes. Her breasts were large, and they bounced at her slightest movement, which was fucking unfair. How was I supposed to fight that? Let alone her Lure.

Gabrelle's skin reflected the light, highlighting her sinuous motion and grace. The dusty pink hair between her thighs was like a beacon against her dark skin, and I could barely keep my eyes off it. Especially since I was on my knees at eye-level with it. I was hard, my cock raging and pounding like a drum. Even though this was messed up, my mouth on her pussy felt so fucking good I wanted to die.

"Tell me you love me," she said, spitting the words like darts.

I didn't know if she was Luring me or not. All I knew was I wanted to confess my undying love for her, even though I hated her. Her betrayal with Erevan and the Stone had wounded me, and this humiliation was even worse. But despite it all, I still wanted to lick her, to fuck her, to tell her I would love her until I died.

I gazed up at her, past her taut belly, her full breasts, to her dusty pink eyes. "I love you, Gabrelle." The flat blue ceiling beyond her was a foil to her luxe pink hair, which fell about her face in waves. But her eyes were unreadable.

"Good," she said, and I wondered if there was any tenderness between us. "Now fuck me."

Those weren't the words of a fae in love, but I was helpless under her power—with or without Lure. Her pussy was so close that I wanted to lean into it again. I licked my lips, wanting to taste her again, but she ordered me to fuck her with my cock, so I would.

I got back on my feet and gripped my cock in my left hand. My shaft was already slick with pre-cum, and I bent my knees and pressed the crown to Gabrelle's pussy and slowly eased inside. She was warm and wet, and I slid in easily.

She moaned as I entered her, and despite everything, despite her treachery and my anger, I would have done anything to make her moan like that again. She was hot and wet, and it was everything I could do not to come the instant I was inside her. Her Lure tingled against my skin, or maybe that was her fingernails.

I knew I was being manipulated, that she was using her Lure to control me. But I couldn't help myself. Her pussy squeezed my cock as I slid in, massaging me and coating me in her juices. I exhaled, and it felt like the most extraordinary relief.

"Fuck me hard," she said, rocking her hips against mine.

I thrust into her, my cock going as deep as it could. I wanted to hit her cervix, touch her womb and make her pregnant so she would never leave me.

"I love you, Gabrelle," I whispered, holding her tight against me. She wasn't Luring me, wasn't forcing me to say it. I just needed to tell her. Even if she couldn't see it, I knew she wasn't really an ice princess, and even if she didn't love me, I still loved her.

Her eyes widened when I spoke, and she went weightless, collapsing against me, so I had to support her weight. I froze inside her, my hard cock spearing her, and stared into her pink eyes.

"I didn't make you say that," she whispered.

"No," I murmured, "you didn't."

My left hand was on her lower back, my other on her ass, holding her up while my cock pulsed and throbbed inside her soft, tight pussy. Her breasts were squashed against my chest, and her breathing was uneven.

"So..." she panted.

I pulled her tight, wanting to meld with her, needing more of her. All of her. "I love you, Gabrelle," I repeated, staring into those fathomless eyes. Our words echoed through the Hall. It was designed so nothing could happen inside the central square that the observers didn't see or hear. Here, in the Realm of Fen, we held no secrets.

Our grunts and moans had ignited the passion of the observing fae, and most of them were fucking now, but when I told the trickster that I loved her, most of the other fae stopped and watched us again. Their crown prince was declaring his love for a foreign princess, even while she degraded him.

Her plum lips parted. I wanted to dive forward and claim them to stop her from speaking because I didn't want to hear her tear my heart apart. "Thorne," she said, and I steeled my spine against her rejection. "I love you too."

Gasps echoed around the room, and my mouth fell open. I lunged at my princess and breathed into her mouth, moaning and tasting her while my cock pulsed and throbbed inside her.

Her body reanimated, and she could support herself with one leg around my waist as she writhed against me, grinding and moaning. She was so fucking perfect, a goddess of beauty and goodness. I forgave her for betraying me—she was scared, terrified of becoming herself.

"I'm sorry," she said, resting her head against my shoulder.

I smiled into her hair while I squeezed her ass and thrust into her pussy. "I know."

"I was afraid," she said, and I sighed against her hair as I tried to hold back my orgasm. I didn't want to come yet, I wanted to be inside her forever.

"I know," I whispered, and I knew she needed to hear that, to be told she wasn't a monster. I wasn't being Lured to do any of this anymore. It came from me. "I don't care what you did because I love you."

"I love you too."

She wrapped her other leg around my waist, and our mouths locked again, our tongues intertwining as I thrust deeper and deeper into her. Her heat was radiating through me, igniting me from the inside out. We moved together effortlessly, as if we had been made for each other.

Our movements quickened, pressure building as we moved

faster and faster. I could feel her pussy trembling around me. She was so close to orgasm that it emanated from her like an aura. I tilted my hips and plunged deeper, eliciting a loud moan from her. My balls tightened as I felt her coming around me, crying out with her head thrown back.

I followed her, spilling into her with a guttural moan as I shuddered through the most intense orgasm of my life, my feet planted firmly on the stone floor, the only thing keeping me grounded.

After holding me for several long moments, Gabrelle unwrapped her legs from my waist and slid to the floor. I held her tight until her breathing returned to normal and our bodies slowly softened.

Around us, the observing fae finished their love-making or fucking and settled down again on the seating, adjusting their clothing with small smiles and quiet chuckles.

Gabrelle nodded at me and stepped away, opening a gulf of cold air between us. She looked alone and vulnerable, and I knew I had to leave her to complete her Ascension alone, but the idea was terrifying. Fear crept up my spine as I watched her pick up the rags of her purple jumpsuit and discard it. She was about to kill herself. Cold sweat formed on my skin, and I knew I couldn't be there. I couldn't stand by and watch my lover kill herself while I did nothing to help.

I had to leave the Hall of Echoes and see her when she was done.

I dressed, pulling on my dark suit pants and shrugging into my pale blue shirt, not bothering to do up the buttons. The cold sweat coating my skin grew hot and sticky as my fear turned to panic. I had to leave. I gave Gabrelle a quick nod and a tight smile, then turned to the nearest doorway—the one they took the dead bodies out.

I was practically jogging across the floor when Gabrelle's voice rang out, loud and clear. "Wait."

She wasn't using Lure, but I was helpless against her anyway. I turned on the spot with an apology and an explanation on my lips, but she held up a palm to stop me. "I need you for the next part."

Her eyes were soft, her inner beauty shining through, and I nodded. Of course. I would support her if she needed me, even if it was torture.

"I've figured out how to ascend into Lure," she said.

"Yes?"

"You need to kill me."

I backed away, blood pounding through my ears. "What? No." I could barely stand to watch her die, let alone do it by my own hand.

"Kill me, Thorne," Gabrelle said, and this time her voice was so thick with Lure that my feet started crossing the square of their own accord.

"No, Gabrelle," I said, fighting to remain calm and composed, dying on the inside. "I would rather kill myself."

"Kill me," she repeated, her words more Lure than oxygen.

My feet kept closing the distance between us, and my heart thudded. "Why me? Choose someone else."

Her eyes were soft and filled with tears. "I'm sorry, Thorne. But you love me, so you will resist the most. That will make my Ascended Lure the strongest it can be. It has to be you."

That might be true, but it didn't stop the whites of her eyes from showing as my hands closed around her throat, or the sickly-sweet pulse of fear that wafted from her skin. And it didn't make the tears dripping from my chin any less salty, or the feel of her windpipe crushing and breaking beneath my fingers any less visceral. The truth didn't stop the gurgling from the corner of her mouth as her lungs screamed for air, and it didn't stop my heart from breaking as she went limp under my grip.

I laid her gently on the bluestone floor and stepped away, watching her naked corpse, staring at her face and chest, willing them to animate.

Watched until she was nothing more than a lifeless husk.

Jayke

I sat in the chilly Hall of Echoes, watching the show with a smirk. I usually avoided the Ascension rites in Fen because these fae had iron rods up their asses and, outside of the Wild Hunt, didn't know how to have fun.

But when Leif Caro told me Gabrelle Allura would be ascending today, I'd had my fastest Flier, Peterson, bring me directly to Isslia, and I'd only just made it in time.

I wasn't technically the heir to the throne in the Realm of Caprice, but I had every intention of being the next king. King Athar and his mortal wife, Bree, were childless and old, and when they passed onto Mortia's realm of death, I would fight tooth and nail to take the throne.

Not for myself. Not because I wanted the power. But for Caprice, because the alternative was that the next king would come from the other noble House in Caprice, House Davin. And they would drive Caprice to rot and decay.

So, I cultivated all of my powerful friends, and the heirs to the Realm of Verda were among my favorites. Not only did they wield a lot of influence over Arathay, but they were fun to hang out with. And Gabrelle Allura was particularly easy on the eyes, so I had rushed here at the word of her Ascension.

Damn glad I did, too. She lay on the floor, completely naked, her curves open and vulnerable. Incredibly, she was even more fuckable like this than when she coated herself in seductive smiles. Gaia-be-fucked, I could suddenly see the appeal of necrophilia.

The power plays in this grimy Hall of Echoes were almost as intriguing as the dead beauty queen on the floor. I was an astute political operator—another reason I should be the next King of Caprice—and I could read the currents of conspiracy as easily as a scroll.

Crown Prince Sanctus was madly in love with Princess Allura. He would give up his throne for her; that much was clear. Erevan Reissan watched the whole scene unfolding with as much intensity as I did, and I could see the machinations of his brain fizzing and whirring as he tried to figure out how he could end up as the King of Fen.

Personally, I didn't care how it played out. I had little love for the fae of Fen—they were dour, uptight, and boring, and I had as little to do with them as possible. But it made a good show.

Thorne Sanctus was pale and trembling, staring at the dead body of his lover in shock. Couldn't he see she was just manipulating him? Every fae in the Hall could tell she was using him for her pleasure and to come into her full power, that she had coerced him into loving her so that when he killed her, her Lure would be strong.

Every fae except him. He stared at her corpse as though his whole future depended on her successful Ascension, as though he would lie down beside her and stick a knife in his own belly if she didn't rise.

With shaking hands, he picked up the ruins of her purple jumpsuit and draped them over her body, hiding the best of her curves and covering her pussy.

"Damn shame," I muttered, turning to Leif to share the joke, but the shifter prince was ashen-faced, his long silver hair hanging limp and his jaw open, staring in shock at his dead friend.

"Gaia, haven't you seen an Ascension before?" I muttered. But, of course, Ascensions in Verda took place behind a swirling fog, so the corpse wasn't visible to the onlookers. I supposed Leif wasn't as used to dead bodies as I was.

Erevan Reissan descended from his seat in the tiered grandstand and stepped into the central square. I hadn't been to many Fen rites, but I knew that was unheard of. I swallowed a chuckle—this ceremony just kept giving.

Rage filled Thorne, his hands fisted at his side, and his face went red, his jaw shaking. "You," he said as Erevan approached the body, "You did this." The crown prince grabbed Erevan's collar, lifted him off his feet, and punched him in the jaw.

Erevan stepped away, wiping his face to look for blood, clearly in pain but grinning anyway. "This is all Gaia," he said, gesturing broadly around the Hall.

"You broke us up," Thorne shouted.

"Nope," Erevan shook his head and spoke to the crowd like a performer at Solstice. "That was Gabrelle who betrayed you. Or have you already forgotten? One public screw and you're her mindless fuck-toy. You'd make a terrible king."

Thorne gritted his teeth, curling and uncurling his fists like he was practicing...or reliving how he'd murdered his lover. "You said the Stone or the kingdom," he hissed.

I leaned forward in my seat. That was news. What the hell was he talking about?

I whispered to Leif. "What Stone?" but the wolf shifter didn't answer. He was just looking at Gabrelle as if he could stare her back to life. She'd been under a long time. With all this entertainment it was hard to be sure, but I thought she should have Ascended by now...if Gaia would allow it.

Erevan stepped forward, and Thorne moved between him and Gabrelle's body as if to protect her.

Erevan smiled broadly, inviting the whole Hall into the conversation. "And I meant it, Thorny. I'll keep the Stone, and you can be crowned next month. Or you take the Stone and keep it forever, and I will be King of Fen forever."

Interesting. Whatever this Stone was, it was worth a kingdom. That made me want it, of course, but that was a matter for another day. I was also fascinated by the deal Erevan was proposing. Between him and Thorne, Erevan was clearly the smoother operator, the more astute politician, so he must have a plan. I doubted he would give up the throne that easily, not when he could have the Stone *and* the throne.

Perhaps the Realm of Fen was more interesting than I gave it credit for. Here, you couldn't lie. Which made fae more inclined to believe your words, so I tried to read between them.

Erevan said he'd allow Thorne to be crowned next month... but presumably, he would overthrow him soon after using the power of the Stone, whatever that was. The alternative was Thorne getting the Stone, and Erevan would be king forever.

Tricky bastard. My estimation for Erevan went through the roof. He didn't care about the Stone; he just wanted the throne, and he had figured out a way to get it, no matter what Thorne chose.

The crown prince stepped forward with a menacing growl, his ugly scar red and angry, cutting down one side of his face. "Will you agree to a Binding?"

Erevan pretended to think, but I could tell he was dancing with glee on the inside. Of course he would Bind on that agreement because it ensured him the throne.

"Yes," he finally said, and I almost laughed. Leif was still staring at Gabrelle, oblivious to the machinations, but he was usually pretty clueless anyway. Ronan Mentium was more of a surprise—he was a savvy operator and would usually see through ploys like this, but his attention was also glued to Gabrelle, his black eyes barely blinking.

I leaned forward, resting my elbows on my knees, and watched it play out. I'd never seen a Binding before, so I was curious.

Sanctus held his palms up and bid Reissan to recite the words of the Binding. As he spoke, blue light emanated from Sanctus's palms, and every word that Erevan spoke became a physical object in the light and rose to the vaulted ceiling like doves of smoke.

Reissan hissed in pain, and the whole room watched as a brand appeared on his arm, a snaking black chain that circled his forearm, showing the completion of the Binding.

His promise could only be broken through death, and any attempt to break it would result in severe pain and weakened magic.

Erevan grinned. "Do you want the Stone, Thorne?"

Obviously, it would be easiest for him if Sanctus took the Stone in front of everybody, so Reissan could be crowned next month. Otherwise, he'd have to overthrow Thorne later using the Stone's power, which would be more of a hassle.

Thorne looked between Reissan and Gabrelle, lying still on the floor. Anguish lined his face as he watched her in silence. When her eyes finally blinked open, Thorne's expression flitted through emotions, starting with relief and ending in anger. Beside me, Leif and Ronan whooped and grinned, and Leif howled at the ceiling.

Thorne's eyes narrowed, and he didn't wait for Gabrelle to fully rouse. He looked at Erevan. "Keep the Stone, Reissan. I want the kingdom."

Gabrelle

The full-length mirror in my cramped bathroom showed a confident fae with a killer outfit. I'd chosen a strapless, backless white gown studded with diamonds, with diamond-shaped cutouts around my torso and thighs. The white silk was studded with diamonds, which also glittered on my dark skin. They would catch the light brilliantly.

In Fen, the Ascension party was after the rite, which I'd always thought was backward. But now I was glad because I could fully enjoy myself without fearing my imminent death.

In the hours since my Ascension, my body had been filling with power. A faucet had opened above me, and warm energy dripped into me straight from the gods, running through my limbs and transforming every cell in my body. I was a goddess.

Everything was within my reach. I'd never been helpless, but now I was unstoppable. My reflection was heightened, sharpened, and brimming with confidence, and the fae staring back at me from the mirror could take over the world. But it was nothing compared to the change inside me. I smiled, and Arathay smiled back.

Ronan waited for me in my bedroom, wearing a black suit with an open neck that fitted him perfectly. I could see his mind just as clearly as his body, laid out for me like a buffet. He briefly admired my appearance, then his thoughts returned to Neela, who occupied the central space in his conscious mind. Around the edges, his subconscious swirled and danced in a blur, but I knew I could pierce any part I wanted.

His brief thought about my appearance began vanishing, turning into smoke, and I decided to try an experiment. I focused on the disappearing idea and channeled a trickle of my Lure power into it, trying to make my magical tendril tiny so he wouldn't notice.

Ronan jumped, his eyes wide, and stared at me. "You look hot, beauty queen," he said, then the image of Neela reformed immediately in his mind and took center stage.

I retreated from his mind with an amused smile, and Ronan narrowed his black eyes at me. "Stay out of my mind."

"How could you tell?"

"You're not exactly subtle."

Well, that was interesting—I thought I'd been extremely subtle and had used the merest trickle of my power. I must be stronger in Lure than I ever imagined possible.

"We're going to need a new pact," Ronan grumbled, still looking at me warily. He was referring to the no-sex pact between the heirs, which had been established to prevent future wars. A no-screwing-with-each-other-using-magic pact was probably even more critical as we Ascended and got older and stronger.

We went to the throne room for the Ascension event. The first thing I saw was King Bastian's lightning bolt tattooed in glistening silver into the shaved part of his head, a striking contrast against his shoulder-length black hair. The King of Caprice ruled the realm alone, which must be a lonely job, although perhaps his mortal Queen Bree had more influence than everybody realized. Together, the ancient fae male and the aging human female looked regal and proud.

"Fucking Athars," Jayke Sansett growled, following my gaze. House Sansett and House Athar were two noble Houses in Caprice, although they never shared the rule. And their hatred of each other was legendary.

But I wouldn't stand around and let Jayke shoot his mouth off. "Queen Bree has always been kind to me," I remarked.

"To your face, maybe," Jayke said, making me wonder if there was more to the Athar-Sansett rivalry than I knew.

Ronan tugged me toward our friends, and I followed behind, noting the swells of each fae's mind as we passed. I had to shut down a mental wall to keep myself from being overwhelmed by all the thoughts and beliefs swirling within the throne room.

I made it to Lief and Alara with my mind firmly closed.

"Trust these tightwads to call it a ball instead of a party," Leif said in greeting. He wore a striking silver suit that fitted him perfectly, and he was clinging to Alara, who wore a black gown that highlighted her vibrant orange hair. They made a gorgeous couple.

The throne room looked impressive. The pillars of smooth bluestone that supported the snowflake-carved ceiling were wound with white ribbons and bows that steered just the right side of tasteful. More white ribbons were strung in mid-air, filling the vast space above us and making the room less austere than usual. But nothing could reduce the severity of the white throne with arms and legs shaped like jagged icicles that stood empty on the central dais.

I scanned the room for Thorne. I'd missed my friends these past few weeks while I'd been in Fen, but Thorne's absence was a physical pain, even though it had been much shorter.

GABRELLE

With my new power swirling inside me to overflowing, there was no room for embarrassment, but I was still aware that my actions during my Ascension were...unusual. Apparently, Thorne had waited until I returned to life, then stormed away, scowling. He was always scowling, so that was no surprise, but I needed to see him. To see what he was thinking. He had told me he loved me, but he'd also called me a bitch, so I wasn't sure where we stood. And him storming away before I awoke wasn't a good sign.

Leif and Ronan were telling Alara all about my Ascension.

"I still don't understand why you made the crown prince kill you," Alara said.

I glimpsed the hole in her understanding; it was a murky patch inside the part of her consciousness that was thinking about my Ascension. Without digging further, I withdrew. Even without a pact, using Lure on my friends was wrong—I would reserve it for my enemies.

"Because Thorne loves her," Ronan explained. "So forcing him to kill her against his will was the strongest use of Lure. It's given our beauty queen freakishly strong powers."

Leif slammed down a glass of Fen Fizz, which was just like Fae Fizz but without the flavor. "I love you, babe," Leif told me, still clinging to his mate. "I would totally have killed you. It would have been my pleasure."

"Er, thanks, I guess," I said, grinning. I felt powerful but also at ease in myself, with less pressure to smile like a princess and more freedom to grin like an idiot.

But I couldn't relax completely until I saw Thorne. What was he thinking? How was he responding to our weird, public Ascension sex?

Ronan and Leif were talking about the Stone of Veritas. They figured that stealing it from Erevan Reissan would be easier than heisting it from Elyssia Castle because Erevan might be a dick, but he wasn't cursed.

"If it wasn't for the damn Binding, I could just Lure the Stone from Erevan," I muttered. Ronan had filled me in on the Binding ceremony that had taken place over my dead body. Literally. I wasn't sure what would happen if I Lured the Stone from Erevan—he would be effectively handing it over to me willingly, so would that mean he was entitled to the throne of Fen?

"Fuck it," Leif said. "Who cares who gets the Fen throne as long as we get the Stone of Veritas?"

I cared.

Then I saw him. Thorne entered the room wearing the most exquisite suit I'd ever seen, a far cry from his usual tasteless slop. The suit was a deep navy blue with pinstripes in a glossy, pearl-like sheen. The thin lapels of the jacket were impeccably tailored and hugged his broad shoulders. His trousers were cut slim and tapered to the ankle, hinting at his trim physique. His crisp white shirt was open at the collar, revealing a flash of bronze skin. He looked more powerful and confident than ever.

He caused a stir. Fae turned to look at him, drawn to his impressive figure and curious about how he would behave. Any fae who'd missed our public fuckfest had undoubtedly heard the gossip by now, and many were pegging it as a humiliation for him. For me, it had felt more like a declaration of my love, but I didn't know if he'd see it that way.

He saw me and headed straight for me, stalking gracefully through the crowd. My heart stuttered, and I resisted the urge to dive into his mind, refusing to be like my mother. I would never use Lure against those I loved.

"Gabrelle," he said, and the formality in his tone broke my heart.

"Thorne," I replied, not bothering to hide my sadness.

"Congratulations on your Ascension."

I searched his face and traced his scar with my gaze, waiting for more. Finally, I said, "Thank you for killing me."

Leif interjected with a whoop. "Weird conversation, guys."

I straightened my shoulders. I had decided—no more hiding behind a mask of indifference. I no longer wanted to be the ice queen unless it suited me politically. I wanted the power not just to hide my emotions but to express them. So I took a deep breath. "I love you, Thorne. I hope one day you'll forgive me for what I did. It was wrong, and I have no excuse, but I was scared. I'm sorry."

It took me a moment to understand Thorne's reply, and I stood at him, blinking while he talked. "I forgive you, trickster. And I love you. So. Damn. Much. Everything you do is for your realm, you are selfless and powerful, and I admire everything about you." He pulled something out of his pocket. "I hope you can use this for your realm too."

The Stone of Veritas pulsed in his open palm, an ethereal blue glow that lit up his face.

Gasps skittered around the throne room as everybody realized what this meant. Thorne had swapped the crown for the Stone.

Erevan Reissan would be king.

"Yes!" Leif punched the air and howled, then I heard him growl into Alara's ear. "Let's go fuck in the bathrooms, babe. We need to celebrate." They didn't even wait for the Stone to change hands before they ducked through the crowd, already smelling of arousal.

Ronan looked after them longingly, and I didn't need to poke around in his mind to know he was missing Neela. Jayke Sansett from the Realm of Caprice let out a loud whistle and wandered closer, peering to see the Stone in Thorne's hand.

I closed Thorne's fingers over the Stone, enclosing his hand in mine and soaking up his warmth. "Are you sure about this? We can find another way to get the Stone."

He put his other hand around me, clasping me. "I've never been more sure about anything in my life. I don't care about the throne, I never have. That was Mother's passion, and Arrow's. Not mine. I only wanted to continue my family legacy, but I want you more."

The heat flowing from his hands into my body rivaled the power still trickling into me from Gaia. "But Erevan's a dick," I muttered.

Thorne grinned, and the whole room sparkled. He was hot when he was scowling and moping, but with a smile, he was irresistible. "Even a dick can be a good ruler, as someone wise once told me," he said, recalling my earlier words to him.

Honestly, Erevan would make a good king. He had decent policies, was good with fae, and was single-minded in improving the realm. But that didn't make this the right decision for Thorne personally. "Are you sure?"

He squeezed my hands where they were still clasped. "If I'm King of Fen and you're Queen of Verda, we can never be together. We would have to lead separate lives in separate realms, and I don't want that."

My breathing was faster, and tears welled in my eyes and slipped down my face, leaving ugly tracks down my cheeks. Real, fat tears, and I was shedding them in public. And I didn't give a fuck. "You would give up your kingdom for me?"

Thorne's breath was hot and minty, and when he leaned in close to whisper in my ear, he set off an avalanche of goosebumps down my body. "I would do anything for you."

His lips collided with mine, hot and passionate, and the whole throne room disappeared as my world focused on Thorne.

Thorne

A few months later, Alara and I were impatiently counting down the hours at the Lakehouse. As the only two non-heirs, we had gotten into the habit of waiting at the Lakehouse while the heirs competed in their trials. While I understood the need for the contests, they felt too brutal.

"I'm sure they're fine," Alara said for the fifth time. Quickly followed by, "They should be here by now."

"They'll be here any minute." I sat in a spartan gray armchair with clean lines and no fuss, which the Lakehouse had grown for me in the past few months that I'd been living in Verda. Apparently, growing personality-based furniture was a good sign, indicating that the Lakehouse, and therefore Gaia, accepted me in the realm.

Which was just as well because I wasn't going anywhere. The day that Erevan was crowned King of Fen was the best day of my life—the start of the next chapter, where I could be myself and not just a continuation of a legacy. Mother would be disappointed, I was sure, but she would also understand my choice. She was a practical fae, and I believed she would have come to agree that Erevan was the better ruler, leaving me free to be Gabrelle's lover.

The heirs had met in Rosenia Forest, as usual. At this year's first trial, soon after I returned to Verda with Gabrelle, Alara had tried to accompany Leif to the trial. Apparently, Gaia had ejected her, shooting her fifty feet into the air on a puff of wind and setting her down at the forest's edge.

Since then, Alara had joined me in the Lakehouse to wait for the heirs to finish up. From my seat, I could see out the floor-to-ceiling glass wall, over the deck, and across the vast lake. The lake shimmered like liquid glass, reflecting the stars and moonlight on its surface. It was broken only by the ripples from the wind and the gentle waves lapping at the shore. Peering across the lake, looking for a sign of Gabrelle, I inhaled deeply, using the scent of wet earth and moss to ground me and the undertone of pine and wildflowers from the surrounding forest to calm me.

The sound of the front door opening had Alara and me on our feet instantly.

Neela stumbled through the door, covered in dirt. I scanned her face for tension. Today's trial was the last for the year, the trial of inner magic, so I expected Gabrelle to do well, given that she'd recently Ascended. But obviously, House Flora had come first.

"They're fine," she said in greeting, and I felt Alara relax beside me. "It was a time trial, and their challenges didn't look too hard. Gabrelle was just staring at some random fae dude, I guess she was tackling his brain or something. Leif was following a scent trail, I think. Anyway, they won't be far behind me."

As if Neela had summoned them, Gabrelle and Leif rushed through the front door, laughing.

"I almost had you," Leif said. "You were a millisecond faster. That shouldn't count."

"Every little bit counts, wolf boy," Gabrelle said, swanning along the corridor in her brown hunting leathers, looking badass. She saw me and beamed, then wrapped me in a delicious passionfruit-scented hug and pressed her lips to mine.

"How do you smell good even after a day of trials?" I asked.

She lifted a perfect shoulder. "It's all part of a day's work."

I pressed my palm into her lower back and pulled her against me. I would never understand how I'd gotten so lucky to win such a fantastic female's heart.

Leif and Alara were making out ferociously as if they'd never had sex when I knew for a fact they screwed many times a day. Gabrelle and I exchanged a glance. "Wolves."

I did some quick calculations in my head. "That puts you on ten points for the year, trickster," I murmured into Gabrelle's lustrous pink hair.

"What about me, Thorne?" Leif asked, breaking away from his kiss. "Eleven points, right?" I nodded in confirmation, and Leif punched the air. "First place, baby." He threw back his head and howled, and Alara joined in.

I covered my ears while Gabrelle rested a hand elegantly on a dining chair and waited for them to stop. "Well done, Leif," she said. "But don't get used to it."

Gabrelle and Ronan typically came in first and second place, but Leif had been paying more attention since he'd become the Alpha of his pack. Alpha of every pack in Verda, as I understood it.

"I'm coming for all you assholes," Neela said, inspecting her fingernails.

Gabrelle grinned, and Leif barked a laugh. "Unlikely, mortal," he said playfully.

Warmth spread through me, all the way to my fingertips. Having Gabrelle safely back from the trial gave me the headspace to relax and appreciate how full my life had become. I used to be close to Arrow, but since she'd died, I was alone.

Not anymore.

Dion was the next to arrive at the Lakehouse, looking grumpy and covered in mud.

"Two points for you, Dion," I said as he brushed past me and headed straight to the shower. He emerged ten minutes later wearing jeans and a fitted T-shirt and headed straight to the kitchen.

I trailed him in. "I've been waiting for you to get back," I said. "I'm hungry."

"So cook your own damn food," he grizzled, pulling cheese and vegetables out of the fridge.

"But you enjoy cooking for others," I said, trying to figure out where I'd gone wrong in this social situation. I still wasn't used to navigating in a realm where fae said the opposite of what they meant or lied even to themselves.

"Yes," Gabrelle said, laughing, "but he doesn't like having that pointed out." Dion grizzled again, so Gabrelle crossed over and tousled his hair until he was grinning. I would never stop admiring her natural ease with the other heirs and the deep bond they'd forged through the years.

Of all the heirs, Dion Dionysus was the most resistant to change. He'd barely looked at me for the first few weeks I was here, but after the Lakehouse grew my chair, he slowly started accepting me. The fact that he now responded when I addressed him was a win.

Ronan finally blew through the Lakehouse door, his clothing ripped and blood pooling in every step.

"Fuck!" Neela ran to him and ripped his shirt off.

"She's keen," Leif remarked.

Neela ignored the jibe and inspected Ronan's injuries. "What the fuck happened, toy boy?" she demanded angrily as though he'd deliberately torn his own flesh.

He shrugged slightly, clearly not too severely injured. "I failed to cheer up a snuffle tuff." He limped across to his black leather armchair and sat down heavily. "Not one of ours," he told Neela, whose hands had flown to her mouth.

"We need to get you to a Healer," Neela said, inspecting every inch of his skin. "You're covered in gashes."

"Yeah," he nodded solemnly. "Snuffle tuffs can be real bastards."

Neela stepped back and put her hands on her hips. "You probably provoked it." She had a strong connection with a couple of snuffle tuffs, who she even allowed to live with her. Gabrelle once told me it was because they looked like grass and Neela was a Grower, but I was pretty sure she was joking. Lying, kidding, it was a fine line and not one I'd had much practice navigating.

Ronan snorted. "No. It definitely provoked me."

"Unlikely." Neela tried to tug Prince Mentium to standing. "We need to go to a Healer. Up, boy."

"His injuries aren't too bad," I interjected. "Nothing some bandages and a restorative meal from D can't fix."

Dion nodded. "Exactly right," he said, and I figured I'd won some brownie points with him. Neela cleaned Ronan up, and he emerged from the shower looking fresh and lively, with none of his insides on the outside.

As Dion clattered around in the kitchen, the rest of us chatted about the trials. Gabrelle and Leif were already planning their training for next year's contests, and Neela was determined to beat everyone.

I listened to their conversation, but my thoughts drifted to Arrow and Mother. They wouldn't have liked it here—too much frivolity and "joking" lies for their taste. But it suited me perfectly, much better than Court life in Fen. Here, I could relax. The faeling who'd spent hours doodling and telling stories in the shed in the Wizen Woods was at home in a realm with endless creativity. I'd spent so many hours maligning the Realm of Verda for being a hive of liars that I'd forgotten the flipside. Imagination.

And, as Gabrelle kept telling me, the truth was relative. One fae's truth was another fae's lie. Lure could be used to make someone lie or to reveal their truth. Lies could tear friends apart or bring them closer. And some of the biggest liars I ever met lived in Fen. Nothing was as simple as I used to believe.

And, as I watched Gabrelle smile and joke with her friends—my friends—I knew that with her, my life would be so much more than I ever thought possible.

Gabrelle

"I have a surprise for you," I said, brimming with excitement. Thorne had uprooted his entire life to be with me in Verda. He'd given up his realm, his home, and his throne. So I wanted to carve out a little piece of Verda just for him.

"Do I like surprises?" he asked, warily following me out of our wing of the Mirror Palace and into the expansive gardens. He wore tailor-made chinos and a light fae shirt, courtesy of my Dressers, and his grace and strength shone through with every step.

I laughed. "I guess we're about to find out."

We strolled through the gardens, taking in the beauty of the roses, tulips, and faelils that were in full bloom. The sun was setting, and the sky was a mixture of pinks and oranges that gave everything a warm hue, glinting off the reflective palace walls and casting liquid shadows on the ground that danced in time with our steps.

Every now and then, I peered over at him, watching his eyes widen with wonder as he took in all the plants around us. He was straight-backed and formal and seemed out of place compared to all of this natural beauty, but I knew that was part of why he loved it so much.

"So, is this the big surprise?" he asked, curiosity lighting up his eyes as we ventured deeper into the gardens. He seemed especially taken with the waterfall that cascaded into a small pool just beyond the rose bushes.

I laughed. "No. This is the garden. Just a bit further."

We explored several more winding pathways before we reached a clearing surrounded by towering trees and thick shrubbery. In front of us stood a tiny shed that looked like it had been through many seasons. Its roof was sprinkled with moss, and its gray boards were cracked and peeling, but it still looked inviting in some strange way.

Thorne's eyes sparked with recognition. "It looks exactly like..."

"Your old fantasy shed," I said, beaming.

He grinned and yanked me into a deep kiss. "My fantasy shed. I love that."

"Come on," I said, pulling free, although part of me wanted to stay in his arms. "Take a look inside."

The outside of the shed looked battered, but I had restored the inside to a perfect shine. It was full of musical instruments from Thorne's rooms in Fen—plus some extras I'd added to his collection.

He walked over to the intricately carved faeboe from Fenwick and ran his fingers over its surface. "Ah, this is where it all started."

I cocked out a hip. "Er, no, it began with you trying to kill me during the Wild Hunt."

His blue-black eyes darkened to coal, and he stalked closer to me. "Next time, I might carry through," he growled.

I giggled. Damn, it felt good to laugh. I no longer felt like I had to play the princess every damn moment of the day. "Tell me you'll kill me."

He raised an eyebrow. "Do you have some new kink I need to know about?"

I grinned. "Just say it."

He grabbed my hips and pulled me against him, and his hard cock pressed into my belly. He leaned forward and whispered dangerously into my ear. "I'll never harm you." I barely contained my giggle as he cleared his throat. "Sorry, a force of habit, truth and all that. Let me try again." He leaned in again, his breath hot on my ear. "I'll kill anyone who hurts you."

He pulled back, his eyebrows so high they almost hit the ceiling. "Shit. I've forgotten how to lie."

My laughter was high and ringing, echoing around the music room. "I warded the shed so nobody can speak a lie within its wall. Well, I had Mother's best Weaver ward it for me. Anyway, if you ever feel overwhelmed by all of us scheming Verdans, you can come here and relax." I beamed up at him, hoping he liked it.

He stood there, a blank expression on his face, and a sense of panic crept over me. Had I made a terrible mistake? Maybe he didn't want to be reminded of his life in Fen and everything he'd given up.

"Is it okay?" I asked gingerly.

Thorne looked around at the instruments, taking them in with wide eyes. He gazed at the hammered silver drums, the shimmering lutes with strings of glowing gold, the ivory whistles, and the twinkling chimes. I scanned his face, my heart hammering.

His gaze finally landed on mine. "It's perfect." He held out a hand. "Shall we play?"

"I'd be delighted."

I moved to the intricately carved faeboe, which first drew

my eye back in Fen. I blew into one end, and the sound that emerged soared through the room. Thorne joined in with a tinkling arpeggio on the gold-stringed lute and his deep, soulful voice.

The music was a dreamscape, and every note held a promise.

Without missing a note, Thorne nodded to the doorway, still playing his lute and singing. I followed him outside, and we wandered through the gardens with our instruments, playing and laughing as we went. It felt so good to be out in the open with music spilling out of my soul. I'd missed that so much.

As we reached the willow tree, Thorne gently set down his lute and motioned for me to come closer. His eyes were bright and alive, and he looked at me like I was the most beautiful thing he had ever seen. And I knew he saw what was inside me, not just on the surface.

We were beside a fragrant rose garden, and I could hear the soft murmurs of crickets hidden in the bushes. His fingers brushed my hair back from my face, and he smiled down at me.

"I'm so glad you showed me this place," he said softly. "It's truly incredible."

My heart swelled as I gazed up into his blue-black eyes, and suddenly all I wanted to do was devour him. I leaned into him, pressing my lips to his neck, then slowly making my way up his jawline until our mouths met in a passionate kiss that sent sparks shooting through me.

I tugged at his shirt, and he pulled it off, tossing it aside so I could run my hands over his smooth, bare chest.

He had the lean, muscled body of a skilled fighter, thighs and arms that bulged with power. He was large, and yet he was gentle and caring with me even when he was demanding.

I loved every part of him, even the scar that decorated his face.

"You're perfect," I whispered. "You're perfect for me."

His eyes darkened as he advanced on me, and he snapped the buttons off my dress and worked his way down my body, peppering every inch with his lips. I moaned at the warm wetness of his tongue against me, and he groaned in response, pulling me against him so my nipples grazed against his bare chest.

Thorne lifted his head and watched me with glittering eyes as he slowly unfastened his pants, his gaze trailing down my body until he was looking at me from between my parted thighs. His cock was long and thick, straining for me, making me even wetter.

"You're so ready for me, aren't you?" he murmured, sending shivers through me. I gasped as his fingers slid between my thighs to my hot, wet pussy, already thick with desire. He pressed a finger deep inside me, and I arched my back, crying out at the delicious ache it caused.

He looked at me with such tenderness my heart ached.

He moved his mouth over me in a warm, sensual kiss, his tongue circling my pussy as he massaged my clit. It was just the right amount of pressure, the right amount of heat, the right amount of everything. He knew me better than I knew myself.

I struggled to keep my eyes open as his mouth brushed over me, kissing and caressing. I clung to him as he slowly licked me, gently teasing my clit, delighting in all the things he made me feel.

My back arched as I gasped for breath. Thorne's eyes were dark as he gazed up at me, moving his mouth over me, memorizing every curve. My muscles tightened as I gave myself over to the pleasure.

"Come for me." His tongue flicked out, and I bucked under him, screaming his name as a rush of intense ecstasy overwhelmed me.

I was still shuddering and gasping when he lifted me up and pinned me against the tree. A sharp ache flared in my back, quickly replaced by pure pleasure as he sunk his huge cock deep inside me.

"I love you too damn much," I told him, almost weeping with emotions. He'd broken my walls so thoroughly that the only thing holding me together was him.

"No," he said, thrusting his hips against mine, driving his cock as deep as he could. "You love me just right." He pushed again, drilling into me and claiming my lips with his. "And I love you, trickster," he murmured into my mouth. "Now and forever."

Those burning blue-black eyes watched me as he slowed his rhythm, pushing into me sensually, lovingly, then kissed me, claiming my mouth. He sank his fingers into my hair, drawing me closer until I gasped for breath. His strong, muscular body pinned me against the tree, and I wrapped my legs around him, moving with him in a slow, sensual dance.

I loved him. I loved him so much I didn't know what to do with it. We fit together like we were made for each other.

His cock filled me completely, stretching me wide as pleasure burnt through my core. I rested my head against his shoulder, panting as I gripped his strong shoulders. He did it slow and easy, taking his time to make it last.

When he slid his hand between us, I gasped and opened my eyes to see him stroking my clit. His face was a mask of concentration, his gorgeous blue-black eyes locked on mine.

His mouth was open as he watched his cock push in and out of me. He looked so hot seeing himself like that, so completely in charge, and my pussy squeezed around his cock.

Watching him was so hot, and I moaned as he caressed me. A violent shudder tore through me as his hands swept over my body, gentle and assured, and he sank his face into my neck and gently licked at my soft skin.

I moaned softly against him. "I love you so much, Thorne. More than I thought I could ever love anything. You're my everything."

He let out a low groan and thrust harder, deeper. The deep, throbbing ache inside me built as his cock pushed me higher toward climax, and he groaned as my pussy clenched around him. His thrusts became more urgent, his fingers moving more quickly, and my body tingled as we raced to the brink of release.

"I've never felt like this before," he whispered. "You're in my blood, Allura."

That sent me over the edge, clenching around his cock, my body shuddering with pleasure. There was nothing for me except Thorne. I moaned his name as I trembled around him, tears slipping down my cheeks. He licked them away, brushing his lips against mine as he thrust deeply inside me, then slowly withdrew, only to push into me again.

The orgasm continued to roll through my body, leaving me breathless. It was so intense it hurt, but Thorne looked at me like he was in agony. I realized he was holding back, holding onto a reserve of energy to ensure I came first.

I rolled my hips to encourage and let him know I was still with him. He growled as he plunged into me with one last, deep thrust, and I dug my nails into his back as he collapsed against me, his whole body shaking.

We were both panting and trembling as we sank to the grass, but I didn't care. I didn't want to let go of him. I held him against me, and he wrapped his arms around me, holding me against his chest.

Epilogue

We strolled along Piccolo Street, which thronged with shoppers during the day and clubbers at night. Music blasted from every bar we passed, some of it actually decent. Gabrelle steered me into a tavern called the Ogre's Nose—it wasn't exactly the most appealing spot among the places we'd seen.

The other heirs were already here, and we joined them in a booth.

Neela sat on Ronan's lap on a wooden chair. "Are they short of chairs?" I asked, and everyone laughed at me.

"No," Gabrelle told me. "Mentium and Flora are just short on manners."

Leif and Alara were snuggled close on one side of the booth. Dion sat on the other, looking sour, so Gabrelle slid in next to him and ruffled his hair. I pulled up another chair and tucked it between Gabrelle and the Ronan-Neela pile.

"Why do you come here?" I asked, taking in the smoky room. Low lighting, dark wood, with lousy music playing from the enchanted ceiling. The place smelled fruity, like someone had overcompensated for an underlying stench by spraying the area in watermelon juice. "It isn't very nice."

Alara threw back her head and laughed. "You're so right, truth boy! I've always thought that, but I wasn't game to ask."

EPILOGUE

I arched an eyebrow. "Truth boy?"

Leif shrugged. "Truth boy, truthenstein, truth or dare... we're workshopping."

"Do not call me truthenstein," I said. "I don't like it."

Leif and Ronan reached across the table and high-fived. "Truthenstein it is!"

Gabrelle patted my leg. "Don't worry, you'll get used to them."

"Probably," I agreed. "So, tell me why we come to this dingy place to drink. There must be nicer places in Verda City."

Dion took a sip of ale. It must have been his first sip because it turned his hair and eyes a deep amber as he talked. "It's called tradition," he grumbled. "Look it up. We come here every year when Gaia releases our cumulative trial scores. And traditionally, it's just the heirs," he added with a pointed look at Alara and me.

Ronan smirked. "Someone needs to chill."

"Someone needs to get laid," Leif added. "I can hook you up if you want, D. I've got plenty of wolves who would lower their standards if I ordered them to," he joked.

Dion grizzled and took another swig of his beer.

Neela downed a shot of Fae Fizz. "Double D's just pissed because I'm ahead of him in the rankings now." She looked around at all the heirs. "I'm coming for you all, assholes."

Ronan was still first in the final rankings, on a cumulative average of twelve points. He'd only scored ten this year and was on a downward trajectory, and I didn't doubt Neela might overtake him eventually.

But my magnificent princess, Gabrelle, might surpass him first. She was firmly in second rank, and her score of ten this year cemented her overall score of eleven. With my support behind her, she would do even better next year.

"Don't fight, guys," Leif said magnanimously. "You're all losers in my book."

Neela cursed, and Ronan scowled while Dion flipped the bird. "Leif's right," I said. "He scored the most points this year."

"He's still only third overall," Gabrelle snarled, and I smiled at her venom. I loved seeing her emotions on the surface. She was still an expert at concealing them if she needed to, like during political events or talking to her mother, but she was free and loose around her friends. Around me.

The biggest mover of the year was Neela, which was no surprise. She'd only been in the fae realm for three years, so her spellwork and physical skills were still improving. Her first place in the inner magic trials had bumped her annual score to nine, bringing her cumulative total to seven points, one ahead of Dion.

"Another round of drinks," Neela called to a serving fae, who came over and took our order. "We're celebrating my future triumph," she explained to the confused-looking fae. "I'm going to rank first one day."

"Yes, Your Highness," the poor female said, unsure how to handle a table full of drunk royal heirs, then she scurried away to fulfill the order.

"Only if you have enough time," I said, and every head swiveled to look at me. "Only one more of your parents has to die before you're all elevated to the thrones, right?"

A chorus of groans met my observation.

"Happy to volunteer my mother," Gabrelle said, deadpan, and my lips twitched. Gabrelle and her mother still had a lot of issues to resolve. Chantelle was delighted her daughter had ascended to Lure but less pleased about all the recent honesty

EPILOGUE

she'd been spouting. Still, they would work it out. Or not. Life had a way of surprising you.

I never thought I'd end up living in Verda and hanging out with the heirs, but I'd grown a lot this year. And it all started with Arrow's death in a twisted way. Good and bad, black and white, truth and lies, none of it even existed, as far as I could tell.

A spellbird whizzed across the room and nose-dived into Dion's ale. "Fuck Gaia," he muttered, fishing it out. "What now?" He unfurled the wet paper and read the message.

"Who's it for?" Leif asked, suddenly tense. He was probably worried about his den, which had been brutally attacked in the past.

"All of us," Dion said.

"Oh dear, that can't be good," Ronan said.

"Fuck," Dion exclaimed. "It's about Caprice."

I knew that Bree Athar, the Queen of Caprice, had died a couple of months ago, shortly after she'd attended Gabrelle's Ascension rite. But that was old news.

Dion put the sodden spellbird onto the table. "Bastian Athar is dead."

Whoa. The monarchs of Caprice had both passed on. Would that affect us here in Verda? Nobody looked too upset, so I asked what might otherwise have been a crass question. "They didn't have any kids, right? So what happens to the throne?"

Leif raised his glass, "Jakey-boy for king," he yelled. Ronan clinked his glass against Leif's, and they both slammed back another shot.

Even Dion smiled.

Gabrelle shook her head, and her pink hair swished across her face. "Jayke Sansett won't automatically become king.

Bastian's death creates a power vacuum, and some other Houses will fight for it. Like Darzan Davin."

Ronan and Dion shuddered at that name. In the land of fae, where the ruler of Brume was known as the Dread King, evil Unseelie Fae lived to the south, and Shadow Walkers were invading from the east, it was hard to get a shudder out of anyone.

"Clearly, this Darzan Davin dude sucks," Neela said. "Have I met him?"

Ronan shook his head. "Nope. Count yourself lucky."

"Well, they'll seek our opinion, and we can all throw our support behind Jakey boy," Leif said.

"To Jakey boy!" Ronan called, and everybody cheered.

It didn't matter to me what happened in the Realm of Caprice. I was happy here with my trickster princess and her lying, wonderful friends.

* * *

Hi, I hope you enjoyed A Court of Verity and Lies!

The fourth book in the series, A Court of Caprice and Decay, features the charismatic wannabe king, Jayke Sansett, in (you guessed it) the Realm of Caprice. This is actually the first book I wrote in the series, but I decided to publish it fourth...you'll see why when you read it. It's a lot of fast-paced, twisty fun!

Get A Court of Caprice and Decay now.

Free novella

If you'd like a FREE NOVELLA set in the same world, sign up for my newsletter at zaradusk.com. It's a prequel novella set in the Realm of Caprice, where the weather is affected by the fae king's mood...and the king is NOT happy. A moody king, a badass heroine, and a beautiful but dangerous world—what's not to love?! This tells the story of Bree and Bastian Athar.

By signing up for my newsletter, you'll also get all the latest info about new releases, some character art, and other good stuff.

xxx Zara

About the Author

Zara has a pretty sweet life – hubby, kids, and a kick-ass Dyson hairdryer. But that doesn't stop her from inventing new worlds and having steamy affairs with her book boyfriends. Angels and demons and fae, oh my!

Lucky Zara, she gets to spend hours with those sexy beasts every day. The rest of the time she's working in health, negotiating with her kids, and beating her husband to the remote.

But mostly it's angels and fae.

Come along for the ride with Zara and her feisty heroines. You can provide the mulled wine.

You can connect with me on:
- https://zaradusk.com
- https://www.facebook.com/zaraduskauthor
- https://www.tiktok.com/@zaradusk

Subscribe to my newsletter:
✉ https://dl.bookfunnel.com/jtbq9u1oeu

Also by Zara Dusk

Fast-paced, twisty fantasy with plenty of smut. Bad men and badass women, some of them with wings.

Before he can return to heaven, she must die

A Fallen Angel hunts a mortal woman who lives in the Undercity because she is the key to his return to heaven.

But she is driven by wild revenge and won't fall easily.

Enemies to lovers steamy fantasy romance at its best, with captivating characters in a spellbinding world.

Complete series.